His kiss was hard and cruel, his fingers tangling in the hair at the base of her scalp. It was a kiss meant to punish. To convince. But when her hands settled on the smooth wool of his jacket, they didn't push him away.

They pulled him closer.

A sudden release of tension weakened his knees. He opened his lips with silent desperation. He didn't want her to push him away. He needed this too much. Comfort. Solace. *Her.* Things he'd sworn he had no need of when they parted. "A good man would walk away," he said.

He cupped the back of her head, his thumb soothing the delicate skin below it. His other hand followed her buttons down her back to her bottom. "I'm not a good man any longer."

Anna Randol

Sins of a Ruthless Rogue

A V O N
An Imprint of HarperCollinsPublishers

This is a work of fiction. Names, characters, places, and incidents are products of the author's imagination or are used fictitiously and are not to be construed as real. Any resemblance to actual events, locales, organizations, or persons, living or dead, is entirely coincidental.

AVON BOOKS
An Imprint of HarperCollins*Publishers*
10 East 53rd Street
New York, New York 10022-5299

First Avon Books mass market printing: April 2013

Avon Trademark Reg. U.S. Pat. Off. and in Other Countries, Marca Registrada, Hecho en U.S.A.
HarperCollins® is a registered trademark of HarperCollins Publishers.

Printed in the U.S.A.

10 9 8 7 6 5 4 3 2 1

To my sister, who told me this was her favorite book even when it shouldn't have been. And as always, to my husband, who I'll love forever and three days

Sins of a
Ruthless Rogue

Prologue

Swift Paper Mill, England, 1807

Olivia crept around to the back of the mill, the note held tightly in her hand. "Clayton?"

No answer. Perhaps he hadn't expected her to understand his code so quickly. Although he should have. The note was short. None of his usual words of adoration. It had taken her only five minutes to figure out that he wanted to meet her at their tree behind her father's mill.

She leaned back against the trunk and adjusted the hem of her dress so she was quite artfully arranged. Feeling rather daring, she edged the bodice an inch lower, too. Clayton's birthday was next week and she had promised him a rather special present. She saw no reason not to give him a small preview.

"Olivia?"

Her heart tangled and flopped in her chest as it always did at the sound of his voice. She was running to him before she remembered her plan to remain by the tree. But she closed the distance anyway and wrapped her arms around his neck.

He didn't swing her about and kiss her. Instead, he held her fiercely and buried his chin in her hair.

"Whatever is amiss, Clayton?" She drew back slightly and ran her hand along his jaw. She loved it when there was just a hint of a beard there. None of her father's other clerks could even grow beards yet. "If Tom has been complaining about delivering your notes again, you can just tell him that if he wants to remain a footman—"

"This isn't about Tom." His dark brows drew down, making him appear far older than his seventeen years.

Heavens, but he gave her delicious shivers.

She peered up at him from under her lashes. It always made him laugh. He said it must be difficult to see anything that way. He was looking far too serious for a tryst. "Well then, whatever could you want to see me about?"

He cupped her cheek. "I wish I'd brought you here for kisses. I wish I could just carry you away."

Clayton was often too serious, but she'd never seen him distressed. "Your mother? Did she have the gall to come home?"

"No." He stepped back and ran a hand through his dark hair.

He'd stepped away from her? He never wanted distance between them. He always wanted to be holding her hand, kissing her, or stroking her hair. "Clayton?"

He reached into his plain black waistcoat and pulled out—a banknote? She couldn't help her sigh of disappointment. If that was his idea of a gift, he'd failed miserably. After all, the mill printed banknotes for the Bank of England. She'd seen so many she thought she'd go cross-eyed. She much preferred her gifts to be shiny and wearable.

Clayton handed her the money. It was a fifty-pound note.

She blinked. That was far more money than he'd make in a year.

"It's not real," he said.

She turned it over. "Yes, it is." She knew enough to recognize the mill's work.

He took it back. "I need your word you'll tell no one what I'm going to tell you."

"Very well."

"No. Truly, I need your solemn promise to keep this secret no matter your temptation to speak."

Her stomach grew hollow. "I already promised, did I not?"

He closed his eyes, his forehead wrinkling in pain. "This banknote is real, but it shouldn't exist. The mill was contracted to print a thousand notes in this amount. Yet we printed one thousand and ten."

"That must have been an oversight."

"I went back over the records. This isn't the first time Swift Mill has made more banknote paper than the number of notes we need to print."

She was the one who took a step back this time. "Surely, in case there are errors or . . . or . . ." But she could think of no more reasons.

He closed the distance between them. "Listen to me carefully." He cleared his throat. "Your father is the one who does the final count of the banknotes. I found this and nine others in his office."

Papa? Clayton must have made a mistake. Besides, Papa was already wealthy. He'd have no reason to steal banknotes.

He held her close when she would have jerked away.

"You must be mistaken."

"I'm not. I've had my suspicions for months, and now I know your father is responsible. I have the proof I need."

She shoved at him, but he wouldn't let go. "The proof you need for what?"

"I have to go to the magistrate. This is theft." His voice shook. "And treason. Listen, Olivia. I'll do my best to shield you from this. I'll marry you, carry you away from the scandal."

He'd marry her? *Olivia Campbell. Olivia Campbell.* She'd practiced saying it so often that the name tumbled through her head a dozen times before the rest of his words registered.

Scandal. Her father. Magistrates.

Her hands trembled and it was suddenly difficult to swallow. To breathe.

He pressed a kiss to her lips. "I'm sorry to burden you with this. But I couldn't stand the thought of you finding out any other way. You must understand I have no other choice. I have to do what's right."

She might have said something. She might not have. She honestly had no idea as she watched him stride away.

Clayton was wrong. The foolish boy. She pressed her hands to her icy cheeks. He'd be humiliated when the magistrate uncovered whatever the real truth of the situation was. Her father would dismiss Clayton and it would be far more difficult for him to see her.

She didn't doubt he'd found something. Clayton was brilliant and far more clever than anyone she'd ever known. But he was mistaken in this.

Perhaps her father had suspicions about what was going on at the mill as well. That would explain why he had the banknotes.

That made perfect sense. She'd just have to ask her father what he knew about the money in his office. He'd probably be impressed that Clayton had such keen insight into the workings of the mill.

She ran all the way to her father's study.

Chapter One

Olivia Swift straightened her spine and glared down at the squinty-eyed man. As much as she rejoiced in what each new hire meant to the success of the mill, she loathed that she had to prove herself each and every time. "My father gives his orders to me and I bring them to the mill. If you have issue with that, you're welcome to seek employment elsewhere."

Grimmon's eyes narrowed until they were mere slits in his face. "I don't see why your father don't hire a man to deliver the orders. There's better places for a woman to be." His leer clearly demonstrated where he thought that was.

Then his face cleared, his expression sliding into a crude semblance of subservience. "But if that's how things are run here, I suppose I can handle it."

Olivia didn't need to look to know that Thomas,

the mill's chief machinist, was standing behind her. But while she might resent the instant respect the huge, bald man received, she wasn't fool enough to reject it. After all, finding a skilled vatsman like Grimmon at the wages she could afford had proved nearly impossible. She had to at least give this man a chance to come to terms with the unusual arrangements at the paper mill before she threw him out on his offensive, smirking face.

But one chance was all he'd get. "You'd best handle it. It might be difficult to find another mill owner willing to overlook your fondness for the bottle."

Grimmon tugged once at his limp neck cloth and nodded.

After he'd walked away, she finally turned to Thomas. "You shouldn't do that. I need to know the men will follow my orders when you're not around."

Thomas shrugged, the stiff motion tugging at the scar tissue that covered half of his face and neck. "Doubt that time will ever come. They don't have to take orders from you for much longer." He had that warning look in his eye again. Thomas was one of the few men who'd remained at the mill all along, even during the rough years before she'd become involved. Even when the mill had been reduced to making paper by hand and its only customers had been a handful of dry goods stores in neighboring towns. As quick as he was to support her, he'd made it clear that as soon as the mill was capable of fulfilling its contracts, he'd hold her to her promise to hire a manager to run the mill.

Olivia wanted to rub the ache at the base of her

skull but refrained. He was right. Her presence
complicated things for the men. Raised too many
questions about her father's health. Yet she couldn't
turn the mill over to a foreman. Not yet. Not when
success was still uncertain. "I will remain until
the contract with the Bank of England is secured
again."

Olivia strode past the hissing, clanking machines. She paused for a moment at the huge metal
cylinders that slowly carried the drying paper to
the end of the line. Each fresh, white inch was a
pound in the pocket of the town. Proof that she'd
succeeded in restoring the mill.

"Miss Swift! Miss Swift!" Colin, the junior
clerk, scurried toward her. His spectacles had
fogged in the perpetual damp from the steam en-
gines and slurry vats. He yanked them off and
scrubbed them against his sleeve, then replaced
them with practiced ease. "I just received a missive
from the Treadmine Stationers. They've canceled
their order."

"All of it?" Olivia rested her hands on the pipe
that carried water to the boiler. "Did they say
why?"

Colin shoved his spectacles back up his nose.
"No, just that they had no desire to do business
with us any longer."

That made the second cancellation today. She
took a deep breath. All businesses were plagued
by setbacks. She'd been expecting difficulties. She
didn't fear them. And she wouldn't let them stop
her. But perhaps she should cancel her plans to
attend the town festival and go to London instead.
"I'll visit them this afternoon—"

"Miss Swift!" Her lead vatsman ran to her side. "The headbox is near empty, and the rags haven't arrived."

"None of the shipments?" Without the rags, it didn't matter whether they had contracts or not. If they lacked the cloth to break down for fibers, they wouldn't be able to make paper at all.

The vatsman shook his shaggy head of red hair. "Nae a single solitary thread."

"This has to be a simple mix-up," she said. "Or they met with an accident along the road. Colin, send one of the ragboys out to see—"

A well-dressed man stepped between her and Colin. Not now. She didn't need any stationers arriving unannounced to examine the quality of the mill's stock. Or worse, someone from the Bank of England. She'd answered all their questions perfectly last week.

But she pasted a bright smile on her face. Looming disaster or no, she couldn't afford to offend potential customers. Her eyes slid up a gray waistcoat, across a surprisingly broad chest, and fixed on a set of piercing, steel blue eyes.

Eyes that belonged to a dead man.

She stumbled back a step. Only Colin's awkward grab kept her on her feet.

The dead man took her other arm with his strong fingers. And even though he wore black leather gloves, his hand was definitely warm. "Miss Swift has been overcome by the heat. She'll recover in her office."

Colin shifted, clearing his throat. "Who exactly might you be?"

The deep voice that had haunted her nightmares

for the past ten years spoke. "Clayton Campbell. I used to work here."

And with that simple statement, her madness was assured. Her vision blurred and grew dark around the edges, but she couldn't afford to let her employees see her weak—not twice in one day—and so she managed to remain upright. "It's fine, Colin. I'll be in my office."

She let Clayton escort her inside. As soon as the door shut, she lifted her hand to his face. The tall, angular boy she remembered was gone, replaced by a lean, hardened man. His cheekbones were more chiseled.

He's alive.

The slight shadow of stubble on his jaw, dark. She hadn't allowed herself to imagine how he might look as a grown man. But even if she had, she wouldn't have imagined this. He was at once more flawed and yet utter perfection.

He's alive.

She traced the line of his nose. The shell of his ear. She wanted to explore every change and remember a hundred details she'd forgotten. Examine him closely enough to convince herself this wasn't a dream.

He. Is. Alive.

The man she'd condemned to the gallows.

Clayton hadn't moved. Not once since she'd touched him. She finally met his gaze. His eyes were dark, cold. "Remove your hand from my person."

She stumbled to a hard wooden chair and sat, staring up at him. "Clayton, where have you been? I thought you were—"

"Dead?"

And with that one icy word, she knew she shouldn't have sat down. He'd towered over her when they were young, but now he dominated. His face twisted in disdain.

This might be a miracle, but it wasn't a joyous one.

"Where have you been?" She clutched edges of her gray woolen skirt in her fists.

Clayton lifted a brow, the look that had been quizzical and endearing on him as a young man now condescending. Cruel. "Hell."

"But they hung you. My father saw it."

"Did he?"

The lead in her stomach expanded until it also encased her heart. Her father had lied about that, too. Another lie. Another— Sweet mercy. "Have you been in prison all this time? Or"—her words seemed to stick in her throat—"transported?" Could she have done something to help him? Gone to the authorities and told them the truth?

"I didn't come for a reunion."

But that didn't mean she could let the question go. She'd loved him once with everything she'd possessed. She had to know.

Know what she'd caused.

She forced herself to stand. "What happened?"

"You gave up the right to ask that question."

"What happened that night—"

"I wish to speak to your father." Clayton spoke right over her, as if she hadn't just been about to speak the words that haunted her every thought. Influenced her every choice.

"Clayton—"

"Do not flatter yourself that I've spent my life dwelling on your betrayal. Or that I want to revisit it now."

"I do."

"You don't always get what you want, Diamond."

How dare he. How *dare* he say those things, then use that name. She'd loved it when he'd given it to her as her code name. Sparkling. Bright. Precious. But now in his scorn it meant pampered, shallow, greedy.

She was none of those things any longer.

"Shall we go meet with your father?"

His words grounded her back in reality. "You cannot."

"So I discovered yesterday."

Olivia gave thanks for the discretion and stubborn loyalty of her butler. "My father isn't a well man. He sees no one."

"He saw the representatives from the Bank of England."

How did Clayton know that? "That was an exceptional case."

"Returning from the dead might also be considered rather exceptional."

"I won't allow it." She would tell him what she told all the others. "Whatever you need to say to him can be said to me. I'll relay the information."

"Still his loyal watchdog, I see." His gaze was derisive.

But she would not flinch, not from his disdain. Not from his anger. While she was no longer loyal to her father, she *was* loyal to this mill. "Do you have a message to relay or not?"

Clayton smiled, a slow stretch of his lips over gleaming white teeth. "Tell your father that I'm here for justice. Everything he has will soon be in shambles at his feet."

"This mill has crumbled over the past ten years. Isn't that shambles enough for you?"

"Bad luck isn't the same as justice. The mill is set to begin printing for the Bank of England again, is it not?"

She couldn't deny it when he already knew the truth. "Yes."

"That is what brought me back. Not you. Your father may have stopped me from speaking the truth when I was younger. But he will not repeat his crimes."

"He won't."

Clayton rested his shoulder against the door frame. His relaxed pose was completely at odds with the intensity of his gaze. "As I recall, you were certain of his innocence last time as well. The Swift Paper Mill will never print banknotes again."

For the first time, the real truth of this situation settled heavily on her chest. There was nothing between them now. Her memories of him were all she'd ever have. And now even those did nothing but open her heart to allow each of his barbs deeper.

She couldn't tell him the truth. Not when he'd use that knowledge to destroy the mill out of pure hatred. Oh, he might deny it. But ten years ago he'd wanted to stop her father for the sake of justice. This went much deeper. "The mill is bigger than my father. Far more lives are in the balance."

"Then they can rebuild what they will out of the ruins."

What had she ever seen in this man? How could she have missed this cruelty? Perhaps her father had been right about one thing in his miserable life—Clayton hadn't been worth her time. Or her heart. "You've waited all this time for revenge?"

"This isn't revenge."

She planted a finger on his chest. "This is *exactly* revenge. Otherwise, why not go to the authorities?"

Clayton knocked her hand away, and for the first time, she could see the hot anger roiling behind his gaze. "The gallows are too good for your father."

"In other words, you have no proof." She stopped and took a calming breath. "Let it go, Clayton. I give you my word that the past will not be repeated."

"Your word?" His voice sliced like a fine-edged knife. He ran his gloved hand over his jaw. "Do you have any idea what happened to my father after I was convicted? Did you even go look for him?"

She knew the stricken look on her face gave away her answer. "I was fifteen." Yet she'd never checked on him in more recent years, either, despite all her attempts to make restitution. Apparently, she hadn't changed as much as she liked to think. "What happened?"

But his brief flare of emotion had been extinguished. "This mill is finished."

The whirr of machinery outside the door slowed to silence. It was only the missing rag shipments, she assured herself.

But then Clayton smiled.

No.

She'd arranged everything to perfection. Even if Clayton had attained the level of genius his youthful abilities had hinted at, he couldn't stop her.

He drew a stack of papers from his jacket pocket. With slow deliberation, he dragged them in a feathered caress along her cheek. The papers were thin. Cheap. Definitely not from her mill. "Do you know what these are?" he asked.

She shook her head, not trusting her voice. Or her temper.

"Every debt that you owe your creditors now belongs to me. And the first of them comes due . . ." He glanced down at the top sheet. As if he didn't remember every number and every word on each page. " . . . next Tuesday. I hope you have the cash on hand to pay it."

She exhaled. She would. She'd made sure the shipment to Treadmine would be delivered before the debt to the coalman came due.

The shipment that had just been canceled.

No amount of determination could hide the trembling in her voice now. "You cannot do this."

Clayton strode to the door. "It is already done. And tell your father that from now on, I'll deal with him and him alone. Deliver *that* message."

Chapter Two

"Yes, but perhaps move the tables into the sun?" Olivia directed the men as they moved the tables out of the tavern into the crisp autumn air.

The harvest festival. This was supposed to be a grand celebration. The first village festival in ten years. The first of many more to come.

If Clayton had his way, it would be the last.

Children scampered around the square, chasing a metal hoop.

Women had set up tables with savory pies for sale, brooms, knitted caps, pins, and carved wooden toys.

It was all arranged to perfection.

And would never happen again if Clayton had his way.

Mrs. Wilkerson pressed a mug of warm cider into her hands.

"Thank you." Olivia tried to hand her a penny, but the woman shook her head.

"Not after what you've done."

"Please take it." After all, Olivia might have re-vived the town only to let it be crushed again.

After a moment's hesitation, the other woman pocketed the coin. "That member of Parliament, did he agree to support your idea? The one about separate rooms in the prison for the children?"

"He said he would think on it." Which was far more than she'd ever gotten before.

Mrs. Wilkerson was one of two women in the town who'd lost a son to the British penal system, so she followed Olivia's reform activities closely. Work Olivia had started to rectify the horrific in-justice she thought she'd caused.

"Them fancy friends of yours coming to the fes-tival?"

Olivia would hardly call the Society for the Humane Treatment of Child Criminals fancy. They were little more than an odd collection of two barristers, a Quaker, a retired vicar, and a handful of concerned women. But she *would* call them friends. And recently they'd begun to make progress on their reforms. "I let them know they're invited."

A few might come. They saw the mill's restora-tion as a grand experiment to see if they could keep young lads from the country from falling into the stews of London.

Mrs. Wilkerson handed mugs to two men who'd stopped to get some cider. Both worked at the mill. Olivia had arranged for the men to have the half day off months ago. So she'd been able to shut down the machines at the mill early without any questions. One thing in her favor today.

Colin came over to the table, one of his little sisters perched on his shoulder. The little girl pointed a chubby finger at the cups. "More?"

He put the girl down. "Do you mind watching her for a minute, Aunt Lucy? The competition's about to start."

"Competition?" Olivia asked.

Colin adjusted his glasses. "Cheese rolling."

Olivia blinked. She couldn't have heard that right.

Mrs. Wilkerson ladled a dribble of the drink into a cup and handed it to her whimpering niece. "You had to have seen it as a girl."

Olivia had never attended the festival as a girl. But she didn't remind them of that. She liked that they'd forgotten she'd once declared that only poor mongrels bothered with the town.

She'd been seven. Her father had laughed and patted her on the head.

Another man and his wife came to buy some cider.

Mrs. Wilkerson shook her head at Colin. "I don't think I can watch your sister. Where's your mum?"

Colin glanced over his shoulder. "Still helping get the children arranged for their songs."

"I can watch her," Olivia volunteered.

They both stared at her. "Aren't you busy with the festival?"

But things looked like they were running smoothly now. "Not for the moment." She set down her cup and picked the little girl up. "We'll be fine. Go."

Colin hesitated, then ran across the square to where some men were gathering atop a hill.

"Yellow." The little girl pointed to the fallen leaves swirling after him.

"Yes. Yellow and orange and red." Olivia pointed out the other colors and moved toward the tables that had been pulled outside the tavern. She rested her cheek for a moment on the girl's soft curls. "We are not going to let the big, mean man take this all away from us, are we?"

"Mean," the little girl agreed.

Handsome, though. But oh so cold.

Clayton's reappearance should have soothed her conscience. But she'd managed to think of her guilt as something in the past. Now it had been thrust in front of her face. Glaring. Ugly. Fresh. When she thought him dead ten years ago, she'd prayed to discover that it was all a mistake and that Clayton was alive and unharmed. She longed for the crushing weight of her guilt to be lifted.

Now he truly *was* alive, and her remorse remained as heavy as ever.

But while she might owe him a debt she could never repay, that didn't mean she would allow him to do as he wished. She'd changed since he knew her last. She hadn't backed away from a struggle since the day she'd been too cowed to follow her father to the courthouse. Since the day Clayton had died.

A new schoolhouse stood proud and straight. The smell of fresh paint still lingered in the air. The inside still needed a little more work, but she'd managed to arrange for the exterior to be finished in time for the festival.

"It's a fine thing you've done. You've set things right." The vicar's gnarled face beamed down at her. "This is all thanks to you." He lifted the little girl into his arms.

They were the words she'd been waiting to hear for three years. Ever since he'd come to her in London and told her how bad things had become at the mill. And in the town.

But now they meant nothing.

She'd been striving to make amends for the death of a man who wasn't dead.

"You were the one who made me see my responsibility to the town." It had been the second time he'd saved her.

The vicar patted the little girl on her back, swaying as the schoolchildren began their song. She longed to tell the vicar about Clayton, but how could she when he was glowing with so much happiness?

She studied the faces around her. The Johansen family, with seven blond boys whose names she couldn't keep straight. Mr. Grupp, who finally had bought a new sign for his tavern to replace the one that been lost in the storms five years ago. There were even a few new faces, people who'd come to spend their money at the festival and the families of the new hires at the mill.

The vicar left her side to return the child to her mother.

A man stopped in front of her and doffed his hat, revealing greased black hair. "Sorry to bother you, miss. But a man visited you at the mill today. I think he might be a friend of mine." He had an accent she couldn't quite place. "But I wasn't sure if it was him."

"Clayton Campbell?" she asked, suddenly eager for someone to share in her shock. In her joy.

The man nodded, but there was no astonishment. "It *was* him. Did he come to look for work at the mill?"

"No."

The man's gaze seemed far too intent, his eyes almost predatory. Olivia stepped back. "How did you say you knew him?" she asked.

But the men were finished with their competition and they swarmed past cheering, pounding each other on the back, and shouting congratulations.

"I came in second!" Colin shouted to her.

She smiled at him, but when she looked back the strange visitor was gone. She stood on her tiptoes, trying to find where he'd gone in the crowd, but she couldn't locate him.

The men gathered around the cider table. The children had finished their song so they threaded their way through the group until they found their families.

She refused to let Clayton destroy all this. The boy she once loved wouldn't have been able to hurt all these innocent people. She would just have to do a better job of showing him exactly who'd be hurt by his actions.

A shiver of something dark coursed through her. Part of it was fear, but part of it was anticipation.

To spend time with him again—

But she didn't delude herself that she could change his feeling about her. What she did hope was to change his mind about the mill. Even as a youth, Clayton had always been too dedicated. Too determined. He had a rather overdeveloped sense of right and wrong. He'd once walked a mile back to a store because they'd given him seven sweets when he'd paid for only six.

There was only one way she'd ever found to dissuade him—his heart.

He cared for things deeply. That wasn't something that could be changed, no matter what he'd suffered. She had to make him think of the mill not in terms of justice for past wrongs but in terms of the lives it helped now.

Before, it had been possible to coax him to change his point of view. It had taken a whispered word. A smile. A caress.

Olivia doubted Clayton would let her near enough to do any of those things.

But he had listened to logic. Always to logic. And saving the mill was logical. It was right.

She'd spent the last eight years working to convince lords, magistrates, and members of Parliament to help children who couldn't even vote. She'd charmed benefactors and political hostesses into funding charities that helped the very street urchins who'd robbed them.

She would handle a former clerk.

Clayton glared up from the papers on his desk. He'd hoped the numbers would soothe him. But they only left him more dissatisfied. From the paltry stipend the Foreign Office had paid him a little more than a year ago, he'd made a fortune, lost a fortune, then made it back again. High-stakes investing was always a gamble, but with careful study it was much less so.

Normally, studying out his investments and planning his next ones soothed him.

But today he could barely keep his eyes on the page.

The numbers were as unsatisfactory as everything else had been that day.

Because he'd gotten nothing accomplished. That had to be the real reason for his discontent. He'd delivered a warning to Olivia.

But unlike ten years ago, he wouldn't try to protect her from what was coming. She'd made her choices. Unlike last time, her father—or even Olivia herself—would be unable to stop him from justice.

Yet one thing had been far too much like the last time he'd seen her.

She was still the most beautiful creature he'd ever beheld.

She'd matured well, time turning her imperfections into assets. The softness of her youthful form had settled into lithe, graceful curves. Lips that had been too pouty now tempted under angular cheekbones. High-arched eyebrows now lent sophistication rather than surprise.

And her wide eyes, the color of the sky, no longer sparkled with an innocence and naïveté so complete it had been as blinding as it had been beautiful.

But it didn't matter. He no longer desired her.

If he'd let her soft hand linger on his face a moment too long, it was because he'd been shocked at her audacity.

His butler, Canterbury, entered the study, wearing a rather improbable puce-colored hat. "Was justice satisfied today, sir?"

"I only delivered a message." Why did he feel obligated to explain himself to his butler? He'd spent a decade as a member of Britain's most feared team of spies—the Trio. He'd revealed less information under torture. Yet somehow, this man made words spew from his mouth at a glance.

Madeline and Ian, La Petit and Wraith respectively, the other two members of the Trio, would have mocked him mercilessly, but there was something about the old servant that made Clayton feel guilty. Even when he was certain he'd done nothing wrong.

He'd inherited the impertinent butler at the marriage of Madeline Valdan, now Madeline Huntford. He still wasn't sure precisely how *he'd* been the one to end up with the servant. Ian was the one who knew Canterbury from a past life.

"You were able to meet with Mr. Swift then?" Canterbury asked.

"No. I spoke to his daughter."

"Ah."

That was precisely how Clayton felt about the whole thing. He hadn't lied to Olivia earlier. At least not much. While he might have thought of her a smattering of times, he'd never had any intention of seeing her or her father again. He'd been far too busy staying alive to hatch intricate plans of revenge.

Until he'd seen the notice in the *Times* six months ago that the Swift Paper Mill was in contention to secure the contract with the Bank of England despite Mr. Swift's infirmity.

Never while Clayton drew breath. He'd given up ten years of his life to protect Britain. He wasn't going to let it be cheated by the likes of Arthur Swift.

"Did she say when you could call on him?" his butler asked.

Clayton tapped at the rows and columns before him. Perhaps that was the root of his dissatisfaction. He'd allowed the Swifts to dictate to him as they'd always done.

He wouldn't make that mistake again.

Chapter Three

It took Clayton only a short while to ride the five miles to the Swift house. Even with surprisingly few windows lit, the huge, Palladian-style estate lorded over the surrounding land.

He waited for a minute in the courtyard after dismounting, but when no groom came to take his horse, he tied the reins to a tree. Perhaps they'd seen him coming.

Indeed, it looked like they had. The front door stood open. Clayton expected to be met by armed footmen, but as he mounted the steps, he saw the soles of two booted feet partially visible in the doorway.

He took the last three steps at a run, his knife already in his hand.

The man lying sprawled inside the doorway was the butler. A huge swollen lump disfigured the left side of his forehead. Clayton dropped to the floor beside him and shook him gently, but the man remained limp. At least he was breathing.

Clayton scanned the surrounding area. Blood

was pooled on the far side of the entry hall, then smeared in a crimson trail into the corridor as though the injured person had tried to drag himself to safety. He followed the path of the bloody handprints. From the amount of blood, the victim couldn't have survived long.

Years of witnessing grisly violence, and at times meting it out himself, should have allowed him to analyze scenes like this without any emotion. Yet this time, his heart hammered so loudly in his ears that he couldn't hear his own footsteps, let alone signs of an approaching attacker.

If *she'd* been the one killed—

It wasn't Olivia. It was one of her footmen. And he was dead. Knife wound to the chest.

Hell. He wanted to call out for her, shout until she appeared unscathed from her room. He might despise her, but even he wouldn't wish this on her.

But Olivia wouldn't have been the type to hide in her room if she'd heard an altercation. She'd have been out to investigate before she realized the foolishness of her actions.

He kept silent. The attackers were most likely gone, but he wouldn't risk giving away his location any more than was necessary.

What had happened? It must have been a robbery. The entry was completely devoid of silver candlesticks and the other glittering things that used to adorn it. But the attackers had entered through the front door. If it had been thieves, why not wait until the middle of the night when they could have entered with stealth?

He worked his way down the corridor, checking each room as he passed.

But the entryway wasn't the only area that had been stripped. The parlor and the study were perfectly untouched, but the rest of the rooms were almost completely bare. And odd things had been left behind. Brass candlesticks. Why would a thief have left behind the most easily sold items?

He knew from his research that the mill had disintegrated due to neglect until its sudden revival two years ago. Was the house's condition a result of that?

The thought of Olivia selling off luxuries bit by bit should have pleased him. A sort of divine justice if he was fool enough to believe in any.

But the thought didn't please him.

What had happened to her after his arrest was no concern of his. His business was with her father, not with Olivia. He hadn't even bothered to look into her life when he'd researched the mill.

He didn't care.

He opened the door to the library, and a woman screamed. Clayton's hand tensed on his knife. But again, it wasn't Olivia.

An older maid huddled in the darkness in the far corner of the room, shielding her face with her arms.

Sheathing his knife, Clayton kept his approach as smooth and calm as he could so he wouldn't frighten her further. "Be quiet. I'm not going to hurt you. What happened here?"

The maid quieted, although the whites of her eyes still gleamed in the thin shaft of light from the open door. "You're not Russian. You're not, are you?" Her voice was tiny and tight with fear.

Clayton shook his head, his feet suddenly too slow. His thoughts muddled. Russian? What the devil was going on? "No, I'm not. Are they still here?"

Her head jerked from side to side. "I think they all left. They took her and they left."

"Who did they take?" His voice must have been harsh because the maid shrank from him.

"Miss Swift."

He'd taken two steps to the door when his training reasserted authority. He couldn't go charging blindly. He didn't know who'd taken Olivia or where to. "How long ago?"

"I don't know." She rubbed her palms on her cheeks. "I was thinking I had to hurry and start the coals for the warming pans. I do it every night—I never thought—"

"When do you normally fill the warming pans?"

"At seven."

It was past eight now. She was definitely in shock, but he needed all the information he could get. He helped the maid sit. "Who were they?"

She bit her lip. "I don't know. I don't—"

Her gaze grew unfocused again and Clayton spoke before he lost her entirely to her terror. "Are you hurt?"

Her hands flew to her throat. "No. Not me." She pressed her knuckles against her mouth. "They took her. Might have had a coach. I think I heard one. Oh, you have to help her."

He'd passed a dozen carriages and carts on his way here. She could have been in any one of them. But Clayton knew he needed patience to get the information. "Tell me exactly what you saw and heard. Everything. Any little detail might help me find her."

The maid yanked her hands away from her mouth, planted them in her lap, and drew a stuttered breath. "I don't know how much help I'll be. But—I was cleaning out the hearth when I heard a commotion in the entry hall. I poked my head out to see what was amiss. Two fellows had knocked Mr. Burton on the head. Perry, he's the footman, tried to stop them, and the black-haired man just pulled out a knife and stabbed him. Right in the chest."

She began to tremble, so Clayton rested his hand on her shoulder. "Can you describe them?"

"One was tall and mean-looking, huge bushy beard. Like some sort of beast. The other was leaner, handsome, black hair. Very neat. Both of them looked foreign. They spoke in Russian."

"How do you know it was Russian?"

For the first time a hint of spark returned to the maid, and she glared at him. "I've been serving this house and its guests since before the master got sick. He was always entertaining all sorts of foreign men of business. We had Russians many times. I know the difference."

"Did you recognize any of the words?"

"Not the Russian ones, but they kept speaking about something in French. La Petot?"

"La Petit?" He had to force the name out.

"Yes! The dark one told the big one something about a La Petit."

"Then they took Miss Swift?"

The maid nodded, her chin wobbling. "I think so. I was—I was hiding in here so I couldn't see. But I heard her yelling."

If Olivia was yelling, that meant she'd left here alive.

"Where was her father? The other servants?"

The maid's head tilted slightly, but then her face cleared. "Not here tonight, sir. But they should be home soon. Oh, they said one thing I did recognize. East End."

The docks. He strode over to the desk and scribbled a quick note on a sheet of paper. "Have this delivered to Ian Maddox at The Albany when the others get back."

He was out of the room running toward the front door before he heard her answer. If the kidnappers thought Olivia was La Petit, one of the most hated spies in all of Europe, then her life was in danger. When they found out she wasn't La Petit, she was dead.

He leaped onto his horse and galloped to where the driveway met the road. Why had they taken her? Olivia looked absolutely nothing like Madeline, the real La Petit.

The only thing that connected the two women was him. The kidnappers must somehow have assumed she was Madeline because of his contact with her. But why the devil had they only wanted La Petit? They must have known where Clayton was as well. They must have been following him.

Damned sloppy.

And who could have taken her? The Trio had been to Russia only a handful of times and every time had involved Prazhdinyeh. But the violent group of revolutionaries had fallen apart with the death of their leader a few years ago.

His hands clenched on the reins, stopping his mount. He slid down to examine the tracks at the end of the drive. It was too dark to see much, but the most recent wheel indentations cut toward London.

Hell, it couldn't be Prazhdinyeh. They no longer existed.

But some of its members might. And all of them wanted La Petit dead. And she soon would be. Or at least Olivia in her place. After they tortured her for information.

If he'd still been a praying man, he would have prayed to make it to the harbor before they sailed. Instead, he pushed his horse into a dead gallop.

Clayton's hand tightened on the man's throat. "Come now, Archie. You know every ship that enters and leaves this port. Even the ones the harbormaster knows nothing of. I will ask again. Where was the ship headed?" Witnesses had seen two men matching the description of the Russians carry a sleeping woman aboard a ship minutes before it sailed. They must have planned the kidnapping to coincide perfectly with the tides.

"We were even." Archie coughed. "I don't owe you anything. Not anymore."

Clayton pressed his thumb harder into the thief's leathery windpipe. "Then I'll owe you one."

Even though he was on the edge of oblivion, interest entered Archie's eyes. "You . . . make . . . a deal? You never . . . make deals."

"And I won't again. Three. Two—"

"St. Petersburg. The ship was Russian. Worthless cargo. It was set to sail to St. Petersburg."

Clayton dropped the man, who slumped to the ground next to the boarded-up warehouse, gasping and rubbing his neck. "Don't forget that you owe me—"

"I don't forget." Not a single bloody thing. Ever. In his whole life. Not the way Archie's throat had spasmed under his hand. Not the haunted agony in Olivia's eyes when he'd announced his plans for the mill. "Where can I get a ship? Tonight?"

Chapter Four

For a moment, Olivia was certain she was blind. She knew her eyes were open. Her lids scraped over her dry eyes with each rapid blink. Yet the darkness remained black. Complete. Not only were her eyes dry, but so was her throat. She tried to reach for the cup of water she kept on her end table, but pain burned in her wrists and shoulders.

She couldn't move her arms. She tried to force them, but gasped as the movement seared like fire across her wrists. They were bound behind her. Her ankles were tied as well.

This wasn't her bedroom. She was on her side on some sort of lumpy mattress. How long had she been like this? Where was she?

The door slammed open. "She is awake?" a voice asked.

She flinched away from the intense light filling the doorway. After several seconds, her eyes adjusted, and she realized it was only a lantern.

"She should drink something then?" another voice asked. It took her a few confused minutes to understand the words. Russian. The voices were speaking in Russian. And to think she'd given her governess endless grief for forcing her to learn it to impress her father's investors.

Two men entered the room. A thin one with dark hair held the lantern. He might have been handsome if not for the cruel twist of his lips. The other man was so massive he had to duck and hunch his shoulders to fit through the door.

The mention of water intensified the dry, swollen ache in her mouth. She wanted to beg for it, but she kept her cracked lips closed. She didn't know what these men wanted. She couldn't afford to appear weak.

"She doesn't get water until she gives me answers," Lantern Man said. "Now tell us the key."

She thought of a dozen keys in that instant. The keys to her home. To the mill. But they'd broken into her house, so those keys could be of no interest to them. The new steam equipment at the mill was expensive, but it would be impossible to move. "What key?" At least that's what she tried to ask. The words were so raspy and choked, she didn't know if the men understood. Her Russian accent had always been horrible. It had infuriated her father to no end.

Lantern Man hung the light on a peg, reached over to a table behind him, and poured water into a clay cup. He must see that she'd need water if she was going to talk.

She couldn't stop her own lips from parting in anticipation of the cool liquid.

Lantern Man tipped the cup and poured it onto the floor.

The air whooshed out of her lungs.

"Don't lie, Petit. I know what you took from Vasin."

Why had he switched to French for the endearment?

Nothing made sense, and she had to struggle to hold on to each thought.

But she did know she hadn't taken anything. "I don't know what you're talking about." She hoped her words were correct in Russian. She'd never used it for anything more than chatting over tea. But surely, she could speak clearly enough to make them understand they had the wrong person. "I do not know Vasin."

Lantern Man lowered his face until it was inches from hers. With a start, she recognized him. The man who'd spoken to her at the festival. This had something to do with Clayton. The man's breath smelled of alcohol and pipe smoke. "Your associate led us straight to you. His brief visit to your house. Your strange meetings with various government officials."

Her work with the Society? But that had nothing to do with Clayton.

"Then we found these. In code, are they not?" He tossed a small stack of envelopes onto the bed next to her. They were tied with a green ribbon.

Her love letters from Clayton. A bittersweet reminder she'd never been able to throw away.

These men had been in her room. They'd searched through her things. And she hadn't even known. Her skin felt like it had been smeared with mud.

Lantern Man continued, "You can say what you

want. Your actions have already proven your identity."

She closed her eyes. The drug they'd given her tempted her back into oblivion. This had to be a dream. None of it made any sense otherwise.

A hand clenched in her hair and viciously shook her. "I know you are not asleep, Petit."

"The count didn't tell us to hurt her, just get her." The other man spoke, his words hesitant.

"Shut up, Blin. You were not brought for your thoughts."

"But she says she doesn't know." Blin's words were emphatic.

She cried out as Lantern Man shook her again. She opened her eyes and tried to pull away, but that only made the pain worse.

"She's lying." His face was nothing but shadows and menace.

She had to try again. "I'm not who you think I am."

"And you just happen to speak Russian? No. You English learn Italian and French. You don't dirty yourselves with Russian. And why did Campbell help you by buying up all your mill's debts?"

Help her? "He wants to destroy me."

But both men ignored her. Blin's brows drew together under the heavy line of hair that hung across his forehead. "What if she's not the spy, Nicolai?"

A spy? That's what those things somehow proved? But it still didn't make sense.

Nicolai dropped her head back on the bed. "Then she's of no use and we kill her. Eventually." He ran a finger down her cheek.

Olivia would have spat at him if her mouth

wasn't so dry. She wanted to close her eyes again, but she refused to let Nicolai know how thoroughly he'd cowed her. She might not be able to fight him, but neither would she just give in.

Blin stepped toward her, his beefy hands tugging on the ends of his beard. "The count will be angry if she's hurt too much to talk."

"The count doesn't frighten me. I've known him since university."

"Then you know he likes to be obeyed."

Olivia didn't recognize the word Nicolai used as he backed away, but she assumed it was vulgar.

"Then *you* take care of her. I'm not a nursemaid. But do not untie her. Remember what I told you." Nicolai slammed out the door.

Blin stood silently by the bed for a minute, then trundled over and poured her a glass of water. He reached for her, and she flinched, but then let him help sit her up enough to take a drink. His huge hand dwarfed the cup. "Nicolai says he thought you'd be prettier, but I think you're very pretty." She thought it was an apology of sorts, or at least an attempt at kindness.

The water tasted like mold, but she drank every drop. Blin then pulled a crumbled piece of bread from his pocket and offered her a small chunk. The bread was hard and tasted worse than the water, but she ate all of it, too, bite by humiliating bite, unsure if she would get more. He then carried her to a foul-smelling chamber pot in the corner.

Afterward, Blin lowered her back onto the bed. She knew her face was in flames, but it didn't seem to bother her captor at all.

Her heart rate finally began to slow, and for the

first time, she noticed a certain motion in the room around her. She looked again at the planks that made up the room. There was a lap of water somewhere on the other side of the walls.

Sweet heavens. Her moment of calm twisted into something sick and unrecognizable.

She was on a ship.

"How long was I . . . asleep?"

She'd had drugs forced down her throat while Nicolai had pinched her nose shut until she'd had no choice but to swallow. But Blin seemed kind and she didn't want to antagonize him. Also, she had no idea how to say *unconscious* in Russian.

"Almost a full day."

Then there was little chance they were still in a harbor. "Where are we going?"

The half-rotted pine chair creaked as he sat. "To the count."

There were far too many people in this conversation that she didn't know. La Petit. Vasin. The count. "Which count?"

Blin folded his arms, revealing long scratches on the back of one of his hands. She'd given him those when he carried her away from her house. Olivia wasn't sure if she felt proud or guilty. If she'd wounded Nicolai, she'd have felt no remorse whatsoever.

"Nicolai said to tell you nothing. He said you were good at tricking things out of people."

Olivia cursed whoever this mystery woman was. If only she had some of her skills. But as it was, all Olivia could do was flounder. "But I'm going to meet the count anyway, so it doesn't matter if you tell me."

Blin rocked slightly in his chair. "The count is my master."

"He hired you?"

Blin frowned slightly. "I work his estate."

She'd forgotten that Russian landowners still owned their serfs. "Nicolai, too?"

"No, he is his associate."

"Why are you taking me to him?"

Blin scowled. "You stole papers."

"I didn't steal anything!"

He stood. "Nicolai said you'd say that. He said you'd lie."

"I'm not lying." Blin was her best chance. She had to convince him. "I'm not a spy. You kidnapped the wrong woman."

He didn't seem to like the word *kidnap*, so she pressed harder. He might have been only following orders but he needed to understand the full ramifications. Blin might not be the brightest of fellows, but he wasn't a fool. She suspected he was more easily persuaded than anything else. She would have to turn that to her advantage.

"You kidnapped me. You and Nicolai drugged me and threatened me. Those are crimes."

"I don't have a choice."

"Perhaps not. But now you do. You could untie—"

The door opened and Nicolai stalked back in. "Enough, Blin. Come."

"She said she isn't a spy."

"Think." Nicolai cuffed the big man on the back of the head. "If she's not a spy, then why did she have all those coded messages from a spy?"

Blin nodded slowly.

"Come, Blin."

He followed Nicolai from the room—or rather, cabin.

She had coded letters from a spy? She didn't know—

Ah, that was what Clayton had been doing for the past ten years.

Clayton swore as he wove his way through the dark streets of St. Petersburg. The ship he'd commandeered should have been faster than the kidnappers' frigate, but the winds had been wrong through the Oresund Strait and he'd had to wait to be towed through by the rowers. Then it had taken him time to track down the man in Cronstadt who could provide him with papers to get off the island that served as the port and actually into St. Petersburg.

According to the harbormaster's records, Olivia's ship had arrived yesterday morning.

He was only a day and a half behind now. But he knew from experience what a hellish eternity a day could be.

After all, it had taken only minutes for the French to flay the skin from his back. An hour for them to break every—

Clayton tugged his greatcoat around him, banishing the memories. He had survived. The French had been defeated.

Olivia had been with her kidnappers for sixteen days.

The deadness in his chest only grew. If he needed proof that there was nothing resembling a soul left in him, this was it. No panic. No desperation. Those had been lost to him long ago. Now there was only a void that deepened with each passing day.

He would find her. Then he would destroy her kidnappers. It was as simple as that.

The mud had begun to freeze with the evening air, leaving an icy crust that crunched under his boots with each step. The cold increased the ache in the misshapen bones in his right hand until he had to tuck it into his coat for relief. Unfortunately, his coat and gloves had been designed for an English autumn, not for the start of a Russian winter.

The door to the Hammer and Anvil stood wide open despite the temperature. Clayton strode in and took a seat. He didn't attempt to look for Daisy. She didn't miss a thing that went on at the inn. She certainly wouldn't miss him.

Like most of the inns and hotels in St. Petersburg, this one was run by a foreigner—in this case an Englishwoman.

But unlike most, the Hammer and Anvil had a rather different clientele. Sooner or later, every unsavory fellow in Russia made his way through here. And she gleaned information from every single one.

As he'd expected, Daisy slid in across from him before the barmaid had fetched his food. While her dimpled cheeks and graying curly hair might have given her the look of a hearty farmwife, she had the heart of a shark.

Perhaps that was why they got along so well.

"Cipher. I didn't expect to see you here ever

again." Her accent bespoke her Welsh origins, but the slight gloss of Russian hinted at just how long she'd lived in St. Petersburg.

She pushed a glass of vodka toward him, which he ignored.

"You're working, then," she concluded.

"Has Prazhdinyeh re-formed?"

She tapped her fingers on the table. "They were never gone. Hatred of the czar won't be stopped by the death of one revolutionary. Someone else picks up the pieces and keeps going. I've been hearing about them for months."

"Where? Who is behind it now?"

She waited a few moments. "You remember how this works, right? You give me something of value and then I see if I can help you."

Clayton considered what he could give up. "They tried to kidnap La Petit."

Daisy pinched her lip as she thought. "Did they succeed?"

"No." There was no reason to tell her about Olivia.

"Interesting." He could see her tucking away that information to be sorted out later. "Now, who their leader currently is, I cannot say. But many supporters have been visiting the estate of Count Arshun." She sketched out brief directions where to find it on the edge of the city.

"What are they planning?"

"Ah, I do not know that, either. But it's interesting timing. At the birthday fete of the Grand Duchess Ileana Narcosky later this week, a portrait of the imperial family will be unveiled."

"Why is that interesting?" The imperial family

was always having some painting done while their people starved.

"It is of the *entire* family. Uncles. Cousins. Nieces. The artist traveled all over Russia for the past three years to gather sketches of them."

Clayton waited. Daisy never said anything without purpose. "It is said that the artist then painted the portrait under the czar's personal direction. Everyone is curious how the czar views them."

"They will all attend the fete to find out their level of imperial favor."

"Every last one. They haven't all been together like this since the coronation of Alexander. Many people in my inn find that of interest."

Revolutionaries who detested the monarchy were stirring at the same time there was to be an unrivaled gathering of royals.

Daisy continued. "Now what *I* find of interest is, if the revolutionaries didn't get Petit, why are you here?"

"They have something that doesn't belong to them." He could see her curiosity, but she didn't press further. She knew when to hold back.

She frowned. "Prazhdinyeh is different than before. More wild. Unruly. Unless I am mistaken, you don't have your associates with you this time?"

While he would have given much to have Madeline and Ian with him, he could save Olivia on his own. "I'll get what I've come for."

She shrugged, not overly concerned with his demise. "*Dobre vecher.*" She stood after wishing him a good evening, apparently done.

He, however, was not. "You still owe me." He pointed to the bullet hole in the rafter, a reminder of when the police had stormed the inn. It had taken all the Trio's skills to save her from execution.

Daisy paled. "You're a cruel man to remind me of that."

He didn't contradict her. "I need supplies."

Chapter Five

Olivia pressed her face against the tiny pane of glass, trying to get a better view of the courtyard below. The carriage had arrived this afternoon. Bright and new with a golden crest on the side. Count Arshun had finally returned, accompanied by a group of three well-dressed associates. Two of them appeared to be young and one an older, portly man. She didn't know where he'd been for the past two days. Blin hadn't known that detail.

Arshun had been followed by several carts full of long wooden crates. They were unloading them below. She couldn't tell what was in them, but the men strained under their weight.

Suddenly, there was a loud shout from the side of the courtyard. One of the crates had been dropped. Pipes? No.

Rifles. Muskets.

She stepped back, seeking comfort from the rough woolen blanket wrapped tightly around her since it offered little warmth. Blin had fought to get her the thin gray scrap of material. Coal for the small stove in the room was out of the question.

The count was here and he wouldn't expect her. He'd expect La Petit.

She studied the distance to the ground from the tiny window. Even if she managed to break the glass and squeeze out, the drop to the ground would kill her.

Perhaps that wasn't a bad option. After all, it would be quick and her choice. But she couldn't bring herself to do it, not while there was any hope left.

"Blin?" He was still her best option for escape. He'd been kind to her, standing watch, protecting her from Nicolai and the other men. She didn't know if he slept outside her door, but he was there when she fell asleep and when she woke. Blin might not be smart, but he was good at heart, if stubborn.

"Yes, *baryshnya*?"

She'd tried to get him to use her given name but he'd refused, insisting on addressing her formally as miss. "Have you heard when I'm to see the count?"

Silence.

She pressed her face against the wood of the door. Blin never failed to respond. They spoke of his mama at home on the count's country estate. She knew of the farm, his dog, and his sister Oksana's suitor, his *babushka*'s gout, his brothers' constant bickering. Silly, simple things. But they had kept her sane.

A key turned in the lock. She scrambled back, hoping to find Blin. But when the door swung open, Nicolai entered, carrying a dress of fine blue wool. "You will put this on. Count Arshun wishes to see you at dinner."

Blin had let slip bits and pieces of the horrors the count inflicted on his serfs. She wasn't eager to see him. But dinner meant leaving the room. And a chance to escape.

She must have hesitated too long because Nicolai pulled out a knife. "Unless you continue to claim you're not La Petit . . . then I'll kill you now and save him time."

She took the dress.

His gaze slid over her, and something like panic entered his eyes. "A maid will bring up fresh water and arrange your hair." From what she'd been able to gather, La Petit had been gloriously beautiful and skilled at seducing men. Perhaps Nicolai was beginning to doubt her identity after all.

She prodded at the weakness. "I thought you were certain about me."

Nicolai glowered. "I am."

"Then why are you concerned about the count?"

"He is exacting."

"I thought Arshun was your friend."

Nicolai glanced over his shoulder. "I never claimed that honor. He is my leader."

A maid appeared in the doorway and Nicolai scurried away. She should have been relieved he didn't try to watch her undress; instead, her unease intensified.

"What is your name?" Olivia asked as the maid began to unfasten her dress.

The maid didn't even look up.

"I won't tell anyone you spoke to me."

Nothing.

Well, she wasn't going to learn anything new from this girl. She used the time to try to think of a plan of escape, but all she could come up with was run at her first opportunity.

After the girl finished, Olivia patted the intricate loops twisted into her hair and shivered as the air slid over a generous amount of exposed bosom. She was glad for the moment that there was no mirror in the room. At least she could imagine herself transformed into a temptress.

She burrowed her face in the scratchy woolen blanket one last time, then squared her shoulders. She refused to huddle away. She'd faced down an angry duke outside the House of Lords, she could survive a count.

Surely, what La Petit did as a spy couldn't be that much different from when she tried to convince politicians not to hang children. She knew how to flatter, how to find common ground. She could spin a tragic tale to make men weep.

She'd even mastered fluttering her eyelashes.

She exhaled. She could do this. If the count wanted to find La Petit, she would be La Petit.

Or at least give the count reason to believe she might be. He surely wouldn't expect her to confess. So if she claimed to be Olivia Swift, she wouldn't need to fear contradicting herself.

She'd hoped Blin would escort her, but Nicolai was there as the door opened again. His eyes widened as he surveyed her, then he pulled two metal bands from his coat.

If he thought she'd allow him to restrain her again—

But they were silver cuff bracelets. He clasped the cool metal around the scabs and bruises encircling her wrists.

Nicolai's hands were sweaty as he released her.

"Afraid?" she asked him. "I seem to recall the count didn't want me hurt."

His lips twisted, but he had to fight to keep the expression from trembling. "Nothing will come of it. He will understand my methods. After all, he chose me for this mission."

His fingers dug into her arms as he forced her down a set of stairs. She kept her shoulders slumped but her head up. She'd have only one chance to escape. She couldn't afford to miss it. After that, she'd either be dead or more tightly restrained.

From what little she'd seen out her window, the servants were still occupied with the count's arrival. She hadn't seen a single person in the corridor.

It was only Nicolai.

Her chances were never going to be better than this.

She drove her elbow back into Nicolai's stomach. She jerked away and darted into an empty parlor, slamming the door behind her. She threw a chair against it, then ran to the window. The latch was stuck. She rammed her fingers against it three times. Four.

The chair scraped along the floor as the door opened.

She reached behind her, searching for something. A candlestick. A book. Something to smash the glass. Something to protect herself with.

Pain slammed against the side of her head, and

she fell against a small table, sending it clattering against the wall.

A red-faced Nicolai blurred in front of her. "Fool!" He grabbed her arm, pulling her to her feet. He shook her, making her head snap back. "Do you have any idea—"

He wrenched himself away.

"What is the meaning of this?" A man's voice spoke in French. Olivia twisted toward it.

A well-dressed youth stood in the doorway. He was young, perhaps twenty. Slight, fair-haired, and perfectly dressed. Two hulking servants flanked him.

"She tried to escape." Nicolai's French was halting, not nearly as smooth as his English.

She'd forgotten most Russian aristocrats chose to speak French.

The young man placed a hand on his hip. "She is La Petit." He minced toward them. "You should have brought guards when you moved her."

If this was the count, perhaps she had a chance after all.

Nicolai backed away.

"You more than live up to my expectations." Arshun's eyes devoured her bosom.

What if he thought she'd be willing to bargain with her body? *Was* she willing?

She exhaled, not ready to make that decision. He was young. Perhaps he could be swayed. "I am not La Petit. I'm the daughter of a papermaker."

Arshun laughed like it was a hilarious jest. "Exactly as I'd hoped!" He cleared his throat as if preparing to play a role. "Do not provoke me. I know you can decipher the code." Then he grinned.

Was this a game to him, then?

"I'm looking forward to our time together," he continued, his voice more normal. "I must hear how you seduced our glorious founder. From what I hear, he was a dried-up husk of a man. If you could sway him, I'm intrigued to see what you'll do for me." He grabbed her hand to lift to his lips, but paused with her fingers inches from his mouth. A mottled flush crept up his neck.

He pushed back the bracelet, revealing the wounds left by the ropes. "You marked her. I told you I didn't want her marked." His voice grew louder, like that of a petulant child. "This is how you repay me for my trust?"

Nicolai pressed himself against the wallpaper. "You said yourself, she is La Petit. I had to ensure—"

Arshun snapped his fingers. The man to his right drew a pistol and shot Nicolai through the heart. He fell to the ground, a stunned expression locked on his face.

Arshun just dusted a speck of gunpowder from his sky blue sleeve and offered Olivia his arm.

Olivia's breath came high and fast in her chest, and she wasn't sure until she took her first step that she'd be able to move. La Petit had no doubt seen many deaths. She couldn't afford to give herself away by fainting now.

Don't look down. Don't look down.

She'd hated Nicolai, but now his blood squished in the rug under her satin slippers. She didn't fool herself that she'd be able to keep from retching if she looked down.

Instead, she focused on the glinting silver button on Arshun's waistcoat and accepted his arm with the grace countless governesses had drilled into her. "You are quite the decisive leader."

Arshun's chest puffed. "One has to be." He placed his hand over hers. "Shall we go in to dinner? I'll explain my plans for the imperial family."

Clayton crept away from the open crate. Arshun was gathering weapons. That didn't bode well.

There weren't many here yet. Perhaps one hundred. They'd need to be destroyed.

But first he needed to find Olivia.

Clayton stepped over the servant he'd tied and left next to the crates. The bald man was still unmoving, but the heavy coat he wore should keep him alive until he either awoke or was found by the next patrol of guards.

Hugging the shadows of the house, Clayton inched closer to the brightly lit window. He needed to get a sense of where most of the people were in the house, so when he entered to begin his search, he'd have few surprises. Once he determined the number of servants and Arshun's whereabouts, he could find where they were keeping her—

Right there.

He'd prepared himself to have arrived too late. He thought he'd find her bloody and broken.

He hadn't expected to find her sipping turtle soup and dabbing her lips with white linen. His own stomach rumbled. How many meals had he skipped in his haste to get here?

She smiled at the youth next to her, a pimpled, sallow lad who couldn't seem to look above her neckline. Count Arshun. Clayton had discovered as much as he could in the few hours before he'd rushed here. The count was spoiled, vain, and cruel, hated by his serfs, and ignored by other nobles. But he made grandiose promises to the poor of St. Petersburg.

Olivia smiled and lifted a bite of chicken to his lips.

Had she made a fool of him again? Was this some sort of trap laid for him? To lure him here? Clayton knew it sounded vain, but why else would she still be safe in the hands of the most brutal revolutionary group in Russia unless the plan had been for him to give chase?

The mill had received a sizable influx of capital a few years ago. Clayton had never been able to track where it had come from. He'd assumed more of her father's suspicious dealings.

But what if they had been hers?

Chapter Six

Arshun unlocked the drawer to the desk and pulled out a paper. "Does this look familiar?"

Olivia shook her head. But rather than scowling at her as he'd done with increasing annoyance as the evening progressed, his chin lifted. "You didn't know Vasin made a copy, did you?"

"Of what?"

His scowl returned. "His orders. Directions on how to contact the agent he put in place."

"You don't know how to contact your agent?" Surprise sparked her words. From what she'd pieced together from Arshun's boasting, in one week the czar and his entire family would be slaughtered. Russia would be reborn. And Arshun would be very, very powerful. From the way he'd spoken, she'd thought the outcome a certainty.

Arshun glanced at his guards, who studied the ground by their boots. His words were clipped. "We simply need to know how to order him to proceed. The old fools who would have been able to break the code have been executed or sent to

Siberia by the emperor. Those *durakov* were going to let this plan fade away after Vasin's death, but I saw the genius in it. I dug through the ashes and rebuilt this group piece by piece. The people will rise up with me."

"But only if you can break the code?"

"The agent is only one part of my plan. I am not a fool."

She wondered if Arshun was who the original revolutionaries had in mind when they planned the rebirth of Russia. "You think La Petit can break the code." She reached for the page, but Arshun dropped it into the drawer.

"You will." He lifted her hand to his mouth and dragged his lips back and forth across it. "Perhaps the translation can wait for the morning."

She yanked her hand away and wiped it on her skirt.

She shouldn't have done that.

Arshun hissed and drew a knife, a glittery ornamental dagger, from a sheath at his waist. Olivia tried to retreat but the guard at her back stopped her. Arshun pressed the blade to her throat. "If one of the former leaders I've sent for arrives before you break the code, you will be useless to me." He slid the blade along her neck. The metal burned as he sliced a short line right under her chin.

She cried out, jerking her hand over the wet trail on her throat. The knife now pressed against her cheek. "Cut me again and you'll never know what the paper says."

She would have said anything to keep him from cutting her again. But she shouldn't have said *that*.

Time. She needed more time. She didn't know

if she could break this code. "I will need to be left alone so I can break the code."

"So you can plan your escape?"

"From that room? It's delicate work. I will need to concentrate." She spoke past the vile taste in her mouth. "I couldn't do that with you there."

Arshun checked his guards' reaction before lowering the knife. He removed her bracelets, then lifted the paper from the drawer and handed it to her. "You will have this translated by morning. If you're lying, you die. And I will know if you're lying. Take her to her room."

A few minutes later, Olivia collapsed on the narrow cot, the page clutched to her chest. Sweet mercy, what had she done? She pressed the blanket against the wound on her throat until the bleeding stopped. Then she wiped away as much of the blood from her skin as she could. She had until morning to do the impossible. She'd bought herself a few more hours of life at most.

She knew little of codes, only what she'd learned deciphering the love notes Clayton had once sent her. She'd known Clayton for two weeks before he'd sent her his first coded note.

She'd been utterly befuddled and slightly irate. It had taken her two days to realize the mash of letters was a code, then another day after that to break it.

She'd been giddy with excitement.

She couldn't remember a time she'd been giddy since Clayton's death.

Oh, she hadn't moped or wallowed since those first two years. She'd been pleased. She'd been proud. She'd even been happy.

But never giddy.

Olivia took a deep breath and studied the characters, but after only a few minutes the candle they'd left her sputtered. She should have thought to block it from the draft from under the—

Too late.

The room plunged into darkness.

She'd die tomorrow then. Or be tortured and then die.

She stared into the all-consuming darkness of the room. She had to try to ask Blin to help her one more time. He'd been waiting at her door when the guards brought her back, and he'd paled at the blood on her hands and neck. Surely, he wouldn't want her to die. She hated using his kindness against him, but she no longer had a choice.

She heard voices outside the door. She waited for them to quiet before sneaking over.

"Blin?"

She waited.

"Blin?" The lock rattled and she jumped back, dropping the paper. The door swung open. "Blin, my candle has—"

Even in the darkness she knew the man wasn't Blin. She stumbled, something deep in her gut recognizing the height and lean strength of the shadow before her. "Clayton?"

His voice was nothing more than a murmur. "Come with me."

The last thing Clayton expected was for Olivia to come to a dead halt behind him in the corridor.

"What happened to the man guarding my door?"

She spoke in only a whisper, but Clayton pressed her against the wall with his hand over her mouth before her lips could stop moving.

Her brows lowered and her mouth thinned against his hand. For a moment, all he could think of was how he'd pressed his hand over her mouth to silence her giggles when they'd snuck away from her father's office to steal a kiss.

He lifted his hand away from her mouth, loving the way that her laughter still escaped even through her tightly pressed lips. As if nothing could contain the joy within her. The exuberance with which she lived. She grabbed his hand and pulled him behind a rack of drying paper.

"We should go outside so no one finds—"

But she didn't want to wait. Her mouth found his. It tasted of berries and tea. He captured her small sigh of pleasure with his lips, feeling warmer, more alive for just holding her. He wondered at how she—

No kisses would occur tonight. If they were lucky, they'd escape with their lives.

He kept his gaze away from her mouth as he lowered his hand, instead searching for some sign of treachery, but could find nothing in her shuttered gaze.

"I sent him on an errand." He brought his lips next to her ear. "If you make another noise, I'll leave you to your captors."

She nodded, a shiver shaking her. Her hand tightened on the thin blanket she clutched under her chin.

But he simply motioned for her to follow him again as he walked, slowing only to ensure the next corridor was still clear. They'd navigated one entire floor before a guard walked into their path.

Clayton grabbed Olivia by the arm and marched her toward the slightly confused man, neither acknowledging him nor speaking. In an organization as varied and unstructured as the revolutionaries now appeared to be, it was far better to act like he was following orders.

"The count sent for me," Olivia said, her voice rushed, trying to fill the silence.

The guard's gaze sharpened. "The count's rooms—"

Clayton silenced him with a blow to the head before he could finish putting together his thoughts.

He released Olivia and dragged the man out of sight into one of the empty rooms. "I asked for silence."

Her wide blue eyes stared at his hands. He pushed her in front of him before she noticed the awkward shape of his right hand. Although perhaps he should let her look her fill at what she and her father had wrought.

Clayton continued marching Olivia like a prisoner in front of him. They passed a maid on the stairs, but she didn't give them a second glance. He steered Olivia toward the room he had prepared with an unlocked window, but she froze two doors down. She pointed back the way they'd come.

Clayton shook his head and tried to lead her farther, but she refused to budge.

She would get them captured.

Was that her intention? The first two incidents could have been innocent, but a third?

He never ignored his instincts. Never second-guessed himself. He should stride through the door and leave her to her own machinations.

But she looked so earnest. "I have to go back. They're planning terrible things. There's a paper in my room that might help us find a way to stop them."

"No."

Her jaw set. "Then I'll go by myself."

"Is it worth dying over?"

She hesitated. "It might be."

"I'll wait for you in there." He pointed to his exit point. "I leave in five minutes with or without you." He fully expected her to stop this foolishness. Instead, she whirled away.

Accursed, stubborn woman. She always did like to have her own way.

Clayton waited a moment, then followed.

Because this might be part of her trap. Not because he was concerned about her safety.

The blanket she'd wrapped around her shoulders did little to disguise the soft flare of her hips. Or the distinctive way she moved. As if she couldn't stand to be still for even a single moment.

But that didn't translate well into stealth. Her motions were too furtive. Too darting.

Yet she did exactly as she said, returning to her frozen attic room.

When he heard her start to emerge, he hurried ahead, returning to the parlor and opening the window before she returned.

When she entered, she was alone, a small paper held against her chest.

She'd come back. And without a contingent of guards on her heels. She hadn't betrayed him.

Yet. The night was still young.

At the window, he took the paper from her and tucked it into his jacket. He'd find out why it was so important later. Ignoring the pain in his right hand, he lowered her to the plants below. She was warm through the blanket, far too light, and a dozen other things he refused to think about as he leaped out behind her.

He'd taken only two steps when a shout sounded inside the house. Olivia had been missed.

She lunged and would have bolted, but he held her elbow. If they had a repeat of her actions in the corridor, they'd be found for sure. "Stay low and slow."

She nodded with a quick jerk and then fell into step behind him. Her unquestioning compliance discomfited him, sparking the desire to tuck her under his arm as he might have done in a different time.

Instead, he wove through the bushes; the bare branches jabbed at him even through his coat. With a silent curse, he wrapped his arm around Olivia to shield her from scratches. She had lost weight since he'd last held her. He would have denied possessing the memory if asked, but he could remember precisely how his hands had fit the curve at her waist. The soft slope of her shoulder.

And now when they parted ways, he'd forever remember the way she fit perfectly under his arm.

No good deed went unpunished, it seemed.

Light flared behind them as the front door was thrown open. Heavy boots crashed through the woods behind them.

She glanced up at him, her gasp condensing into fog. He tightened his hold, ignoring the way it melded her form to his. He kept their escape steady and silent until they reached the clearing where he'd tethered the horses.

He tossed Olivia into a saddle. "Ride!"

Chapter Seven

Olivia blinked, trying to focus on Clayton's back as he galloped in front of her. Her hair whipped around, tangling in a knotted mess in front of her face, and her eyes watered in the cold. She desperately wanted to wipe the moisture away, but if she let go of the strange pommel in front of her, she'd be thrown to the ground. She'd never ridden astride and never even seen a high-backed saddle like this.

Besides, she wasn't even sure if she could move her fingers. Her thin blanket was long gone, torn away by the wind. For the first few minutes of the ride, she hadn't noticed the cold, but now it occupied every thought. She kept herself awake by trying to rank the most sweltering heat she'd ever experienced. Under the steam engine's boilers last August was in contention for first place with the summer afternoon she'd been trapped in the traveling coach in Bath while a flock of sheep passed by.

The ride had settled into bone-jarring tedium. She had no idea if they'd been riding twenty minutes or an hour.

Finally, Clayton reined in his horse beside a pile of timber. Olivia pried her hand off the saddle. Her tears had crystallized into brittle, frozen flakes on her cheeks. She tried to scrub them off with the back of her hand, but it shook too badly. In fact, she couldn't feel her hands at all.

That really couldn't be good.

Clayton swung down to the ground in a quick, graceful movement. He frowned when she didn't follow. "We need to get inside."

Inside? Inside, where?

Clayton gestured to the pile of logs, and for the first time she noticed a door in the center. It was some sort of crude hut. She hadn't realized she'd been staring stupidly until Clayton wrapped his hands around her waist and pulled her from the horse.

He grabbed one of her hands and turned it over in his, swearing. "Where the devil's your blanket?"

She shook her head. Words were too slippery to form on her tongue.

He ripped off his jacket and threw it over her shoulders. The sudden warmth buckled her knees. She tried to grab his hand to keep from falling, but he yanked it away with a hiss. Yet before her hip had hit the ground, he scooped her into his arms. He kicked open the door of the hut and brought her inside, setting her on some sort of rough stone bench.

Light flared as he lit a candle, illuminating the room. The inside of the place looked little better than the outside. The cracks between the logs were stuffed with mud and moss. The windows were covered in some sort of hide.

Logs clattered as Clayton threw wood into a stove a little to her left. After a few moments, a blaze flickered. He moved a copper kettle near the edge of it.

Clayton's brow furrowed deeply as he caught her hand again. He sat next to her, then untucked his shirt with a few quick tugs. "Place your hands on my torso."

"What?"

"Unless you want to lose fingers to the cold."

Her hands shook as she edged them under the hem of his shirt. Where was she supposed to put them? His stomach seemed far too intimate, so she settled for his waist. He didn't so much as flinch when she touched him.

But she did. *Sorry*, she intended to say, but couldn't quite manage. All she could feel was warmth radiating from his skin. Glorious heat trapped under the thin layer of his shirt.

But as her fingers warmed, she could also feel the firm muscles along his sides. The slight expansion of his chest with every inhale.

He was inches from her. So close that if she lowered her head slightly, she could rest against his chest. But she didn't give in to temptation.

He hadn't escaped the cold, either. The tips of his nose and ears were bright red from the cold and wind. And here she was stealing his warmth.

"You must be cold, too. You can—" She wasn't entirely sure what she dared to offer. "Put your hands under my coat." Well, his coat. "I'd offer you my stomach, but women's garments are far less accommodating about that sort of thing."

He didn't smile. Instead, he lifted a gloved hand.

"I was better prepared. Can you feel your fingers yet?"

Unfortunately, yes. They stung as if she'd plunged her hand into a barrel of needles. She flexed them, then shifted experimentally, her hands skimming up his ribs.

Clayton sucked in a deep breath. "I'll fetch you another coat." He untangled himself, then retrieved a neatly folded bundle from a pile of supplies in the corner of the room. The pile reeked of a barnyard. He shook out a thick jacket of sheepskin and added it to her shoulders. "The *peech* should be warm in a moment." Her confusion must have shown because he continued, "The stove. It vents the smoke through the space you're sitting on to retain more warmth in the room."

She nodded, finally noticing the barest traces of heat shimmering under her thighs.

"I think you've been spared frostbite, but it will be a close thing. There will likely be peeling at the very least." He reached into his waistcoat and pulled out her paper. "Now would you like to explain what this is?"

She exhaled slowly. "It is a code. Arshun plans to start a revolution but he needs the information on that paper to start it."

"What does that paper say?"

She shook her head. "I don't know. Arshun didn't, either. The code belonged to some man named Vasin. But the count says there's a plan partially in place. Vasin placed an agent in a high-ranking imperial position. But Arshun doesn't know who and he doesn't know how to contact him. But if he can figure out the code, they'll set the plan in motion and the czar and his entire family will be killed." She couldn't let that happen. "Do you think you could break the code?"

Clayton crossed his arms across his chest. "Ah." Shadows clung to the planes of his face, making his expression impossible to read. He prowled toward her. "Why did the revolutionaries kidnap you?"

"They thought I—or rather a spy named La Petit—could break the code. They said she'd done it before."

"La Petit is horrible at codes."

"What do you want me to say? That's what they told me. I only know that she seduced information from their former leader. Information they think she was able to decode."

"Now you're asking me to do it." Tension hummed off him. Was he upset that she knew he'd been a spy? Or that she dared to ask him a favor? But the favor wasn't for her.

She nodded. "Yes. I looked at it, but I think it's beyond me."

"And what will you do with this code once I break it? Wouldn't it be safer if I just burned it now?"

"No." She jumped to her feet as the paper swung toward the stove. "La Petit was only one way he was trying to break the code. There are other copies. He might be able to read it another way."

"So you need me?" A strange undercurrent darkened his words, but she had no idea what he meant.

And she'd had enough of his pointed looks. "Yes. I've said that already."

"Who will you go to if I break the code?"

Then it clicked. Of all the imbecilic, paranoid, ridiculous—

He couldn't really think—

But he did. His eyes glittered with suspicion. Rage.

"You think I am working with Arshun. That my job is to, what? Trick you into reading the code for them?"

"It fits."

Her palm met with his cheek with a crack. Her hand stung but she didn't care. It had been worth it to knock that smug assurance off his face for a moment.

And she did not feel bad that she'd left a perfect imprint of her hand on his cheek. "They took me because you led them to me. *You*. They think I'm La Petit. She's your friend, isn't she?" Did he even care what she'd been through the past two weeks?

"Then why are you unharmed?"

Apparently not.

"Unharmed? This is from where Arshun held a knife at my throat tonight." She ripped the coats off her shoulders and lifted her neck high, showing the dried blood she could still feel there. Then she held up her arms, showing the mass of scabs and the dirty yellow bruises on her wrists. "These are from where I was bound on a ship for over two weeks."

She snatched up the sheepskin coat from where it had fallen and shoved her arms inside, leaving his on the floor. She'd freeze a thousand deaths before she accepted *his* jacket again.

Clayton stared at her long and hard. If she

thought her outburst would spark any remorse in the coldhearted bastard, she was wrong. "All of your injuries are superficial."

"You think I did this to myself?"

"I've seen people do far worse."

What had he seen that— But any pity she might have felt disappeared at his careless shrug. "Would you have been happy if you'd found me broken and near death?"

"I would have been less surprised."

She spun toward the stove, unable to look at the creature who used to be the boy she loved. "How clever do you think I am? I just happened to have a devious plan in case a man I thought was dead returned?"

"They could have told you I was alive long ago."

"If they wanted you, why didn't they take *you?* They knew where you were. They followed you."

"They knew they would never be able to get me to break the code for them." But something flickered deep in his gaze.

"You aren't positive of that, are you?"

"Where did the money for the new machinery come from?"

The change in topic momentarily stunned her, but she lifted her chin. "It doesn't concern you."

"Where?"

That was an answer she could never tell him. She'd been desperate. She'd found the fresh banknotes hidden in her father's belongings when she sold the London house that was to have been her dowry, but she'd vowed never to use them.

But then she'd had no choice if she wanted to save the mill.

There'd been no way to know for sure where the banknotes had come from. They might have been from any of a dozen other investments. It could have been coincidence that they were all fifty-pound notes.

The money Clayton had hanged for.

No. She didn't know that for certain.

"Why should I tell the man who wants to destroy the mill?"

"Because then I might consider trusting you."

"I don't want your trust." Not now. Not ever. Clayton would never understand her actions. Her determination to restore the town.

But spending the money she'd found hadn't been an easy choice. And now looking at Clayton, all that uncertainty and guilt washed over her. What if it *had* been the money—

If it had been her father's illegally printed money, then she'd used it to help the very people her father had hurt. She'd sworn not to agonize over her choice after it was made.

The lines on his face deepened, as if he hadn't slept for days. He rubbed his palm over his jaw. "Nothing about you makes sense, Olivia."

It was the first time he'd said her name since he'd come back. The familiar cadence rumbled through her to the hidden part of her soul that had never let him go.

Part of her wanted to stay angry at him. To rail at him for his distrust and coldness. But every terror she'd felt over the past few days slowly ebbed away. "I spent the past decade thinking I had blood on my soul." Blood that had marked her. Blood that had burned. Blood that had torn aside her naïveté and made her see herself crimson and ugly in the mirror. "I won't spend the rest of my life knowing it to be so."

If only he could believe that her anguish was real. But he still had far too many doubts.

And mingled with those doubts was regret. The discomfort was foreign and distasteful. He'd done truly horrible things in his time as an agent of the Crown. Followed orders that should have kept him awake at night. But he didn't regret those things. He'd never allowed himself the luxury of uncertainty. It reeked too much of weakness.

But looking at the dried blood on Olivia's neck and the wounds on her wrists cracked open pieces of his soul he'd long since sealed.

"Ouch."

The single word stopped Clayton in his tracks. "What happened?"

Olivia shook her head, but her bottom lip was caught tightly in her teeth. "Nothing, just a splinter from the fence. That is what I get for choosing to meet you in the woods, I suppose." But her words wavered.

He settled her on his lap in the grass. "Let me see." He caught her hand, and after a moment plucked out the dark fleck.

"Thank you." But her exhale was breathy, shuddering.

"Hmm . . . I believe more care might be needed." He drew her finger to his lips and pressed a kiss to the reddened spot. "Better?"

Clayton exhaled, trying to banish the memory, but failing to succeed completely. What if he'd still been the kind of man to pull her into his arms, and ask if she was all right? What if he'd kissed the frozen tears from her cheeks and felt her sigh against his lips?

Yet that would have done nothing but show her the power she still held over him.

His training had taught him not to be such a gullible fool.

He didn't want to be dragged back into all this espionage. The Foreign Office was finished with him and he was finished with the Foreign Office. He wasn't bitter like Madeline had been; he was simply . . . done.

Besides, he had no love for the czar. The man had Madeline tortured for three days before Clayton and Ian had been able to get her out. Clayton had saved the ruler's life once; this was the perfect opportunity to rectify that mistake.

Olivia's eyes narrowed. "You still think I have something to do with all of this, don't you?"

He didn't deny it.

She exhaled in disbelief. "Fine. But will you at least help me send word to St. Petersburg so *I* can warn someone?"

Hell, he'd been in this business too long. "I have contacts at the port. We can send word once we find a ship to return to England."

Something passed over her face, a hesitance. A slight pause.

He wanted nothing more than to pluck that thought from her head and examine it. To know for certain whether she worked for the revolutionaries.

"Do you trust these contacts?"

Clayton shrugged. "For the most part."

"Then we must go to St. Petersburg ourselves."

Further proof she was working with the revolutionaries. Otherwise, sending a warning would have been enough. "The revolutionaries will be looking for you."

Her hand lifted to the wound on her neck but then lowered. "I won't slink away and let them win. What kind of person would I be?"

"A living one."

She bared her perfect white teeth but didn't let him distract her. "If there is a chance we can break the code and save lives, we must try. And what good will it do us to understand the code if we're on a ship in the Baltic Sea?"

He had no obligation to scamper around Europe propping up Britain's allies, but he'd pass the code to one of the British spies in St. Petersburg. Even he hesitated before allowing cold-blooded murder. "This isn't my fight any longer."

"I thought you cared about justice."

"Only my own." He let the words sink into her, feeling nothing at the shocked light in her eyes.

"You'll let them die?"

"They aren't what I came for."

"What *did* you come for?"

A dozen answers vied for his tongue, but finally, the truth won out. "You."

She swept her fingers under her eyes, only serving to highlight the smudges darkening them. "Why? When you don't want me?"

Part of him wanted to deny her words. To apologize for his harshness. To tell her of his determination to see her safe. But he didn't believe in apologies. His mother had filled an entire lifetime with them.

Instead, he said, "We need to clean your injuries." Perhaps once he had her warm and clean, his brain would finally be able to return to some sort of logical function. He retrieved some bandages and salve he'd stored in the hut earlier in the afternoon, then poured water from the kettle into a clay bowl.

He pulled his glove from his left hand and squeezed the extra water from the cloth as best he could. He wasn't about to remove his right glove in front of Olivia. It would be an excruciating, slow process that would be best done long after she was asleep. He didn't want her to see what a twisted monstrosity his hand had become.

Because he couldn't risk her realizing the advantage the knowledge would give an enemy.

Nothing else.

Olivia held out her hand for the cloth. "I'll see to them myself."

He found himself loath to give up the cloth. He wanted a reason to approach her again. "I'll do it."

"I would rather not have you touch me."

He couldn't argue against that. He handed over the cloth.

She dabbed at her neck, her jaw tightening as the rough material touched the wound. Her eyes flashed to him, then she turned away.

Her back was stiff as she worked, but that was all he knew. He had no right to expect her to allow him to witness her vulnerability. He went to the bag and pulled out a small flask of vodka. It might eat straight through a man's gut, but it would also ease the pain and help her sleep. "Drink this."

She glanced over her shoulder only briefly. "If I did this to myself, don't I deserve to suffer?" Her voice was too brave. Too bright.

"No." He needed that tension to leave her spine. The trembling in her arms to stop. Damnation, why didn't she take the flask already?

"Will it kill me?"

"Probably not. But it will help the pain." He stood there like a fool proffering the flask.

"Mine or yours?"

"Both."

She finally turned and met his eyes, and for a moment, something like amusement chased away the pain. "Are you going to keep holding that until I take it?"

"Or my arm falls off." He'd just made a jest. He couldn't remember the last time that had happened. "Take the bloody thing."

Finally, she did. And when her deep swallow ended with choked sputters, he took the flask from her and pounded her on the back by reflex. But he didn't know why he then softened his motions to slow circles until her breathing returned to normal.

When she lifted her head, her neck was clean. The wound there was even more visible. More damning. He held out the tin of salve. "Put this on your neck and on your wrists."

She traded him the wet rag for the medicine.

She again moved away as she applied the salve. But this time she couldn't hide a sharp inhale from the touch of the pungent ointment.

If she was trying to cozen him—lure him into

breaking the code—why did she move away? She had to have spotted his moment of weakness. Why wasn't she trying to wring all the sympathy she could from him? He knew from Madeline that sympathy was one of a female agent's greatest tools.

Indeed, he'd never understood just how great until this moment, as each flinch of her body splintered some part inside him.

As she started to treat her wrists, her head dipped forward and bared a small piece of skin above the collar of the coat.

He'd skimmed his fingers across that skin before. Slipped them into the silken hair at the nape of her neck to draw her mouth to his.

He tried to breathe to clear the memory, but the air was thick with the scent of the herbal liniment and wet with the steam from the kettle on the *peech*, refusing to free him.

The air had been steamy then, too.

He'd pulled her behind one of the vats in the mill. "What is it, Clayton?" Her eyes were wide with surprise, her lips soft. He couldn't look away from them.

"Did you mean what you said in the letter?"

"That I dream of kissing you—"

He cupped the back of her head and covered her lips with his own, drinking in her confession of desire.

He'd known they'd have only a few seconds before her father missed her, so he'd stolen his first kiss.

It had been awkward and fumbling. But he'd never tasted anything so sweet.

"Clayton?"

He blinked. Olivia was holding out the salve. He took it and picked up the bandages.

"I will—" He cleared his throat. "It will be easier if I bandage your wrists."

She glanced away but nodded, lifting her arms.

He gently but firmly wound the cloth around her sores. He tried to keep from touching her as much as possible, but even the occasional brush of hand against her skin was enough to send the blood pooling in his groin. He should have kept his damned glove on his left hand.

The silence in the room was awkward. Their earlier interaction ensured it could be nothing else. But awkwardness alone he could have ignored. There was something more crackling between them. Something fueled by the way her tongue moistened her lower lip once, then again. By the way his gaze couldn't lift from that soft, rosy flesh.

Her eyes lifted, her expression aching with the very torment he refused to let her see. He tied the knot with a quick tug and turned away.

"Thank you. For this and for saving me." Her words were soft and tentative. An attempt to pass beyond the bitterness between them. Like a hand reaching to pull him from the darkness.

One he wouldn't take. "If you apply this salve morning and night, it should heal with less scarring."

"How much is *less*?"

He pulled up his right sleeve, where only faint

parallel lines remained from the three weeks he'd spent secured in manacles.

He flinched when her finger brushed where the scars disappeared inside his glove. Why had he shown her that arm? He jerked the hand behind his back.

"Are these from when you were in Newgate?"

"No. These were a gift from the French." He forced himself to look at her. To look at her and not care about the compassion she offered. The concern.

His mother had been concerned about him, too, when she'd bothered to come home. It lasted until she ran off with another lover.

"Were you a spy the entire time you were gone?" Olivia asked.

"Yes."

"Was it . . ."

Thrilling? Cruel? Worthwhile? What would she call it? Why did he care?

But she didn't finish her question. Instead, she asked, "Are we staying here for the night?"

Clayton nodded. He fashioned a crude bed for her as close to the *peech* as he dared. "In the morning, we'll sail for England."

She gritted her teeth, but settled on the bed, tucking her head on her arm. "This isn't quite how I imagined spending the night with you when I was younger."

"Go to sleep."

He waited until her eyes drifted closed, her long eyelashes nearly brushing her cheek. Only once her breaths were deep and even did he grasp the edge of his black leather glove and begin working it down his right hand.

The glove had gotten damp from the night ride. If he let it dry any further, he might not be able to remove it.

Little did Olivia know that the manacle scars on his wrists were the tame ones. He edged the glove lower, revealing the long horizontal scar at the heel of his palm from when his torturer had peeled back the flesh and then entertained himself by plucking at the tendons, forcing Clayton's fingers to twitch and curl.

The thought of Olivia's face had kept him sane while being tortured. Only alone, in the darkest part of the night, would he admit that humiliating fact to himself. Only a weak man would still cling to the memory of a woman who'd proven herself a traitor. Only a weak man would revel in the sight of her now as she slept, his hands aching to brush that strand of hair from her cheek. Only a weak man would break when she began to whimper in her sleep and go to her side, soothing her with soft words until she quieted.

Clayton stood abruptly and strode away. He wasn't weak. When he swore he wouldn't allow Olivia to play him like a puppet, it wasn't a vow he made lightly.

He pulled a dry set of gloves from the bag. The crude sheepskin was hardly fine English leather, but it would do.

He needed to find out who'd connected Clayton Campbell with Cipher and then used that to try to determine La Petit's identity. Madeline had just given birth to her first baby. A little girl, Susie. Madeline had earned her peace a dozen times over, and he refused to let any harm come to her.

Arshun would have the answers he needed. Clayton would extract them from him.

And repay him for the marks on Olivia's fair skin.

Arshun wasn't there.

According to the frightened footman Clayton had pulled from his bed, Arshun and his associates had fled as soon as Olivia had disappeared. Gone to ground like the vermin they were.

Arshun had most likely gone to St. Petersburg. If he planned to strike against the czar, the city would be his destination.

Clayton swore as he pulled the flint from his pocket. Olivia would get her trip to St. Petersburg after all. He had to know that Madeline was safe. And he was willing to do just about anything to do that.

Destroy a group of revolutionaries.

Even save the blasted czar.

Clayton laid the line of gunpowder to the keg. At least the excursion wasn't a total loss. Arshun had been frightened enough to leave the weapons behind.

The few remaining servants scampered away to the village, not even bothering to try to stop Clayton. There were only about a hundred rifles stored in this outbuilding. But Clayton was more than happy to deprive the count of these ones while he had the chance.

He lit the black power.

There were a few benefits to the job, after all.

Chapter Eight

Olivia watched as Clayton approached the old, swaybacked mountain pony in front of the cart. The creature was an odd mixture of brown, gray, and white, the colors sprouting at uneven intervals on its shaggy coat.

The creature snorted in aggravation, its breath emerging in small white clouds.

Clayton slowly ran his gloved hand along the pony's neck, all the time whispering in Russian. She thought she heard him explain about coming snow. The horse's ears twitched twice.

He soothed around the straps, then cleaned the bits of ice that had formed around the horse's mouth. This was the boy she'd known. Patient. Kind. That part of him did still exist. He might have buried it deep, but it was still there.

"Why did you change your mind about taking me to St. Petersburg?" she asked. She'd been delaying asking the question all morning, but she had to know.

He tugged the crude sheepskin cap lower on

his head. The peasant garb should have made him appear comical, like a poor serf, which was what she supposed they were supposed to be. Instead, it emphasized the hard line of his jaw and the sharp angles of his cheeks. "I need to know how Arshun tracked me down."

She exhaled, the band about her chest finally loosening. "Then it wasn't because I asked?"

"No." He pulled a bit of carrot from his pocket.

"Thank heavens."

That finally caught Clayton's full attention. He paused with the carrot inches from the pony's mouth. "I thought you preferred to be at the center of attention."

The pony snapped at the carrot and the cart inched forward.

"Not any longer." Now she did the things that needed to be done even if no one knew she was the one behind it.

"I find that difficult to believe." Clayton swung up into the cart next to her again. The old farm wagon had been designed for only a single driver, so his thigh pressed tightly against hers. The fact that there must be half a dozen layers of cloth separating them seemed to have no effect on the intimacy it created. At least on her side. He didn't seem to notice at all.

"I don't know how I'm supposed to argue against that without proving your point. If I tell you the good things I've done that I haven't taken credit for, I would be taking the credit for them."

Clayton tucked his right hand inside the folds of his coat. "Perhaps you can tell me the truth about why you want to go to St. Petersburg."

The truth? How could she when it would make him hate her all the more? She didn't know if she could sink lower in his estimation, but if it was possible, this would guarantee it.

The truth was that she'd begged to stay in Russia to keep *him* here. Far, far away from her mill. If she could stall him for just a little while longer, the mill would have earned enough money to pay back the debts he held. She had secured enough contracts before she'd been kidnapped—even excluding the ones that had been cancelled and the Bank of England—so things would continue to run in her absence. And unlike her father, she had known the value of excellent clerks. They would keep things functioning until she returned.

But she couldn't tell him her plan. Not when he might change his mind and rush back to England to stop it.

It was mercenary. And calculated. But it was the only chance she'd seen to save the mill.

Instead, she said, "I told you before, I want to stay to try to save the czar."

She *did* want to save the czar. That desire was unfeigned. She'd spent eight years doing everything she could to make restitution for her part in what had happened to Clayton. She didn't want to add more to the tally. Clayton's death had been a wound on her soul that never healed.

Olivia waited by her bedroom door, her reticule in hand. She managed to throw open the door right as her father passed. "Papa?"

He whirled toward her, cane lifted, his square face more startled than angry. Perhaps with a night's sleep he'd be able to see he'd come to the wrong conclusion about Clayton. He'd see that someone else was responsible for the crimes at the mill.

He patted her cheek. "Go back to bed, pet."

"I'm coming with you to the court. I have to see Clayton."

Her father's face reddened. "You will not."

She'd never disobeyed her father. She knew better. Last summer, her father's favorite horse had bitten him. He'd had the animal destroyed before nightfall.

But this was for Clayton. She lifted her chin. "I will."

She'd landed on the floor before she'd even realized her father had struck her legs with his cane.

She clutched the back of her calf, rubbing it frantically with her hands. He'd struck her. He hadn't hit her since she'd been out of the schoolroom.

She tried to stop her cries long enough to talk.

"Papa, Clayton isn't guilty. I know he's not. I have to tell—"

Fire exploded across her shoulders. She cried out, her heaving sobs mingling with whimpers.

"The boy is a criminal. He used you and lied to you. He tried to use you against me to take the mill from me. You will stay here. I will not have you labeled loose for that son of a whore."

He lifted his cane and she tried to raise her arms to protect her face but they shook so badly she couldn't get them up. She tried to speak, to stay brave, but the only thing that would come out of her mouth were pleas for him not to hit her again. Apologies for angering him.

Her father's voice was black with cold rage. "Go back to bed."

She'd get up. Follow after he left.

"If I see you at the court, there will be consequences."

She curled tighter on the floor. Clayton wouldn't be alone. The magistrates would be able to discover the truth. They'd see that her father was wrong about Clayton. That's what they did. Discovered the truth.

Clayton would be fine.

Olivia had to warn the czar.

"So you aren't going to tell me the truth," Clayton said.

"That is the truth."

"But not all of it."

She hated that he could still read her so clearly. She'd never been able to hide anything from him for long. "You come and threaten my mill. Forgive me if that doesn't inspire openness."

The cart hit another rut, and she caught herself by placing her hand on Clayton's thigh. The muscles tensed under her fingers.

Clayton shifted his leg away from her. "You've done nothing but give me lies and keep secrets, and then you expect me to believe the mill is worth saving?"

Yes. That's why she kept them. "Sam Gaines, a fourteen-year-old boy from the village, was hanged in London for stealing a loaf of bread. Did you know his family? His father, Douglas, worked at the mill at the same time you did."

Clayton shrugged.

She had to make him see reason. "Then the vicar pointed out if the boys had jobs to keep them in town, we could keep them safe."

Clayton only turned up the collar of his jacket against the wind. "You realize this argument simply convinces me that your father failed even more people."

She clenched her teeth until her jaw ached. "Twelve new families have moved to the town since the mill has been refurbished. The Diplows convinced their two sons to stay in town to work at the mill. The vicar was able to fix the hole in the roof of the church. I know you remember the vicar. He would lend you books."

"What I remember is being taken from my bed in the middle of the night and being thrown into a cell that was covered in piss and mold. I remember the beating the guards gave me, breaking my rib. I remember the other prisoners trying to strip me of my coat while I was vomiting from the pain." His voice remained perfectly calm, perfectly composed. But a single muscle ticked along his jaw.

She didn't want to know those details. But she needed them. She still had nightmares about what Clayton might have suffered, and now these new images would fill them. But at least she'd be able to tell what was real and what was imagined when she awoke. "I'm sorr—"

"You know I don't believe in apologies."

"Then what am I supposed to say?"

"Nothing. It is a simple statement of fact."

No, it wasn't. And she wouldn't let him pretend that it was. He might hide his true emotions deep, but they did exist whether he wanted them to or not. "Then why did you tell me? To shock me into silence?"

"That isn't—"

"Because that obviously won't work with me. To make me feel guilty, then?"

His jaw clenched and unclenched several times before he spoke. "No."

"But that's the result. You may like to pretend that I'm some coldhearted traitor, but I'm not. When you tell me a story like that, it tears me apart. I would give up anything to have spared you that."

His left hand tightened on the reins. "I told you so you'd realize your sentimental arguments about the mill are useless."

They weren't. Not if they'd provoked this reaction. But she knew pressing him about it would only ensure he steeled himself against it in the future. She switched topics. "Did you have any luck with the code last night?"

"No."

"Would you tell me if you had?"

"Doubtful. But in this case, it's irrelevant."

"Can I see it?"

He pulled the paper out of his jacket and handed it to her. She unfolded it, the thick gloves on her fingers making the movements awkward. The irregular dark scrawl she remembered from the night before covered the page.

"Arshun said La Petit had broken this code."

"She didn't."

"Have you seen it before?" The letters were Cyrillic. That in itself was almost code enough for her. Her Russian reading skills were even more unpracticed than her verbal ones.

He looked up from the road. After his careful disinterest, his sudden focus was almost invasive. Yet heady. She wouldn't be the first to look away.

"Yes, but we never had reason to try to decipher it."

She had to concentrate to keep her thoughts on the code rather than the fact that she couldn't breathe. "Can you now?"

His eyes narrowed. "Perhaps."

"Truly? I need something to tell my superiors soon."

His hand tightened on the reins. "You—"

"I wasn't serious."

Clayton returned his gaze to the road in front of them. "I no longer play games."

But that meant he did remember. He remembered everything. She hadn't even intended to provoke him. It had just slipped out. An old habit she didn't even remember she had. Clayton had been so smart when they were younger that she'd begun to slip outrageous comments into their conversations just to see if he'd catch them. Ninety percent of the time he had. But those other ten percent had been enough to puncture his serious mien and free them both to laugh.

Bolstered by her small victory, she studied the paper.

The corner of his mouth edged up the slightest fraction, but when he glanced over at her, his expression was empty again. "When we arrive at the city gates, remain silent. Can you manage that?"

She wasn't sure if he was teasing her or annoyed. "Are we close, then?"

"More or less."

"Which is it?"

"It depends on what you are comparing it to. It is much closer than England."

She glared at him. "How far away are we?"

"About four miles."

"What's our plan once we arrive?" She'd tried to ask him before they'd left the hut, but he'd ignored her.

As he was doing again.

Olivia settled more deeply into the sheepskin coat, trying to ignore the smell while claiming the small amount of heat.

The cart lurched to the right, sending her tumbling again, but this time toward the edge. She tried to grab the bench, but her hands were holding the paper.

Clayton's arm snaked around her at the last minute, saving her from careening off the cart like the dozen cabbages that splatted into the muck. For a moment, her back was tucked against an impossibly hard and broad chest, his fingers splayed across her stomach. His breath warm on her ear.

"Mud." Clayton climbed from the cart. The rear right wheel had sunk to its axle in the mud. The formerly staid pony pranced in agitation, and Clayton stopped to soothe it before it hurt itself on the shafts.

Olivia gathered up her skirts and followed him. Stuck wagons were something she'd learned far too much about once she'd taken over the control of the mill. So rather than sitting on the cart now, adding her weight, she began gathering sticks and branches to wedge under the wheels.

She'd managed to place three of them before Clayton stopped her. His head tipped to the side. "What are you doing?"

"The sticks will provide traction for the wheel—"

"Why are *you* doing it?" He sounded suspicious.

"I keep trying to tell you that I'm truly not as worthless as I was when I was fifteen."

"You weren't—" He cut off. She wasn't sure if it was because he realized what she said was true or because he'd been about to say something nice. "If you lead the horse, I'll lift."

"It might be easier if we remove the cabbages first."

Clayton shook his head. "Prazhdinyeh will be searching for you. I'd rather not give them more time to find us."

That option didn't appeal to her, either. "I'll speak to the horse."

The pony turned a panicked eye on her as she approached. She tried to speak to it as Clayton had done, in soft, soothing tones, though she ended up speaking English. "We just need you to try to pull." The horse nipped at her with yellow teeth and she skipped back, switching to Russian. "I suppose being female you probably prefer Clayton, but he has to lift the cart—" The mare snapped at her again. "What exactly *do* you say to this horse?"

Clayton left his position by the back. She thought his cheeks reddened slightly but it might have been from the cold. "I tell her what a pretty girl she is." His voice dropped to a murmur. "What a smart girl she is." The horse's ears stilled.

"I'll give it a try," Olivia said, and Clayton returned to his position by the wheel. But rather than use his words, she tried some of her own. "I wouldn't fall for his pretty flattery. I think he used the exact same words on me once."

Clayton coughed.

It felt good to have it out in the open. Their past. That strange awkwardness that existed in the void between two people who had once shared everything, but now shared nothing.

She continued speaking to the horse. "But I wouldn't believe him. He might change his mind and decide that you're involved with a group of murderous Russians. And don't let him kiss you. That won't end well . . ."

Clayton coughed harder.

"On the count of three. One . . . two . . . *three*." She tugged on the mare's bridle. After a dreadful pause, the cart lurched forward and came free of the mud with a wet, sucking sound.

Clayton climbed back into the cart, and after a pat on the pony's nose, Olivia followed. They rode in silence again for another hour, but unlike before, the silence was no longer brittle.

Eventually, they rounded a corner in the forest and she gasped. The city was just . . . there. Spread out below them. Gently divided by dark rivers and then more sharply sliced by straight roads and canals. The sun glinted off golden, onion-shaped spires, only to be absorbed by granite façades that spanned entire blocks. Red and green metal roofs topped walls of pale blues, yellows, and pinks.

"Have you been to St. Petersburg before?" she asked.

Clayton flexed his right hand several times as if it pained him, but when he saw her watching, he tucked it beside him. "Three times. The first time, I killed a man. The second time, I saved a friend. And the third time, the czar made me a baron."

Chapter Nine

"*The* baron said I was to bring the cabbages ruined or not." Clayton gestured with a wide, careless motion, the normal stiffness along his spine absent. He even managed to scrunch his face as he spoke, completely obliterating all traces of his keen intelligence.

The policeman at the city gate nodded, the lower half of his face obscured behind a heavy knitted scarf and the collar of his gray felt coat. "Papers."

Clayton nudged Olivia. "You have the papers?"

What? Did he expect her to—

"Wait, my sweet. I have them." Clayton pulled something out of his vest and handed it to the man.

Olivia held her breath. Clayton couldn't really have orders to sell cabbages. Any moment the policeman would find something wrong and expose them as frauds.

The policeman brushed a few flakes of snow off the paper Clayton had supplied him, then handed it back. "Make sure you have the proper permits before you sell."

"Always. Always." Clayton flicked the reins and moved into the city.

He'd not only been a spy for the last ten years—he'd been a good one.

Olivia waited until they were out of sight before letting her shoulders relax. Their cart rattled down a street of shops, all of which had written signs as well as pictures proclaiming what they sold. A loaf of bread. A woman's shoe. "You are quite good at this, aren't you?"

"Not good enough. I should have grown the blasted, itchy beard."

"A beard?"

"Look around at the peasants."

She glanced around the cart. All the poorer men had thick, heavy beards.

"But the policeman let you past. He couldn't be suspicious."

"They've set someone else to follow us."

She started to jerk around, but Clayton gripped her knee. "The old man by the gate is police as well. He signals who needs to be followed."

She hadn't seen the old man do anything. Who could he have signaled— "The bread seller?"

Clayton lifted a brow and nodded.

It took a minute for the rest of his comment to register. "Someone *else*?"

"Someone has been trailing us since shortly after the mud."

The mud? That had been over an hour ago. "And you didn't say anything?"

"Our tracker is keeping his distance. I saw no reason to worry you."

"Or you assumed I already knew?"

"The thought did occur to me."

How much would it hurt him if she hit him on the head with a cabbage?

"What did the man following us look like?" she asked.

"I never got a clear look." When she was tempted to glance about, Clayton tightened his hand on her knee, but then he winced and drew away.

"Is your hand injured?" she asked.

He tucked it in his coat. "Nothing of import."

"How did you hurt it?" She'd always loved his hands. Except for the constant ink stains, they'd been like the hands of a farm laborer or a dockhand. Strong. Long-fingered. Blunt-tipped. One of her favorite pastimes had been trying to imagine what those hands would feel like caressing her naked skin. She'd thought she'd outgrown that.

Apparently not. A tendril of awareness twined up the skin of her thighs.

"It's an old injury."

"But what—"

"When we reach the *dvor*, we'll leave the cart and lose our admirers in the crowds of the marketplace. Stay close." He pulled on the reins, and the pony stopped abruptly in front of a huge building wedged in the intersection of several wide streets. Elegant arched windows, columns, and balustrades stretched an entire block. Where was the market?

Clayton climbed down and Olivia did the same, not waiting for him to help. She suspected speed would be important here.

He led her straight through the throng of people crowding around the main doors. Old women carried bags that should have been too heavy for a grown man. Thin, sharp-faced wives had their hands tucked into muffs, children tottering around their ankles in thick coats.

The building *was* the market. Or rather the market was inside the building.

Clayton caught her arm to stop her from gawking at the hundreds of shops that filled the space, and led her, instead, into the thickest part of the crowd. Past old bookstores, past shops selling furs, perfumes, and gilded icons. Past shopkeepers shouting that their silver was the finest in Russia.

With every step, Olivia felt eyes on her. "How do we know who to avoid if we don't know who's following us?"

"We don't try to avoid anyone. Our best chance is for them not to know we realize they're there."

A man walking past with a pile of cloaks brushed her shoulder and sent her stumbling. Clayton's tug kept her from stepping on a hound tied to a metal ring outside one of the shops, but the dog barked in their wake.

Clayton swore and pulled her through a nearby doorway that swirled with thick woolen scarves. He tugged down two, one a bright crimson red and the other navy blue. Without a word and only a few coins passed to the proprietor, they slipped out again.

Clayton handed her the red scarf. "Tie this one around your head instead."

"Isn't the red too—" But then she noticed three other women nearby wearing the same color.

Clayton removed his sheepskin coat, revealing a much finer greatcoat, and tied the blue sash around his waist. "Tuck the old scarf into your coat to disguise your shape."

She did as he said.

He paused at a storefront a few feet away. "Buy a snuffbox and do not move." He dropped a few coins in her hand and left her in front of a row of brightly enameled boxes.

She jumped at a hand on her elbow, but it was only a young, dark-haired boy. He beamed at her. "What do you need? Come into the shop to find it."

"Just looking." She tried to mumble so he wouldn't note her accent. She pretended to study a golden snuffbox decorated with a portrait of the czar, who preferred to be called Emperor Alexander.

Where was Clayton?

She glanced around, searching for him, and bumped into a familiar massive chest. She dropped a snuffbox inlaid with a sunset of amber.

"Blin!" She lowered her voice. "What are you doing here?"

"Followed you."

"Is anyone else with you?"

"No. Tracked you. I'm good at tracking. Had to hunt deer to feed my family." He smoothed his matted beard. "I had to make sure you were all right. Sorry the count hurt you. I should've taken you away. But I was too scared."

"I'm fine."

"But your man blew up the count's house."

"What?"

"Part of it at least. He went back to the count's last night and blew up one of the barns."

Clayton had gone back. Had he killed Arshun? Arshun deserved to die, but the thought of Clayton returning to slay him chilled her. "Was anyone hurt?"

Blin shook his head. "Not this time, but Nicolai told me all about the people the Englishman had hurt. Nicolai was scared of him." He shifted, dislodging dried clumps of mud from his boots.

Is this what Clayton was now? A killer who'd been stripped of all the good things he'd once been?

"Are you scared of him? I'll keep you safe if you need me to," Blin said.

But despite Clayton's anger and resentment, she'd never feared him. "No. He rescued me."

She didn't want Clayton to find Blin. She couldn't risk Blin getting hurt and she couldn't risk Clayton deciding that she was a revolutionary. Not before she could warn the czar and not before she could change his mind about the mill. Keeping him here might have bought the mill some time, but she had to ensure he never went after it later.

Blin's stomach rumbled.

She frowned. "When's the last time you ate?"

"I had some of the cabbage you left behind."

She pressed the coins Clayton had given her into Blin's hand. "Get yourself some food. Then go somewhere safe."

He stared at the coins in his hand. "I'm not going."

Clayton brushed the snow off his jacket as he ducked into the smoky tobacco shop. He had to give the bread seller credit; he'd had to go farther than he'd expected before he lost him and could double back to the *dvor*.

The young girl led him into the rear of the shop, where an old, hunchbacked man sat. "I need information on Vasin."

The old man shooed his granddaughter from the room, then took a long drag on his pipe. "I have nothing to do with all of that now, as you can see." He pointed to his clouded eyes and the open crates of dried tobacco sitting around him.

"You were his butler. How did Vasin pass codes between his generals?"

Oborin smoothed his knotted hand over the embroidered blanket covering his legs. "I don't know." He blew out a long stream of smoke. "But my granddaughter will need a job soon."

Ah, that was the price the old man set for his help. That type of arrangement had been Ian's specialty. Clayton preferred threats. "If there is a revolution, it will start at the palace. Your son still works there, does he not?"

Oborin chomped down on the stem of the polished black pipe he held in the side of his mouth and spoke around it. "Despite all his talk of equality, Vasin wasn't one to trust the servants. He always wrote his orders in the library, allowing no one inside while he worked."

It might be a coincidence, but something had caught Clayton's attention. "Always?"

Oborin nodded.

"What if he received a note elsewhere in the house? Where would he go to read it?"

Oborin tapped the pipe on the arm of his chair. "To the library. Even at night. He often had me stoke the fires there at odd hours."

"Were there any books consistently out after that?"

"No. Vasin was fastidious. Never a thing out of place."

Damn.

"What happened to Vasin's things after he died?"

"Things had pretty much fallen apart by then. The emperor took all his lands and property. He would have had him executed if Vasin wasn't nearly dead from his illness already."

Another useless path. Clayton paused before brushing aside the cloth that acted as the door. "I'll see what I can do for your granddaughter."

Oborin slowly removed his pipe. "The few possessions he still retained went with him to his nephew's wife when he fell ill."

Ah, perhaps this path wasn't so useless after all.

Clayton pushed aside the cloth and stepped past a row of ivory pipes. Perhaps he'd been too hard on Olivia. Everything she'd done last night to raise his suspicions could be explained away. It was possible that his distrust of her was making him harsher than the situation warranted.

Where was she?

He'd been certain anyone from Prazhdinyeh wouldn't have been able to follow them through the market, but what if—

Then he spotted her. At the edge of the shop. Speaking to a huge bearded man. One of the revolutionaries he'd seen at Arshun's.

He started to reach for his knife and had taken two steps when he realized she was shooing the man away, casting a worried look over her shoulder.

He'd left Olivia alone for less than an hour and she'd already made contact with the enemy. He'd given her an opportunity to redeem herself and she'd just hanged herself instead.

Chapter Ten

$\mathcal{B}$lin had taken only three steps away from her when Clayton appeared a few feet away. Olivia lunged between them, blocking Clayton from following the big man, allowing Blin to disappear into the crowd.

Clayton grabbed her waist to set her aside, but she gripped his arms, refusing to be moved. "It's not what you think. He wanted to make sure I was safe."

"And I want to find Arshun."

Her grip weakened, and he shook her off him, but then swore. Blin was gone.

She braced herself for his tirade.

Instead, he stepped away from her. He traded his sheepskin cap to a boy sitting in a doorway for one of his marbles. Then picked a low-crowned hat from the shop behind him.

As soon as the hat was on Clayton's head, he stumbled.

Olivia caught his arm again, but he shook her off.

"I will drink when I want, woman!" He spun toward a man selling spirits, and after a few coins disappeared, Clayton held up a bottle with a crow of victory, which earned him bemused chuckles from the men in the shop.

What was he doing? She barely managed to remember to speak in Russian. "I can explain about—"

But Clayton spun her in a circle, which ended with her back flat against the wall between two shops. His chest pressed against hers, his lips brushing in light kisses across her forehead.

Sweet heavens.

He set the bottle down. "Found your revolutionaries already, I see. What did he want?" But his voice was a growl in her ear and his fingers bit into her waist even as his lips continued their soft exploration. Not so sweet, then.

"He protected me at the count's. He followed me to ensure I was all right."

"Was he pleased when you told him I'd looked at the code?"

She pushed against his chest. "It's not like that. I told him I was well and sent him away. Now get off me, you oaf."

But he wouldn't release her. "Don't resist."

If he thought to punish her, he'd picked his method well. His words spurred a dangerous tension inside her. She liked the pressure of his fingers. It was honest. Consistent. Unclouded with any of the layers of civility they both pretended to possess.

She had to fight the urge to lean toward him to increase the pressure of his lips. To feel the stubble along his jaw burn across her cheek.

"What are you doing?" she managed to ask, as she tried again to pull away, gasping in frustration and pleasure when he refused to let her go.

"Creating a scene." Clayton's hand skimmed down her waist and over her hip. But his hand didn't stop there. He tucked his hand behind the back of her thigh and lifted her leg so it rode up the outside of his hip.

"I know you're angry with me—" Her words ended as his hips pressed against her. He was aroused. And despite her frustration, she couldn't help her body's instant response.

"I'm not angry with you."

"You think I am a revolutionary."

"I have all along. Confirmation changes nothing."

"Except now you are mauling me against a wall."

"Mauling?" He stilled, and she regretted her choice of words. But then he rocked his hips again, the action rubbing the sensitive spot between her legs. She bit her lip to contain her moan.

"You have no idea the amount of restraint I am showing right now." His growl swept over her skin like a caress.

"Even though you think I am a lying traitor?"

"I think of you as nothing more than a means to an end." His fingers twisted in her hair. And this time her hips bucked against his.

"What end?"

He exhaled slowly before he spoke. "There's a woman I care about far more than you, and I need to keep her safe. And to do that I need to make the cabbage farmer and his wife disappear."

She didn't flinch at his words, but she did push at him again. "You're drawing more attention to us, not less." How did her hand end up fisted in the lapels of his coat?

His hand slid down her calf and around her ankle. "I need to send a message."

"What? That you're stronger than me. That you can make my body be as much a traitor as you think I am?"

Clayton hissed between his teeth at the space right above where she'd tied the scarf. He was about to kiss her there. Suddenly, the wool of her scarf itched unbearably. His lips would be hot, soothing.

"The message isn't for you."

A man in a gray felt coat appeared out of the press of people. Another policeman.

As she opened her mouth to warn Clayton, the man lifted a baton and swung hard at Clayton's back.

Clayton knew from the panic in Olivia's eyes that someone was behind him. Hell, he shouldn't have allowed himself to be distracted by her response to—

But he didn't have time to finish the thought. His body twisted into action.

A policeman with his arm in motion. Olivia's face contorting with pain as she cried out.

Clayton caught the baton before he'd even realized what it was and pulled it from the other man.

But the policeman didn't resist, his face pale.

Olivia sucked in gasps behind him, and Clayton

risked a glance over his shoulder. She'd clutched her arm protectively to her chest.

He'd meant to draw the police's attention after his switch from peasant to baron, but he'd thought to catch any blow himself.

Olivia had taken the hit for him. "*You struck her?*" What the devil had she been thinking? Why had she chosen now to protect him? She always stepped aside.

But that wasn't true. A memory rose unbidden of restraining her from hunting down his mother when she'd come home, then run off again a month later.

"She's the one who put her arm out. I was just going to tell you to move along . . . sir?" The young man rubbed his clean-shaven jaw, and studied Clayton a little more closely.

Clayton had forgotten to switch completely from coarse Russian. When was the last time he'd broken character while on a mission? Madeline and Ian would have mocked him for days.

Clayton cursed his arrogance. He should have let the original policeman relay his message, but no, he hadn't been able to resist baffling the minister of police by appearing to materialize in St. Petersburg out of nowhere.

He sharpened his accent and lifted his chin. "Baron Dimitri Komarov. I don't appreciate you abusing my servant." He held out the baton with a scowl.

The policeman rubbed at his neck. "This is a public space. There are certain rules—"

Clayton lifted a brow.

"Perhaps if you speak with—"

"No. If the minister of police wishes to speak to me, he can find me at the home of Princess Katya Petrovna."

The man flinched. "I don't think the minister needs to be involved."

"Trust me. He'll want to know." Clayton tucked his arm around Olivia's shoulders and led her away.

"Ow!" She lurched into him.

Clayton couldn't see past the edge of her scarf. "How badly are you injured?" He needed to see her face.

"You put a marble in my shoe?"

He'd forgotten. "It changes your gait. So we won't be recognized."

"Couldn't you have asked me to limp?" Her voice was tight.

"Not consistent enough." He reached out and brushed the edge of her scarf back so he could see her. Somehow, the slight invasion was far more intimate than their previous position against the wall. That had been the spy keeping his disguise. This was Clayton wanting to know about Olivia. "Your arm?"

She turned away. "More bruises to add to my collection."

Why did that admission sit so ill? He and Madeline had taken many blows for each other over the years. And Madeline had been his comrade-in-arms. His friend. Olivia was neither of those things.

But she moaned at his touch and tasted of honey and roses. She refused to cower. And she had the damnable habit of tempting him to smile.

He led her through a different entrance onto

a street and hailed a *droskie*. The driver's enormous overcoat made him seem like part of the ramshackle cart. Clayton haggled for several minutes before dropping two silver coins in the man's blackened fingers. "To Princess Katya Petrovna's," he ordered.

The cart's wheels spun in the deepening snow, then finally lurched forward. Olivia gripped the narrow wooden seat to keep from being thrown. "We are truly going there? I thought that was a ruse."

"No, unfortunately."

"Unfortunately?"

"I killed her husband. I doubt it's something she's forgiven."

Chapter Eleven

Olivia wasn't entirely sure what she expected of Princess Katya. A regal dowager. Or a delicate young girl with blond ringlets.

The woman who sailed down the corridor was dainty, but she was only a few years older than Olivia. Sunset red curls hung down her back. She was dressed in buff breeches with a flowing white shirt and a long emerald vest over the top.

She also spoke with a crisp English accent. "Baron Komarov." She lifted her arm, revealing a pistol. She aimed it directly at Clayton's heart.

"Clayton!" Olivia cried.

He pushed her backward as the pistol fired. Smoke, sulfur, and bits of plaster drifted through the air. Plaster. The princess had fired into the ceiling at the last moment.

"Pleasure to see you, too, Kate."

The princess planted her free hand on her hip, glaring at Clayton. She glanced briefly at Olivia. "I apologize for startling you, my dear. But *you*—"

She jabbed the gun at Clayton. "Six months. Six months—"

Clayton held up his hand. "This discussion should be held in private." He motioned toward the servants who'd gathered in the corridor.

Princess Katya's lips thinned, but she led them into a nearby parlor. She motioned for Olivia to take a seat. "Can I offer you tea? Coffee?"

Olivia shook her head.

The princess shut the door with an ominous click, then rounded again on Clayton. "You soulless monster. You let me think he was dead. I mourned him. *Mourned.* Not that you'd have any idea what an emotion like that would feel like."

Clayton simply stood there, his hands behind his back. As emotionless as the princess claimed.

Olivia wasn't. "He *isn't* a monster."

Both of the other occupants turned to her with eyebrows raised.

Olivia was a touch surprised herself. Apparently, old habits still lingered. But she wouldn't let anyone speak of Clayton like that.

"Perhaps we should be introduced now," the princess said, her face tense.

Olivia stood again. "Olivia Swift," she replied before it occurred to her that perhaps she shouldn't use her real name.

Kate folded her arms. "I don't know what you are doing with this man. But let me warn you, I trusted him once, then he lied to me and robbed me of what I cherished most."

Clayton's gaze finally moved to the princess. "His uncle and the minister of police had to believe he was dead. Your pain was a means to bolster that image."

The princess's hand clenched at her sides.

"I trusted you."

"Unfortunate. You said you only mourned him six months. How did you discover he was alive?"

"I received a parcel containing a book of William Blake's poetry. At first, I thought it was some sort of cruel jest. But then I put the pieces together. Your sudden appearance—a distant cousin I'd never heard him mention. His missing body. The nonsensical reason you gave for him being on the bridge that night. He'd sent me the book to let me know he was alive. So where is he?"

Clayton shrugged. "It's not for me to say."

"Why not? You were the one behind it, were you not? You were the one who came to me with the news."

"I played the part I was assigned."

"Played? Played? Is this a"—her voice cracked—"a game? It may have been to Sergey. It may be to you. But it is not for me." Her lip trembled. "Where is he? Can you at least give me that?"

"For a cost."

Olivia had thought his icy reserve stemmed from his plans for her and her father. In fact, the thought had been rather comforting. It meant the boy she'd known was still in there somewhere, just hidden from her.

But perhaps he wasn't.

And yet, a memory surfaced of Clayton taking a scolding from her father over some small error. He'd stood just as proud and uncaring as he did now. She hadn't thought a word her father had said meant anything to him until she'd sneaked out to meet him later and he'd held her tight until his shuddered breaths had calmed.

If that sensitivity was still there somewhere, he'd hidden it so deeply that she doubted even he knew where it was.

She had to help him find it. When was the last time Clayton had been truly happy? She might not be able to give him happiness any longer, but at least she could remind him to want it.

The princess collapsed on a settee, her eyes pinched shut. "You dare . . . Yes. I see that you do. What do you need?"

"A place to stay. Clothing. An audience with the emperor."

Princess Katya stood, smoothing her long vest. "Tell the servants what you need. I'll see what I can do about the emperor." She seemed to remember Olivia's presence. "He's a beast. Don't ever doubt it."

She strode from the room, her shoulders straight and her chin lifted at a proud tilt.

Clayton paced to the window. "I don't need you to speak in my behalf. I make no apologies for my actions."

"I've noticed." She didn't like not seeing his face, so she moved next to him.

"It will do you no good to appear sympathetic to me." He spoke so matter-of-factly. As if he expected her to change her opinion simply because he'd said so.

"You're right. From now on I'll shriek obscenities at you when we are around others."

His gaze was fixed on some distant point on the horizon. "It might be safer for you if you did."

"Why do you care if I'm safe?"

She thought for a moment that he might admit to some sort of concern. Some emotion.

Instead, he stepped away. "I already saved you once. I have no desire to do so again."

A brisk, gray-haired housekeeper arrived to lead Olivia and Clayton to their rooms.

"The princess say one room?" she asked in heavily accented English as they mounted the stairs.

"Two." Olivia and Clayton both spoke at once, so emphatically that the housekeeper's eyes widened. Olivia couldn't help looking at Clayton, and heaven help her if the tension around his lips hadn't relaxed a touch.

The housekeeper opened a door revealing a pale blue room with intricate plaster moldings and frothy white lace. She darted a glance from Olivia's muddy boots to the carpet. "The footman bring bath?"

Nothing had ever sounded so divine. "*Yes.*"

"Your friend has room through there." She pointed to an adjoining door. "Bath for you, too?"

Clayton nodded and the housekeeper left.

"Are we safe here?" she asked, when Clayton didn't immediately go to his room.

"As close as I can come." Weariness pierced his response so completely that she glanced up at him. But his face was as impassive as always.

"That isn't precisely reassuring."

Clayton bowed. "Knock when you're finished. I'll dress your wrists."

After an hour spent scrubbing layers of grime from her skin, Olivia shrugged into an incredible banyan—sapphire silk adorned with a silver Chinese dragon swirling across the lower half—that had been supplied by one of the maids.

If she closed her eyes, she could almost believe she was home. Not that she'd owned silk for many years, but the smooth slide of the fabric over her skin felt like sanctuary.

Someone knocked on the door. Perhaps that was the maid bringing her clothing?

She crept to the door, trying to convince herself that she wasn't showing *that* much leg, and opened it.

Princess Katya sailed in. "So you aren't his mistress."

Olivia blinked at the bluntness. "No."

Princess Katya cleared her throat. "Then I fear I must apologize for my poor manners earlier."

"No—"

The princess shook her head. "No. It was definitely a *scene*. And the only thing worse than participating in a scene is being forced to witness one between two other people." There was genuine regret in the woman's eyes. "I can promise that despite what you saw, I'm neither insane nor . . . dramatic." The word was pronounced with distinct distaste. "In fact, most people would call me completely unflappable."

"I'm sorry about your husband."

"So am I." She picked up a crystal perfume bottle, then set it back on the table. "And I suppose I owe the baron an apology, too, if he did save my husband's life. But I cannot bring myself to offer that yet. He deserves to stew first. Not that I suppose my words had any effect on him."

"He isn't as cold as he appears."

The princess sighed. "I thought that once, too. Now I have no idea." Her expression lightened. "I realize my introduction earlier was incomplete. I am Princess Katherine Rosemore Petrovna."

The princess held out her hand for a handshake, and Olivia immediately revised her opinion of the woman. There was nothing so refreshing as a lady who was willing to give a brisk handshake. And the name sounded familiar for some—

"*A Lady Pedestrian's Guide to Traversing Siberia*! You wrote that? The book?"

For the year after Clayton had died, she'd been worthless. Both overwhelmed with the sudden responsibility of caring for her ill father and dealing with her grief at Clayton's death. She'd spent every day with a new doctor who promised a cure for her father. She'd arranged for her father to go to springs, visited experts, forced medications down his throat.

All to help the man who'd just killed the boy she loved.

After the vicar had given up counseling her with verses from the Bible, he'd given her a copy of the princess's book. He'd probably hoped to inspire her to do something more than bemoan her fate.

He couldn't have expected her to devour the book. To realize she didn't just have to accept what happened to her. She could make decisions on her own.

Her father had wanted her to appear cultured, not to actually have any knowledge cluttering up her mind. The princess's book was the first she'd read from cover to cover that wasn't mainly composed of pictures. After that, she devoured books, reading everything she'd been able to find.

And for the first time, she hadn't been Swift's daughter or even Clayton's sweetheart. She had been her own woman.

A crease appeared in Princess Katya's forehead. "Yes. I wrote it."

Olivia knew she was babbling but she couldn't help it. *Katherine Rosemore.* She'd read and reread the book until the pages were worn and falling from the binding. "You walked across Siberia. Alone. Without an escort. You never let anyone stop you."

"Yes. To the continued ire of proper society everywhere."

It had inspired Olivia to form the Society for the Humane Treatment of Child Criminals. Rather than sitting about wishing she'd done things differently, she could make things different. The book had given her the courage to keep going in the rough moments. If Katherine Rosemore could eat camels and bargain her way out of a slave market, Olivia could continue to knock on the doors of the politicians who laughed in her face.

"But how did you become a princess? Your father was baronet, was he not?"

Kate patted her trousers. "An unlikely princess, I know. You must call me Kate, by the way." Her eyes grew wistful. "I met Prince Sergey Petrov at one of my talks. He had questions about one of the tribes I stayed with in the Ural Mountains."

"If he's a prince, then is he related to the czar?" Perhaps Kate could take the warning about Arshun's plan and the killer already in place.

"No. The Russians allow royal families from the lands they conquer to keep their titles. Various princes and princesses are as common as *droskies*. Sergey was Latvian."

"Is that why he was working for the English?"

"I don't know. I don't know much of anything except he worked with that bastard you came with."

"He's actually quite brilliant at what he does, if that's any consolation." Getting her out of Arshun's house of armed men had been an amazing feat. As was the fact that he'd found her in the first place. But why was she defending him again?

"Not really. What are you doing with him?"

"He rescued me."

"What did the baron— But is he truly a baron or is that a ruse? What is his actual name?"

"Clayton." He spoke from the door that connected the two rooms before Olivia could decide whether she should reveal his real name. How long had he been there? From the way his gaze lingered on her, long enough to hear her comment about his brilliance.

He'd bathed, shaved, and dressed in a white shirt—open at the collar—and dun breeches. His black leather gloves were back in place even though they were indoors.

Kate's good humor vanished. "I'll ensure you have the key to lock that door before tonight. So, *Clayton*, if I'm being forced to aid you, can I at least know who we're fighting?"

"Prazhdinyeh."

"Ah, I'd wondered why you'd really come."

Clayton tried to keep his gaze on Kate face. Whose idea had it been to dress Olivia like she'd stepped from some eastern harem?

"Vasin is dead." Kate paused. "Truly dead. I saw his corpse."

"Prazhdinyeh has re-formed."

"Who—"

"Count Arshun appears to be leading it."

Olivia flinched at the name, her hand going to her throat.

She was working with the count, Clayton reminded himself. The flinch was most likely an act. He turned until he could no longer see her at all.

Kate scoffed. "Arshun is a sick little weasel."

"Agreed."

"What has this to do with me?"

"You nursed Vasin in his final illness, did you not?"

"Because he was Sergey's uncle."

"He put a plan into motion before his illness. We need to know if he spoke to you of it."

A frown formed on Kate's face. "He was mad by the time I cared for him. Do you think he would have let the wife of his greatest traitor near him otherwise? He never forgave Sergey for working with the British, not even after Sergey's death."

"I'll need to know everything he said in those last days. Every last ramble. Every rant. You were also given his belongings. I'll need anything he left behind."

"I have a few boxes of books in the attic, but everything else is gone."

"Then I'll need those books."

"Why?"

Clayton wasn't about to explain his thoughts on the code and how it might be broken, but he supposed some explanation was in order. "We need to find something before Prazhdinyeh can."

Kate pulled at a loose stitch on the arm of the settee. "Is it something that needs to be found?"

"Obviously."

The two women shared a commiserating look. For a moment, he remembered when he'd stayed up late into the morning trying to beat Kate and Sergey at a game of chess. The two of them against him. The taunts. The tension. The laughter. For a few hours, he'd felt like a man, not a spy.

But those moments were long past. And he wasn't going to put this mission at risk because of female annoyance.

"I'll also need your husband's effects."

"What?" Kate's curls bounced as she shook her head. "No."

"That isn't a request."

"Then ask him yourself."

Olivia spoke before he could. "They plan to kill the czar and his family."

That had been Madeline's role in their interrogations—to be the compassionate one who gained their target's trust. He didn't like that Olivia slipped into it naturally.

"Why do you care?" Kate asked.

He shouldn't have made the mistake of looking at Olivia when she answered. The sincerity in her expression was too damned convincing. And the wet strands of hair drying in soft curls against her neck didn't precisely help his objectivity. "I have to try to stop it. I don't have a choice."

"If he is forcing you—"

But Olivia shook her head. "I cannot let innocent people die."

Did Olivia have to finger the neckline of that blasted robe? She'd pulled it tight to her neck, but each twitch revealed the delicate line of her collarbone. He wanted to run his tongue along it and trace it to the hollow at the center of her throat.

"But what does that have to do with Sergey's belongings?" Kate asked.

Clayton paced to the window. "That is not your concern."

"Not my concern? You want to take the only things I have left from my husband and you dare say—" Her green eyes flashed and she stood. "Fine. You already took everything from me that matters." She tugged at the heavy ruby ring on her thumb and threw it at his feet. It landed with a thud on the carpet, then rolled until coming to rest next to his boot. "There, you can start with that. You told me you pulled it from Sergey's body." She prowled toward him. "You realize that coming here puts me and my household in danger from the revolutionaries."

He made no move to pick up the ring. "You can send us away."

"You know I cannot, you bastard."

No. Not with the information about her husband he held over her.

When Clayton had told Sergey of the plan to save him, the prince had fought against it, refusing to leave his wife. Clayton had thought him foolish and overly sentimental. After all, a woman could hardly be worth one's life.

Yet as Kate prowled toward him, he felt the first flicker of understanding. A slight stab of jealousy for the man who had someone in his life so desperate to keep him.

He'd never had any woman want him that much. Not even his own mother. She was more than happy to run off with her lovers again and again.

He'd once hoped Olivia would fight for him in such a way.

"Perhaps we should stay elsewhere." Olivia pulled the robe tighter, the silk clinging to her rounded hips. Damnation, was she bare under that robe?

He resumed his pacing to hide his body's reaction to that thought. "Prazhdinyeh may try to glean information from Kate as well. If I'm here, I can protect her."

"Don't make yourself sound noble," the princess said.

No, he wasn't noble, that was one delusion he didn't have.

"It appears I must go to my attics." Kate paused by Olivia. "Do you want me to ask a footman to toss him from your room?"

Olivia shook her head. As she lifted a hand to push back a strand of hair, her sleeve shifted, revealing the scabs on her wrist.

Kate gasped. "What happened? If Clayton—"

Olivia spoke before he could decide whether to defend himself. "Prazhdinyeh abducted me. That's who Clayton rescued me from. That's why I'm here."

Kate's bluster and animosity vanished. "Did they— Would you prefer a woman tend you?"

Clayton halted, his hand gripping the door frame. If she wasn't a revolutionary, then her captors might have . . .

He hadn't even asked.

What if—

He stared at the straight lines of a candlestick until his gaze could focus. He'd cut Arshun's bollocks from his body. That wasn't an empty threat.

Olivia shook her head, but her eyes were distant. "No, thankfully. One of the revolutionaries protected me from the others."

Clayton's hand fell to his side. Had she been telling the truth about the man at the market? The same man she'd risked everything to inquire about as they escaped the count's?

Kate caught her arm to look at the sores and Olivia's sleeve slipped further, exposing a bruised, egg-sized lump on the back of her forearm.

That had been his fault alone. Why the devil had she taken the blow? Most people would have flinched *away* from an attack. He might not believe in apologies, but he did make restitution for his mistakes. "Have the maid fetch ice," he ordered.

"I don't need—"

"Fetch it."

Kate was apparently less than intimidated. "Olivia?"

Olivia sighed. "A cold compress would be lovely."

Kate left, with a frown.

"Let me see your arm."

"It's fine," she insisted.

"I'll be the judge of that."

He gently grasped her arm, trying not to notice

the sweet honey smell of her clean skin. He felt along the bones in her arm and after checking thoroughly, released her.

"Believe it or not, I do know my own body."

He would like to as well. Every pale, silken inch. Holding her this afternoon had been heaven and hell. He'd been so angry at her betrayal, and yet as soon as she was against him, that no longer mattered. His only thought had been the woman in his arms. Back where she belonged.

But she didn't. He couldn't let himself believe that. No matter what his lust told him.

"I wouldn't be so proud as to hide a broken arm. Not even from you." Olivia smoothed the sleeve of her robe.

He forced himself to step away, returning to the window. Ordering his thoughts to settle like the heavy, wet flakes of snow that obscured the sill. But they wouldn't. They never did when she was around. "Why did you do it?"

"What?"

"Why did you take that blow meant for me?" Or defend him to Kate. She hadn't known he was listening. He was certain of that.

She shrugged. "I didn't really have time to think."

"I don't need you to protect or defend me." Did she think him weak? "It will not alter my opinion of you."

"And what is your opinion of me? That I am a traitor? That I am trying to get you captured?"

"It wouldn't be the first time."

She planted her hands on her hips. Did she have any idea how that stance made her breasts jut against her robe? "*That is it!* I'm finished letting you hold my actions ten years ago over me. Did I betray you? Yes. But I was fifteen years old. I was little more than a child. I went to my father because I didn't believe your accusations could be true. I never had any idea he would falsely accuse you and have you arrested. I was a fool, yes, but I never meant for any of that to happen."

"Neither did you make it right."

"Make it right? How could I? I was a *child*. And do you have any idea how my father reacted to the news that I'd been involved with one of his clerks? When I asked to go to your trial, he thrashed me with his cane."

His stomach roiled at the image. But then why did she still give her father her loyalty?

"When I saw him next, he told me you'd already been hanged."

"That must have been a relief."

"I *grieved* for you. I thought you'd died, and part of me—" She swung away from him. "Kate is right about you. You *are* a coldhearted bastard. You don't care, do you?"

"You speak to me of caring? Do you have any idea what happened to *my* father after I was convicted of treason?"

She sucked in a breath, and guilt brought tight lines to the corners of her mouth.

"The bank my father had worked at for thirty years turned him out. No one would hire him. Not with a criminal for a son. My father didn't protest. He was never the type that would. He finally found a job six months later sweeping filth from the gutters." The horror in her gaze yielded no satisfaction to him. Only a sharp, stabbing grief that was as new and brilliant as the day he'd learned the news. "He was struck by a carriage two weeks later. It took three days for his mangled body to die. At least, that is what his neighbors told me. I don't know if that's the truth. I don't know how much he suffered. I never got to see him. To explain—" He cut off, his breathing heavy. Unable to put into words the depth of his regret.

She lifted a hand to his cheek. "Clayton—" Her voice contained the promise of comfort that he'd never allowed himself.

He knocked it away. "Damn it. Don't just stand there and take this guilt. Call me a hypocrite. After all, I was too bloody ashamed to go back and see him." His hands gripped her shoulders, his chest felt like it had been pried open and rearranged by an angry child.

Olivia's hands were laced so tightly her fingertips had turned white.

Yes, he *was* a coldhearted bastard. He strode to the window, suddenly needing something to keep him upright. As if that tight bundle of anguish had been the fuel for some internal fire. Now it was gone. Extinguished.

Olivia was silent for several moments. "Will you let me apologize for my part in this?"

He spun away from the window. How dare she assume a simple apology would—

But she held up her hand. "I didn't expect you to." The color hadn't returned to her face, but the determination had again tilted her jaw. "I understand about your mother, why you refuse to allow apologies. But that means you've left me no choice but to stand here as you flay me with guilt." Her hands trembled, but she clasped them harder until the trembling stopped. "That I will not bear. If I cannot apologize for my errors, then you aren't allowed to keep bringing them up."

Damnation, but she was glorious.

And she was right. He might not trust her, but she did have a point.

The thought was like a kick to the side of the head. A much needed one.

He released a slow breath. He'd relied on his own judgment for too long, both as leader of the Trio and in his investments. He wasn't infallible, he knew that, but often only after the fact.

He might not like to be questioned on his decisions and opinions, but he needed to be.

Strangely, it was a bit of a relief to be challenged. To be forced to change his way of thinking. His view of the world was so entrenched, it was refreshing to be lifted up enough to see that there were other views.

And it took a rare person to dare it. "Agreed. I won't mention it again."

Olivia's mouth parted in surprise. "You won't?"

"No."

It would be more humane if he snuffed out the hope in her gaze before it was allowed to flourish. She would no doubt attribute his agreement to some softer emotions he refused to possess.

Clayton would not go back to the boy she'd known. Poor, gullible, and foolish. He wouldn't be like his father, hoping for a wife to stay who never would. Waiting for friends to pay back loans they never intended to. "My plans for the mill haven't changed."

The corners of her mouth slowly lowered.

He felt as if he'd taken a flower and stomped on it with his muddy boots. But if he was a bastard now, at least no one took advantage of him.

"Yet," she said.

"Nothing will change my decision."

"We'll see."

"I—" He glared at the determined gleam in her eye, the slight tilt of her lips. Minx. "You won't pull me into a pointless argument over this."

"Yes, I will."

He grabbed her shoulders, only to freeze. He had no damned idea what he intended to do now. Shake sense into her? But now that his hands were on her, far different images presented themselves. Her body writhing under his as he pressed her against the wall. The moment when her surprise and anger had sparked to arousal.

A strand of her damp hair clung to his gloves. He cursed them. He hated that they kept him from feeling her sleek tresses. And from feeling the silken fabric that separated him from her skin.

The silence stretched. Clayton normally liked silence. He knew the power of it, knew how to use it. He'd never been bothered by the weight of it before.

But now it pressed down on him, threatening to bury him.

"Baron Komarov."

Clayton glanced at the servant at the door.

"Soldiers are here to escort you and Miss Swift to see the emperor. The princess says to tell you that they're armed."

Chapter Twelve

The maid tried to tighten Olivia's borrowed stays, but despite all their fidgeting, Olivia would never be able to match Kate's more buxom figure.

The young maid frowned, tugging at the bottom. Iryna was an upstairs maid, but she'd proven apt as a lady's maid. "I hadn't thought we'd have to use so many pins on the bosom. I'll need to fetch more for the dress."

"No, this will have to do." Olivia didn't want to keep armed soldiers waiting.

But the maid was already hurrying from the room. "No. No. I'll fetch some. The dress won't fit right."

Olivia paced to the window and cleared a small section in the foggy glass with her hand. Below, two closed sleighs waited by the entryway. The poor groom tending the horses slogged in snow up to his knees.

"The emperor cannot know about La Petit."

Olivia whirled, grabbing the curtain and pulling it in front to hide her barely covered bosoms. Clayton stood by the adjoining door.

"I thought that was locked."

"It was."

"You could have used the main door." Olivia dropped the curtain. He'd technically seen more of her when she was in the robe a few minutes ago, and it was rather difficult to avoid feeling ridiculous when cowering behind a curtain.

"I would rather avoid having the servants see us conversing. The less they know, the better."

She hadn't considered that. "You could have knocked."

For a brief moment, his gaze slid from her face and across the display of bosom visible above the cups of her stays.

Her skin heated as if he'd caressed it.

She jerked her hands up to cover herself, but the pressure of her hands against her too warm flesh was even more disturbing than his gaze.

He cleared his throat. "And I brought fresh bandages for your arms."

The last thing she needed was for him to touch her again. She could still feel the weight of his hands on her shoulders from a few moments ago.

She held out her arms and he bandaged them. His attention was quick and impersonal; he was even wearing gloves, for pity's sake, but that didn't stop her heart from skipping every time he touched her.

"How did the czar find out we were here so quickly?" she asked.

"That was why I made a scene with you in the market. I wanted the minister of police and the czar to know I am here." She could have sworn Clayton's cheeks had reddened slightly, but his lips remained in a firm line, unapologetic.

Ah. That piece of the afternoon finally made sense.

"I need your word that you won't mention La Petit."

Another loop of the fabric. Another brush of his leather-encased finger.

Her breath quickened. "Then how will I explain—"

"I'll speak for us. All I need is your word that you won't contradict me."

Another layer. Another touch. She would be mad by the end of this.

Focus. "What will you say?"

"I'll stay as close to the truth as possible."

"Then how will you explain why the revolutionaries kidnapped me?"

He finally looked up from her wrists. "I'll claim it was an attempt to lure me here."

"That *is* what you think."

He regarded her steadily, the lines of tension around his mouth deepening. And she thought for the first time that perhaps he did have some doubts about her guilt after all.

"Then why lie at all?" she asked. "Why not tell them everything?"

"I won't let anyone else connect La Petit with the code." His eyes were intense, determined. Whoever this woman was, Clayton cared for her deeply.

"But you'll tell him of the threat?"

"The emperor will know the full extent of the danger to him and his family."

She supposed that would have to be enough. "How well do you know the emperor?"

"I saved his life."

Some of the tension uncoiled in her neck. Perhaps they wouldn't need to break the code at all. Perhaps once they explained the danger to the emperor, he'd cancel the fete, and her good deed would be done. "Then the soldiers are a formality?"

"Not precisely."

Footsteps halted outside. Clayton disappeared into his room before her door opened.

Iryna rushed her through the rest of her toilette, finally slipping a gown of pale yellow silk over her head.

By the time Olivia reached the bottom of the stairs, Clayton was pounding a rifle-carrying soldier on the back and accepting a drink from a silver flask offered by another soldier in a green uniform. "No, I swear by then General Mozvan had slipped a dozen of the sausages into his pocket."

She almost tripped down the remaining three stairs when he directed a warm, appreciative grin at her. She actually looked down. Surely, neither the yellow dress nor the plain woolen pelisse was stunning enough to— *He isn't actually smiling at you, you ninny.* It was another act.

The soldiers straightened when they saw her. One of them, an officer, she guessed, based on the golden epaulettes on his shoulders, bowed. An amazing feat considering his enormous gut. He spoke in heavily accented English. "Miss Swift, you're as beautiful as your betrothed claims. How are you enjoying St. Petersburg?"

Betrothed? She did trip down the last stair, but Clayton caught her before she landed on her face.

She dug her elbow into him as she regained her balance. "It's positively surprising."

"Indeed." The officer kissed her hand. "You should have no fear of the czar's approval."

"I hope not." She wouldn't let him see how bewildered she was.

"The emperor is usually gracious about approving nuptials. And for a favored one such as the baron, I have no doubt at all. I cannot think why they ordered so many of us to come. Perhaps he wanted to show you favor?"

"Most likely," Clayton said.

The officer might have missed Clayton's slight hesitance, but she didn't. He'd saved the czar, hadn't he?

After she secured a muff from the footman, they hurried outside to the sleigh. The groom arranged furs and heated bricks around them, and then the horses jerked into motion, the runners scratching across the snow.

She could think of no reason the czar would be unhappy to see the man who'd saved his life, but the officer's presence across from them in the sleigh made it difficult for her to ask.

Difficult but not impossible.

She just needed to ask the right questions. "Darling, you must tell me the full story of how you saved the emperor. I'm afraid you've been too modest."

Clayton flashed her a quick glare, but as she'd hoped, the officer seconded her request.

Since Clayton had decided to play the affable nobleman, he had no choice but to comply. "My regiment was assigned to escort the czar's carriage

through St. Petersburg. As we crossed the Palace
Square, a revolutionary threw a bomb through the
window of the coach. I was simply the closest soldier to the door."

The officer spoke. "He's definitely too humble!
What he has declined to say is that he grabbed the
bomb with his bare hands, not knowing when it
would explode, and threw it into the river."

Olivia sucked in a breath.

The officer grinned at her. "So you can see he is
well-favored indeed."

Clayton pulled the fur blanket tighter around
the two of them. When she would have asked another question, his hand rested on her leg, silencing
her.

For the rest of the ride, Clayton chatted nonstop
about the weather and fashion and his recent trip
to England, where they'd apparently met. But his
hand remained on her knee. Four fingers on the
inside of her thigh and his thumb on the outside.
His hand never tightened. Never loosened. But she
could think of nothing else. Had he forgotten it
was there? Or was he prepared to stop her from
speaking again?

The sleigh came to a halt in front of a vast
palace. Unlike the palace she'd seen in London,
this one wasn't separated from the city by gardens
and gates. It dominated the center of it.

White classical columns topped with gold soared
up the heavily ornate exterior, but as if one column
simply wasn't grand enough, a second column was
stacked on the first. Bronze statues stood watch
along the edge of the roof, their identities shrouded
by a thick layer of snow.

The soldiers led them through the huge arched doors into a hall with a checkered floor of white and black marble. High above, painted cherubs and Greek heroes cavorted on a ceiling illuminated by rows of elegantly arched windows. Two staircases rose up in opposite directions only to meet again at a landing at the top.

And she was dressed in a borrowed yellow dress that gaped in the same manner as her stays.

The officer bowed smartly, then passed them off to a set of palace guards, these dressed in scarlet with black caps topped with ostrich feathers.

"Your cloak, miss," a soldier ordered.

She hugged it more tightly around her. "I'm a trifle chilled. Perhaps—"

Clayton leaned close. "It is considered a great insult to keep your coat. It implies you do not think your host keeps his house warm enough."

Lovely. She'd been in the palace for less than a minute and she'd already managed to insult one of the most powerful monarchs in Europe. She gave up her cloak.

They passed through a series of apartments. Paintings by Rembrandt and Caravaggio hung on the walls as if they were nothing more than a child's watercolors.

Determined not to gawk, Olivia kept her eyes downward as she walked. But the floors themselves were intricate patterns of inlaid woods. Some rooms possessed complex geometric patterns and others intricate florals made out of wood of a dozen different shades.

As they passed into a large salon, the Cossack guards who'd been lounging there in their short jackets, loose trousers, and quilted vests rose to their feet and lined up shoulder to shoulder.

One soldier's mouth formed a smirk as he surveyed her dress from the corner of his eye.

But she put back her shoulders and met his eye until he was the first to look away. She might be embarrassed about her dress, but she wasn't going to let anyone imply that she should be.

Every room they passed through after that contained soldiers who presented arms and stood at attention. They passed a dozen types of soldiers. Chevalier guards. Dragoons. Clayton murmured to her who they were, but she couldn't remember half of them.

Finally, they stopped in a hall so immense the entire mill and half the town would have fit inside.

After a few minutes, a large group filed in. Turbaned men in flowing caftans. Elegant men in perfectly cut jackets and ostentatious waistcoats. Men with medals and ribbons obscuring their chests.

"The diplomatic corps," Clayton whispered.

Complete silence reigned for several moments. Dozens of eyes pinned her.

Her father never had any desire to rise in the social ranks, but he'd had big plans for her. Not because he wanted her to be happy, but because he thought it would bring more investors. Yet in all the etiquette lessons Olivia had been forced to endure, she'd never learned what to do when meeting a Russian emperor.

The doors on the far end of the room opened, and a cluster of men entered. Everyone in the hall sank into a bow and Olivia followed, praying her legs would remember how to curtsy.

"Alexander, Emperor of Russia, King of Poland, and Grand Duke of Finland and Lithuania," a deep, echoing voice announced.

She stayed bent low, head bowed, legs wobbling, until Clayton straightened next to her. In front of them stood a slightly balding man of middle height and middle age. He held out his ring to Clayton, who kissed the air above it. A matching moue of distaste curled both men's mouths.

"Baron Komarov. I shall speak in English for your *betrothed's* benefit."

Olivia understood two things in that moment, Emperor Alexander knew Clayton was English, and he hadn't fallen for the betrothal.

"I wasn't expecting to see you in St. Petersburg so soon," the emperor continued. The guards surrounding him suddenly loomed ominously.

"The same thing keeps drawing me back." Clayton's voice was perfectly polite in tone and nuance, yet his words sounded somehow disdainful.

The emperor's gaze sharpened, then he turned to his guards. "I wish to reminisce about old times with the baron. Alone." In less than a minute, the room had cleared of everyone save her and Clayton, Alexander, and three of his aides. "I thought by gifting you with the estate in northern Siberia I was making it clear I did not want you to remain in Russia. What is it you have to say?"

"Prazhdinyeh plans to kill you."

The emperor's appearance hadn't improved in the past year. He now had less hair and more lines of strain around his eyes. "Again? We thought they were destroyed."

"They're gathering again. They're taking funding from Count Arshun."

The emperor glanced over at the thin, cadaverous man to his right, the minister of police, Maxim Igorvitch Golov, before nodding. "We have had our suspicions about him for a time."

"They plan to attack during the grand duchess's birthday fete while the entire imperial family is gathered."

Golov chuckled, the sound harsh and condescending. "If the police do not know of the plot, then it does not exist." Not much escaped the man's notice, but he didn't always share what he knew with his emperor. Criminals disappeared before trials. Informants were tortured.

"You are fallible as always, Golov."

The other man's nose twitched like a rat. "How will they attack then?"

"That isn't entirely clear."

"How many people are involved?"

Clayton spoke through gritted teeth. "We aren't clear on that, either."

Golov's nearly colorless lips lifted into a smirk. "Who do they plan to attack? There will be close to fifty members of the family. Just the emperor? His brothers? His cousins?"

"I don't know."

"Then what do you know?"

"Vasin planted a killer in your ranks before his death."

"Who is this supposed agent?"

"I don't know." He could feel Olivia tense next to him. She'd probably expected the emperor to be terrified of this threat and go into hiding. But Alexander simply stood back and watched the exchange with disinterest.

"Why should the emperor listen to the words of an English spy?" Golov asked.

"Because I'm the one who found out the information. Not him." Olivia stepped closer to the emperor, addressing him directly, that earnest look she'd used with Kate back on her face. "You must not go to the fete."

"I mustn't?" The emperor seemed bemused by her audacity.

Clayton felt slightly better that the emperor seemed swayed by her sincerity as well.

"The danger's real. I spoke with Arshun. I heard what they were planning."

Golov stalked around the emperor until he stood inches from Olivia. "How did you come to be there? The emperor issued no passport for you to come to St. Petersburg, Miss Swift. Highly suspicious."

Clayton wasn't ready to test whether Olivia would follow his advice about not mentioning Madeline. "Prazhdinyeh kidnapped her to lure me here." He gave a brief, edited account of what had happened and the code they possessed.

The emperor glared at Golov.

Golov bowed his head as if contrite, but a vein pulsed along his temple.

The emperor offered Olivia a pat on the shoulder. From a man as reserved as Alexander, even this small touch was shocking. "I am glad you are

well now, Miss Swift. But why did they think the
baron would come after you? I was assured the betrothal story I heard was a lie. Is it true?" He held
up a hand when both Clayton and Golov would
have interjected. "I wish to hear from Miss Swift."

"Clayton and I were sweethearts a long time
ago. When he returned to England, he came to find
me."

Clayton felt a momentary pang at the longing on
her face, a small part of him wishing it *had* happened that way.

The emperor's face softened. "Why this concern
on my behalf?"

"I've done many things in my life that I must
atone for. Once I found out about the threat to you
and your family, I knew I must warn you. I didn't
want your deaths to be added to my transgres-
sions."

La Petit herself couldn't have chosen more perfect words. The emperor was fascinated with reli-
gion and the state of his soul.

And it was close enough to the truth that she
was able to speak convincingly. Golov's eyes narrowed but he didn't question her aloud.

Olivia clasped and unclasped her hands. "You
must not attend the fete," she repeated.

Alexander sighed. "Do you know how many
threats I face every week? This week alone I have
been alerted to two separate conspiracies. Most
amount to nothing but empty threats. The others
are dealt with."

Clayton stiffened. As Madeline had been dealt
with? They'd crushed her under pounds of rock,
beaten her, starved her, made her bathe in the

blood of prisoners they tortured in front of her. The emperor may have declared an end to cruel punishments at the beginning of his reign, but war with Napoleon had changed those ideals.

The emperor rested his hand on Olivia's cheek. "I will be more alert, but I will not rule in fear. That would give the revolutionaries the very control they seek."

"Your entire family will be at risk," Olivia said.

"We will increase the number of guards, but even *I* do not risk angering the dowager grand duchess without evidence."

Golov's tongue flickered across his lips like a serpent. "We'll need the code, of course. Then you may go."

"No." Olivia's voice was laced with enough steel that even the emperor raised an eyebrow. Clayton watched her warily. She used to be soft, like a kitten that needed protecting; this new Olivia was far more alluring than he'd ever thought possible. "If you won't call off the fete, we will continue to work on it as well."

Golov's vein bulged even more. "I hardly think—"

But the emperor chuckled. "Splendid. It is rare I witness such honest dedication on my behalf."

Clayton studied Olivia with new respect. She'd always been determined, but when she was younger, that had manifested itself as stubbornness. He'd suspected she would be incredible if she learned how to use that resolve in the right circumstances.

She was.

But she underestimated the ire of the man standing across from her. Clayton knew just how dangerous that was. "I also need Golov's word that no harm will come to Miss Swift or myself while we're in St. Petersburg."

The emperor frowned. "Of course, you have it. You are under my protection while in this city."

Golov's lips pinched. "Of course. No harm will come to you *before* the fete."

While the emperor turned his discussion with Olivia to the night's ball, Golov leaned in close, his whispered words for Clayton alone. "Did I not take good care of your other female friend?"

Olivia's safety was the only reason he didn't gut the foul man where he stood. "Not quite as well as I took care of General Chilenko."

Golov hesitated for less than an instant, then drew back. "Ah, that *was* you."

The emperor pointed to Clayton. "You will escort Miss Swift to my ball tonight. I will not have it said that I neglected the man who saved my life." He smiled almost fondly. "Or his lovely betrothed."

Clayton bowed. "We'll be there."

"And to ensure I do my utmost to protect the imperial family"—Golov paused, his eyes narrowed and gleaming—"tomorrow, I will work personally with you on the code."

Chapter Thirteen

"You did well with the emperor." Clayton finally spoke to her once they were alone in the sleigh. Bits of snow kicked up by the horses rattled against the boards under her feet.

Then why was he scowling? "I've spent the last eight years trying to negotiate with politicians." Had he not asked about her at all before storming into her mill and casting dire promises? "For the Society for the Humane Treatment of Child Criminals." She found herself leaning forward in the seat, hoping to see some flicker of curiosity or admiration. "There have been real reforms. Women have been separated from the men in the prisons and we've also made progress on having the children separated."

He gave her nothing. "Why are you involved with them?"

"You. What happened, or almost happened, to you was wrong."

He frowned slightly, but it was more considering than disbelieving. "And now that I'm alive?"

"I'll continue to work with them." How could she not? She was relieved to find that now that the shock of Clayton being alive had worn off, her dedication to the society hadn't waned. She might have started the society because of him, but her work there now was because she believed in their mission.

He didn't contradict her but his gaze searched her as if probing for some missing piece.

There was no missing piece for him to find; she truly *had* changed. "The mill employs three boys who'd been convicted of theft in London. We hope to prove that children can be rehabilitated—"

His face hardened, so she let the matter drop. She knew when a man would no longer listen to what she had to say. But the seed had been planted. One more thing that would make him hesitate to destroy the mill. That would have to be enough for the moment.

She tried to steer the conversation to safer ground. "Have you ever been to an imperial ball?"

"Yes."

She gave him a dry look. "Please, don't wax poetic with details."

His brows drew together. "They are long and tedious." He shrugged as if at a loss. "People dance."

It was such a male response that she couldn't help it. She laughed. She tried to stop. She truly did. But it had been so long since she'd truly laughed that her body apparently decided to make up for all the missed moments.

A part of her hoped Clayton might join her, but by the time she managed to regain control of herself, he hadn't even smiled.

But the lines of tension *were* gone from his brow and he'd relaxed against the seat. And was that a smug glint in his eye? She couldn't tell. Had he intended her reaction?

"I try to avoid imperial functions. The emperor and I are not precisely close."

That had been hard to miss. "I thought you saved his life."

Clayton's jaw worked for a moment. He studied her as if deciding whether to trust her with the truth. "Our history isn't as simple as that. Two years before I saved his life, Golov captured La Petit and the czar ordered her torture. It took us three days to free her." Even though no emotion showed on his face, his left hand tightened into a fist.

The warming bricks in the sleigh couldn't prevent Olivia's shiver. She'd spent the last few weeks imagining what torture might await her, but to actually endure it . . .

"She was mine to protect, and I failed her. The things they did to her—" He turned to the frozen river outside the window. A few people had already begun to brave their way across on skates and sledges rather than walking to the bridges. But from the way his hand gripped the seat cushion, she knew that wasn't what he was seeing.

She placed her hand on his knee. He jerked away from the window, his brows clashing together. But his focus was on her, no longer on those memories. "Then why did you save him?"

He shifted his leg, so her hand fell away. "More people than the czar would have been hurt."

He was just so . . . noble. He always had been.

She tucked her hands into her muff to keep from reaching for him again. And despite what he claimed about who he'd become, he still was.

"But why does that make him dislike you?"

"He doesn't like to be reminded of what he did to La Petit. And although he knew what I was, the saving of his life was so dramatic that he either had to reveal there was a spy in his ranks or pretend there wasn't and reward me."

She blinked at him. "Then you *are* a baron?"

"Indeed. I believe they raise camels at my estate in Siberia."

"Camels?"

"Two-humped." This time she was certain a touch of humor entered his eyes. "Very resistant to the cold."

"You're jesting." Her heart skipped a beat. He *had* been jesting. With her. And it was marvelous.

"No. Three hundred and twelve at the last count."

"Is that where you earned your fortune?" She found herself hungry for the smallest scrap of information about him.

His expression shuttered. "The serfs keep their own money. I don't live off the ownership of other men."

Her stomach filled with lead. She wanted to take the question back. To ease the tension on his face.

"Why do you want to know?" he asked.

She shifted, wanted to escape back to his humor from moments before. "It was just a simple question."

"Was it? Or are you eager to ferret out information to help you protect your mill?"

For once she hadn't been. All she wanted was more of him. "Is it so difficult to believe that I just want to know about you?"

"I'm not a man people want to become better acquainted with." The words were filled with bitter pride.

"What if I'm not like they are?" What if she wasn't the villain he believed her to be?

Her short strand of hope stretched thinner and thinner in the following silence until his words shattered it completely. His smile was as grim as a hangman's. "Then you're too late. There is nothing left worth knowing."

"Olivia!" Kate strolled down the corridor as they entered the house. "How did you fare? I feared Clayton would provoke the emperor into ordering your executions."

Olivia pinned a smile on her face. "It was a close thing."

Clayton folded his arms. "She will require a proper dress for this evening's ball."

"More favors?"

Clayton simply waited.

Kate smoothed her vest with a flick. "Fine. I'll see to it."

He nodded once. "I'll return in time to escort you to the ball."

"Where are you going?" Olivia asked. "Surely, there are other things we must see to this afternoon." Since the emperor hadn't agreed to stop the fete, they had to break the code. He must realize this.

"You have known from the start what my priorities are."

Finding Arshun. Keeping La Petit safe.

But where did that leave Olivia?

Solving it on her own. "Give me the paper."

Kate slowly turned her head back and forth between them. "What paper?"

Olivia held out her hand. "The one that belongs to me. I retrieved it."

Clayton's jaw was set. "There's no—"

But she was done allowing him to lead. She understood that he needed to protect La Petit, but he would have to understand that she needed to protect the czar. "Are you afraid I'll solve it without you?"

"It is a possibility. You're clever enough." He withdrew the paper from his waistcoat and handed it to her.

She stared at it for several seconds. He'd actually given it to her. And he thought that she was clever.

But she wasn't so starved for affection that this small morsel of praise could make her heart pound in her ears. It could not make her knees wobble.

Much.

She lifted her chin. "I'll let you know if I find anything."

But he was already striding away.

Kate took Olivia's arm. "Don't you dare gape. He doesn't deserve it."

"I'm not gaping."

"Like a fish." Kate pointedly turned her back on Clayton. "Come." She led Olivia into the nearby parlor. "Now you are going to tell me what that was all about."

She wasn't sure what to say. "The paper has to do with saving the czar."

Kate snorted. "I figured out that much. What is it between the two of you? His eyes follow you like he wants to devour you whole, and yet you both act like you are separated by a frozen mountain pass."

Olivia plopped in a red silk chair. "Worse." She found herself explaining her betrayal, her attempt to rebuild the mill, and his promise to destroy it.

Kate poured them each a cup of tea from the tray the maid had just brought in. "So what had happened to the mill that you needed to restore it?"

Olivia hated this part of the story. "To be honest, I didn't know what was happening with it. My father became ill and we moved to the London house so I could seek help for him."

"Did you find it?"

Olivia poured cream into her cup until the liquid grew cloudy. "I found many who *claimed* they could help."

"Ah."

The single syllable held so much understanding, Olivia's throat tightened. "Then I stayed because I became involved in other things in the city." And because the house by the mill was filled with too many memories. "After hearing of my father's sickness, the Bank of England ended its contract with the mill. The other clients followed."

"What brought you back?"

"The vicar. He came to me and demanded I return to see what was happening to the mill and to the town. He was right. I'd failed the town without even realizing it."

A few employees, such as Thomas, had remained, fulfilling the few orders the mill did have, but there had been no one to bring in new contracts, no one with authority to act in her father's name. Thomas, to his credit, had tried to contact her father, but she'd never bothered to open any of the letters. She'd wanted nothing to do with the business and corruption of the man who sired her. Thomas had also tried to contact her father's solicitor, but the man had apparently spoken of stopping production at the mill entirely, so Thomas had ceased inquiring and continued to do what he was paid to do.

"So you set about restoring it on your own? Where did you get the funds?"

Olivia couldn't bring herself to tell the entire truth. Shame that she'd sworn she didn't feel caged her words. "I sold the London house, then sold off everything else that I could find."

Which was when she'd found those accursed banknotes in her father's things.

Kate's eyes glimmered. "I'm very much afraid I like you. What will you do about Clayton?"

"I'll stop him from ruining the mill."

"And what if you can't?"

Olivia held tightly to her cup and lifted it to her lips, ignoring the heat burning her fingers. "I will." No matter what he thought of her, she had a duty to the people in her town.

"You don't think being in love with him will interfere?"

Olivia choked on her tea. "I am—"

Blast. She tried to regain her breath but couldn't. Her lungs ceased to function properly. Probably due to the obscene pace of her heart.

Finally, she managed to draw a normal breath, and although her heart slowed, it didn't return to normal. How could it? It didn't belong to her.

Kate tapped her spoon on the rim of her cup and placed it on her saucer. "I'm a firm believer in being honest with yourself."

Which was one of Olivia's greatest weaknesses. She loathed herself for it. Yet she could convince herself of the correctness of anything if it suited her goals. In retrospect, she could always see the flaws, how she'd rationalized or ignored an important fact, but she'd learned the art of justification so well she didn't know she was doing it.

"How do you do it?" Olivia finally asked, staring at the intricate embroidery on the table linen.

Kate set down her cup. "You have to be willing to accept yourself and all the flaws inside you. And you have to be willing to accept the consequences of every action you take. We all have ugly bits, but you can learn not to fear letting others see them."

Olivia nodded, still not meeting her gaze. The red pattern on the linen blurred before her suddenly stinging eyes. "But what if they are really, truly ugly?"

"The people who matter won't care."

Kate was a princess. Of course, no one cared.

"I've found that most people aren't honest with themselves because they fear what they'd have to give up if they were." Kate leveled her gaze on Olivia. "So you betrayed him when you were a child. Does it mean you plan to give *him* up now that you found him again?"

"What more can I do? He was sentenced to hang because of me. He spent ten years as a spy."

"He got you kidnapped and dragged to Russia. I'd say you are near even."

Olivia's hand shook, sloshing tea on her skirts. Could Kate possibly be—

But she trapped the pleasant spark of hope before it could wander further than her heart. She hadn't told Kate everything. She hadn't told her about the banknotes that Clayton wouldn't forgive her for using.

And if she was finally honest with herself, she knew she couldn't forgive herself for using them, either.

She busied herself dabbing at the stains. But it was too late for the delicate silk. "There's too much between us for love to work. But does it seem arrogant that I think I can help him not be so cold? Am I too presumptuous? *Especially* when I know there can never be anything between us?"

"Why do you want to help him?"

"Because it's my fault he's closed himself off."

"And?" Kate pressed.

Olivia placed the napkin on the table, picked it back up again and set it on her lap, and then tossed it on the table in a crumpled pile. She rearranged her skirts to hide the spots instead. "And because I love him and this is the closest I can come to showing that."

Sweet mercy. She'd said it out loud. She pressed her sweaty palms against her skirt. There was no taking it back now, no more denying the truth.

Kate nodded. "Then no, I don't think it seems arrogant at all."

Olivia looked up as the clock chimed in the corridor. She was grateful for the reassurance, and the topic was still too fresh, too tender, for her to want to discuss further. "I should work on the code."

"Can I see it?" Kate asked.

Olivia hesitated, but Clayton seemed to trust the princess, at least to a point. He'd chosen to come to her house and told her about the revolutionaries. At this point, Olivia needed any help she could obtain. She unfolded the paper between them. But after a few minutes, neither of them could come up with anything.

Kate stood, folding her arms, and then tapping her chin with one finger. "You can continue to work. I will turn my attention to where I can be useful. Provisioning." She eyed Olivia. "If you're to attend the emperor's ball, you'll need a dress. One slightly better than that. I know we had to find you one at the last minute, but I cannot think of a single positive thing to say about that dress."

Olivia smoothed one of the gaping sections of the gown. "It smells better than sheepskin?"

Kate snorted and circled the chair where Olivia sat. "We can do better than that. I didn't have much time to work with your wardrobe before, but now I have a whole four hours."

"I don't want to trouble—"

"I built a shelter in a blizzard with less time. I can certainly outfit you. My maid's sister is a fabulous modiste."

Kate called her maid and took Olivia's measurements. "I was thinking I should hold a dinner in your honor tomorrow. If you and Clayton are to be favored by the emperor tonight, it will look odd if I don't host a few select engagements. How did

Clayton explain you to the emperor, by the way? I don't want to contradict your story."

Olivia looked up from the code, her cheeks hot. "As his betrothed. He claimed Prazhdinyeh used me to lure him here."

"Why would they want him?"

She'd asked him that same question, but now she could supply a dozen reasons. The soldier's recital of Clayton's heroics only reinforced what Olivia had always known—Clayton was invaluable. "The code."

Kate sighed. "He'd be good at that, wouldn't he?" Her voice was resigned. "I always told him he was wasted as a common soldier. But it turns out he never was one. So how do you plan to free the heart of a man who doesn't think he has one?"

Olivia lifted her shoulder, her smile as fragile as old parchment. "I'll simply convince him he's still the man I always knew him to be."

There were no revolutionaries.

Normally, that wouldn't be a matter to cause disappointment, but considering Clayton stood across the street from Arshun's St. Petersburg house, it was disheartening.

Clayton hadn't expected to find Arshun there, but he'd held out some small hope that after he raised a ruckus on the doorstep, one of the servants would be suspicious enough—and knowledgeable enough— to send Arshun word.

But after an hour standing in the snow, Clayton had to concede that they'd been telling the truth. They didn't know his whereabouts.

He curled his toes in his boots, his hands in his gloves. Three times. Then four. Despite all the tricks he knew to avoid frostbite, this time had been a near thing.

And had gained him no information at all.

With a sharp slash of his hand, he filled the circle of compacted snow that marked the spot he'd been occupying with fresh powder, smoothing it until it was indistinguishable from the snow around it.

Once assured his feet were capable of movement, he quickened his pace until he was running, until his toes burned from the sudden intrusion of blood flow as his circulation returned to normal. Clayton kept his steps confined to snow that had already been packed down. It would make him difficult to follow, but it also made for several teetering moments.

A *droskie* swished on the snow behind him, the driver slowing hopefully as he approached.

But movement had cleared Clayton's head for a blessed moment. He couldn't think about the revolutionaries or the count or Olivia, without risking slipping on the snow and ending up in the nearest snowbank.

He waved the driver on and took a breath so deep his lungs stung with a hundred icy pinpricks.

Soon the princess's house appeared ahead. The sweat on his cheeks chilled, but residual heat from the exercise lingered, allowing him to check the perimeter of the house.

Olivia would be there waiting for him, her delicate neck bent over a desk as she studied the code.

He stared up at her window and caught a flicker of movement.

Not at a desk, then. Perhaps she paced back and forth, her lower lip trapped by her teeth as she thought.

Another flicker at the window confirmed his suspicion.

There would be a slight wrinkle in her nose. Occasionally, she'd tug at her ear. Her steps would be small and graceful, yet quick enough to be purposeful.

He found himself holding his breath until she passed by the window again.

What was it about her that blinded him to better judgment? She was like a spark in the flash pan. Deceptively small, bright, beautiful—yet capable of creating many an explosion.

He hadn't meant to fall for her all those years ago. She had been his employer's daughter. Rich, a touch spoiled, unattainable. And he'd had no plans to become serious with a woman ever. He'd been too angry and bitter at his mother. But something had drawn him to her like a drunkard to a tavern.

And apparently, he still had the heart of a sot, because here he was staring up at her window in weather cold enough to freeze hell.

He ordered his gaze to trace the perimeter of the house instead, searching for any oddities, any hint of danger or—

There was a circle of compacted snow by the west wall.

Precisely like the one he'd just concealed at the count's house.

Clayton kept his gait casual as he approached the area, but he silenced his breathing, listened for the slightest creak of snow or crunch of ice.

Most of the house was hidden from that vantage point by the thick woven branches of a larch tree.

Except for Olivia's window.

His fists tightened until the seams of his gloves bit into his skin. Someone had been watching her.

Footprints led away from the spot. Clayton followed them, his hand finding the hilt of his knife. The prints were fresh, the edges hadn't yet hardened with ice. He reached the end of the wall.

There.

The scraping of snow against snow.

He spun around the corner, his training making his adjustment instantaneous as he sighted his target, just standing there, waiting. He was huge. He caught the man's lapels as best he could with his right hand to keep him from fleeing.

Although with as much pain as his hand was giving him, he hoped the man didn't try.

Clayton had to raise his knife five inches to be even with the gap between the man's sheepskin collar and his scarf. The man's head was covered in a rough hat. His arms swung as he stumbled back in the snow. But when Clayton pressed the tip of his knife harder against the man's throat, the fellow stilled. He closed his eyes tightly, like a child hiding from a monster.

With the man's height and girth, he could be only one person. The man Olivia claimed was her protector. What in the blazes was he doing here? Had he come to pass information to Olivia?

Or take her news to Arshun?

The man opened a single brown eye. "Aren't you going to do it then?"

"Kill you?" Clayton's voice was low and threatening.

The man's throat convulsed under the knife. The sliver of face visible over the top of his rough woolen scarf would have blended with the snow. "Just don't hurt her. She thinks you are good." The other eye opened, both now soft and pleading, a deer caught in a hunter's snare.

That wasn't the plea Clayton had been expecting. He—

The big man knocked the knife out of Clayton's hand.

Damnation. He'd been distracted like a raw recruit. He dodged a fist that hammered toward his head, but when he reached for his other dagger, his foot slipped in the snow.

A vise clamped around his neck, cutting off air. The man's gloved hands were so wide he could fit only three fingers around Clayton's neck.

But three fingers were effective.

Black dots pulsed at the edge of Clayton's vision, and he found it rather depressing that he might die staring at a limp, muddy scarf.

The man's eyes were hesitant. And his fingers were loose enough that Clayton could still draw a tiny amount of air. "You're a killer like Nicolai said. You must have fooled her."

"Don't . . . kill . . . innocent . . . women." Each word cost precious oxygen, but the fact that he wasn't dead yet renewed his hope. Desperation gave him a spurt of energy. He kicked out. His foot connected with the side of the man's knee, sending them both falling tangled into the snow.

The mountain made no attempt to grab him

again. Instead, he sat up and dusted snow from his coat and his gloves. The scarf had fallen away from his face, revealing a thick mustache and a coarse, matted beard. "You don't kill innocents?"

Clayton drew his knife from his boot, but kept it by his side. "Never."

"Oh." A pause followed. "Then why didn't you take her home?" The man's words were the opposite of his fighting. Slow. Deliberate. As if he feared stumbling over them.

He reminded Clayton much of one of the other inmates in gaol. A simple but kind boy who'd taken up with a gang of thieves. But he'd given Clayton a piece of bread to clear the vile flavor of vomit from his mouth.

The memory made Clayton soften his tone. "She didn't want to go yet. What is your name?"

"Blin."

Clayton climbed to his feet, but when Blin would have followed, Clayton stopped him with a firm hand on his shoulder. "Why were you watching her in her bedroom?"

Blin's face turned crimson around his beard. But his eyes were earnest. "I wasn't looking at her like that. I was just watching to make sure she was safe."

"From what?"

He poked at the snow with a finger. "You and Arshun."

Clayton didn't like that he'd been lumped with the count. And cold began to gnaw on his intestines at the thought of Arshun coming after Olivia.

Because if she wasn't a revolutionary, the count

might. Arshun wouldn't like being thwarted. He'd be humiliated and hurting, ready to strike out to regain some sense of power.

And Clayton had left her alone.

His gaze flashed to her window, but it couldn't be seen from here. He'd seen her in the window, he reassured himself.

That also meant his best chance of finding Arshun was to catch whoever came for her.

He discounted Blin. The man hadn't killed Olivia when he had her alone in the market. Or when Clayton had left her in the house. Neither had he killed Clayton moments ago.

But there would be other revolutionaries. "Have you seen the count?"

Blin's head shook from side to side. "Not since you blew up his h-h-house." The man was shivering so badly it took him three tries to say the final word. He buried his hands in his beard, fingers tangling in the curly mess.

"How long have you been out here?" Clayton asked.

The man's shoulder lifted. It was wide enough to hold a sack of flour. Maybe a sack and a half. "Since you left with the soldiers and came back."

Over four hours. "When did you plan to contact her again?"

"I didn't. She told me to go home."

Devil take it. The more time Clayton spent with this fellow, the more he believed his claim.

But if he believed Blin, then he'd have to believe Olivia wasn't one of the revolutionaries.

He wasn't quite certain of that.

But he *was* certain this man was going to lose

his toes if he kept standing in the snow in those felt boots.

"Come." Clayton pulled Blin to his feet.

"Come where?"

"Into the house. I will find you a place in the kitchen to keep warm."

The man's shaggy brows scrunched together, and his eyes were wary. "Why?"

Because if he was innocent as Olivia claimed, Clayton owed him a deep debt for keeping Olivia safe. Dark horror at what could have happened to her without this man slithered up his spine, coiling tight around his ribs.

Perhaps she *had* been quick enough to keep herself alive with Blin's help.

"Because Olivia would want me to."

Chapter Fourteen

Not being a particularly religious man, Clayton had never thought to be divinely punished for his past sins.

He was fast altering his opinion.

He'd heard voices in Olivia's room when he'd come upstairs. So he did what he'd been trained to do—spy. He'd meant to crack open the adjoining door to get a visual on the occupants, then ease it closed again and simply listen for anything interesting.

He had a dozen things he hoped to glean. Ensuring she was safe. Making sure she wasn't passing information. Watching her interact with others to see if her interaction with him was false.

Now he just wanted to remember how to breathe.

The modiste stripped another gown from Olivia with a click of her tongue. "The alterations would take much too long."

Every bit of Olivia—from her lush lower lip to the honey and cream of her skin—made his body ache as it hadn't in years.

Today in the market he'd thought he'd lose control like a green youth at the feel of her. But that interaction had been clouded with anger, suspicion.

Now there was nothing to distract him from the thud of his heart against his rib cage or the swell of her bosom that peeked over the cups of her stays. The sudden itchiness on his palms or the sweet curve of her waist. The pressure in his groin or the brush of a curl across her cheek.

" . . . quite chilly. I expect the port to freeze over completely in a matter of days." Kate and Olivia chatted nonstop about everything from books to ancient tribal customs. Now they'd moved on to St. Petersburg.

"The ocean freezes?" Olivia asked.

"Entirely. People take sleighs across the ocean from St. Petersburg to Cronstadt. Although once a count waited too long and . . ."

The talk was quick and witty. Both women were relaxed and constantly doubled over with laughter.

Because he wasn't there.

The door jerked under Clayton's hand and he forced his grip on the handle to soften. He was being a fool. There was no reason to be watching. The women could be heard perfectly well through the closed door.

The modiste slipped another dress over Olivia's head.

Clayton stilled.

All three women sucked in a breath.

The high-waisted ivory silk skimmed over her form like she'd been dipped in cream. The bodice drew the eye with dozens of seed pearls that shimmered. Long, elegant sleeves covered the bandages on her wrists. The neckline was so wide it fully displayed the smooth line of her shoulder.

There she was. The creature of money and prestige. The girl who'd once had her father change the upholstery in the coach to match her dress. The girl who threw out a pair of slippers because they didn't have *enough* gold thread. The girl who turned up her nose in revulsion when she found Clayton eating something as common as porridge.

He should have despised her.

But hell if he didn't want to trace his fingers over each pearl. He wanted to weave a dozen more into her soft hair. He wanted pearls to dangle from each of her delicate ears.

After a lingering strum of her fingers down the side of the bodice. Olivia shook her head. "I'll go with the blue satin."

Impossible. Clayton had to let go of the handle to keep from charging into the room and demanding to know if she was insane. It was obvious she adored the gown.

"But the ivory was made for you," Kate said. Clayton thought that was a rather blatant understatement.

"I'll wear the blue."

"If it is the cost," Kate said, "it is truly nothing to me. It would be a pleasure to buy it for you."

"I appreciate your kindness, but it's not necessary." She sounded entirely sincere, but her fingers dropped to the silk skirt once more. "A simple dress will do."

He'd never known Olivia to deny herself any treat. In fact, she'd often demanded them. Nothing had made her happier than when he'd saved enough to buy her some trinket.

Then again, she'd been wearing that cheaply tailored dress when he'd found her at the mill. And not once had she complained about the peasant clothing and poor-fitting gowns she'd been dressed in since.

She had changed. There was no denying that truth now. But how much of her was good and how much was him wanting her to be so? Wanting an excuse for his fascination? Looking for a reason to be able to take her back?

Was this the pull his mother had over his father? Clayton had never understood how his father could keep taking her back. Once she'd even had her former lover drop her off on the doorstep, and his father had still allowed her in. If this was the tug that he felt—

No. He didn't understand it. He wouldn't.

Clayton returned his focus to the other room. Olivia resisted the arguments of both Kate and the modiste, and soon she was left alone to rest. She stood and stretched, hands high above her head, back arched. Then with unconcerned, leisurely deliberation, she slipped off her dressing gown and then her stays, leaving her clad only in her shift.

She reached down to grasp the hem and slowly, so slowly, lifted it. It skimmed past her knees. Clayton could hear nothing but his pulse echoing in his ears.

If he valued his sanity, he'd move away now. The thoughts of what she might do alone and naked shuddered through him.

The linen lifted another quarter inch, revealing the pale skin of her thighs.

At least close your eyes. Give her privacy. He was no longer a lad waiting by the window of the mill to catch a glimpse of her as she arrived with her father.

Another quarter inch . . .

But she dropped the shift, letting it fall back to her calves. "Was that enough of a show for you?"

He scrambled rather gracelessly back to dodge the door swinging open from her adjoining room.

He tried to look nonchalant, perhaps a bit imposing, though he doubted how effective he was with either. His breathing he could control, but not the heat that colored his face, and not the lingering hunger that possessed his body.

"Learn anything?" she asked, her hands planted on her hips, a single brow raised.

That he could see the outline of her nipples through the thin, white linen. That they were a dusky pink. That they were jutting in the cold. Why the devil wasn't she wearing flannel?

"That's what you wanted, wasn't it? To spy on me and find proof that I'm working for the revolutionaries?"

"How long have you known I was there?"

There was a flush of something on her cheeks as well. Amusement? Arousal? "You groaned."

"I did not."

Now there was definitely amusement on her face. "The first time my dress came off. And you had the door practically halfway open by the end."

Absolute disaster. But he wasn't about to let her know that. "Why didn't you get the dress?"

"I did get a dress."

"The white one."

Her bare toes dug into the carpet, and she fingered the linen of her shift. "I didn't need it. And Kate is already beyond generous to let us stay here despite the risk we pose. Why do you care?"

Why *did* he care? Why was he still upset she didn't choose the dress she loved? He reached out a finger, tracing it along where the neckline of the ivory dress had fallen. Over the rounded slope of her shoulder, across the sharp angle of her collarbone, ending at the slight valley that dipped between her breasts. "Because I don't know what to make of you."

Her chest lifted and fell with shuddered quickness. "I am a woman. A woman who has made some terrible mistakes." Her eyes dropped from his, and regret and something darker crossed her features. "But I am a still just a woman."

She lifted her eyes to him again, and their gazes locked. The blue of her eyes was nearly gone, hidden by the black of her pupils.

Clayton jerked his hand away and clenched it behind him. Did he have so little pride? That all she had to do was gaze up longingly at him and he'd throw himself at her feet? He refused to return to being the same lad who jumped at every footstep in gaol because he was convinced she'd gotten help and come for him. "Did you have any luck on the code?"

She blinked twice and her breathing slowed. She rubbed her arms as if to warm them. "No. I think I need your help. I tried the things I know, but I can't find any pattern to know where to start. Did you find Arshun?"

"Not yet."

"How will you?"

By using Olivia. Either she was working for the revolutionaries and she'd eventually try to make contact with them . . .

Or the revolutionaries would try to find her.

Either way, Clayton had his bait.

Chapter Fifteen

"*If* you need to use the chamber pot, I'd hurry and do it now before your glowering escort returns," Kate whispered behind her fan. She'd changed from breeches into a simple yet elegant gown of crimson silk edged with black fur. "Really, the man is taking his role of overprotective betrothed far too seriously."

Olivia couldn't keep her gaze from sliding to where Clayton stood conversing with a group of soldiers. His eyes lifted immediately, sweeping over her before returning back to the group.

Her hand skimmed the neckline of her ivory gown. When the box from the modiste had come an hour ago, it had contained the ivory dress rather than the blue. There was no time to try to exchange it. When she'd asked Clayton about the switch, his lips had lifted in a satisfied smirk.

"Shall I ask the empress to have him locked up for the rest of the ball so you can dance with someone else?"

Kate, Olivia had quickly learned, was a favorite confidante of the empress.

"No. In fact, I believe I can dance with someone else right now."

One of the gentlemen grouped around Kate offered Olivia his hand and led her to the dance floor.

When she returned at the end of the set, she expected Clayton to be waiting, but he must have felt like he'd played his role of betrothed well enough. For the next hour, she danced with half a dozen men and was introduced to countless more, but Clayton made no attempt to return to her side. He always stood somewhere nearby, however, just close enough that she could never draw a full breath of air, that her shoulders could never unknot.

Olivia surveyed the crowd swirling around the glittering ballroom, trying to shake him from her thoughts. She was attending an imperial ball. Something far beyond the dreams of a mill owner's daughter. She wouldn't let him consume all her attention. When she returned home, her friends would want details. For instance, the lush tropical trees that lined the walls. Despite the two feet of snow outside, ripe oranges and lemons dangled from the branches.

But even this made her think of the time Clayton had tucked a peach blossom in her hair.

And there he was again, his shoulder propped against the wall with negligent grace. He appeared to be in conversation with two blond women, but his gaze was pinned on Olivia. Despite the hopeful entreaty she put on her face, his gaze shifted past her and he stayed with his current companions.

The room suddenly became oppressive with perfume and sweaty bodies. Her throat burned with each inhale.

"I think I need some air," she whispered to Kate.

Kate cut off the angular young cavalry officer who argued with her about the value of mountain ponies versus purebred Arabians. "I can go with you."

Olivia shook her head. She just needed to get . . . away.

She forced her way through the crowd before Kate could protest. She stepped on three sets of toes, and had to use her elbows twice before she was able to stake claim to a small open window in the corner of the ballroom.

The air inside the insufferable ballroom was so warm, it turned as thick and heavy as smoke as it fled into the night sky.

Olivia rested her hand against the sill and debated sticking her head all the way out. Behind her, women tittered and men murmured; the cadence of the language and the occasional enthusiastic exclamation were the only things that set it apart from its English equivalent.

She sucked in the icy breeze, ignoring the goose bumps that rose over her skin. It did clear her head somewhat.

She couldn't let herself be disappointed. She'd made progress with Clayton. The fact that he'd arranged for her to have the dress she admired could only be good. He *was* softening. She refused to give up.

Hands clamped on her waist.

"What the devil were you thinking, going off by

yourself?" Clayton whirled her about and pulled her tight against his chest. His face was pale, yet arranged into angry slashes. He exhaled with measured control as if trying to master his rage.

She shoved against his hands, but he wouldn't be budged. He'd ignored her all evening, then thought he could castigate her for going to the window? "I didn't leave the ballroom." It wasn't as if she'd even walked more than a few dozen feet away.

"Why didn't you take Kate with you?"

"Because I wanted a moment alone." She glared at him. "Which you are spoiling. So *good evening.*"

Clayton knew he was overreacting. But damnation, he hadn't been able to find her. He caught Olivia's wrist and tugged her through the door to the right and out into the corridor before they attracted even more attention.

Her breasts strained against her bodice with each breath and her hand dug rather painfully into his damaged hand, but he still couldn't let go. It was as if his body hadn't yet registered what his eyes knew.

She was safe.

It was with vague surprise that he realized he'd pressed her against the wall in a deserted parlor. He released her arm, moving his hands to the wall on either side of her head. His calming breaths did nothing but bring the scent of her deeper into his lungs. Until he knew he'd never be able to walk past jasmine without searching for the underlying scent of this woman.

She was innocent. She wasn't a revolutionary.

He finally had to accept it. Apparently, his heart had already believed it. When he'd lost sight of her, he hadn't thought once about her making contact with the revolutionaries; his only thought had been that he'd failed her. That someone had hurt her. That he should have warned her about his fears. That he shouldn't have placed her in the ballroom like a rabbit before the hounds.

He ran his hand down her cheek, only to earn a glare.

"*Dobre vecher*, if that makes what I said clearer," she said.

"I shouldn't have let you out of my sight. I was . . ." Was he truly about to admit this? Yes, apparently. " . . . concerned."

Her gaze softened, and after a hint of deliberation, she caught his hand, trapping it against her cheek. The tension eased from her spine. And her lips softened, nudging upward to a satisfied angle.

It should have pleased him, but it didn't. She shouldn't forgive him. Not that easily. The warmth of her skin through his gloves was like a brand of guilt.

"Ask me." The words rasped from him. "Ask me why I was so concerned."

She blinked, her brows drawing together. "What?"

"Ask me about my plans for the evening. Ask me how I'd hoped the revolutionaries would come after you so I could catch them."

She paled and pressed herself hard against the wall. Away from him. But then something in her face shifted. A new determination set her jaw, and she cupped his face. "What if I asked why you're telling me your plan now? Why not continue to sit back and observe?"

Because the thought of anything happening to her had eaten at him like acid. And there was no way in hell he'd ever intentionally risk her again. "Because I want you too damned much."

But he had to make her see that he wasn't noble. She wasn't the only one to make mistakes. That the light in her eye was misplaced.

So he kissed her. His kiss was hard and cruel, his fingers tangling in the hair at the base of her scalp. It was a kiss meant to punish. To convince. But when her hands settled on the smooth wool of his jacket, they didn't push him away.

They pulled him closer.

A sudden release of tension weakened his knees. He opened his lips with silent desperation. He didn't want her to push him away. He needed this too much. Comfort. Solace. *Her.* Things he'd sworn he had no need of when they parted. "A good man would walk away," he said.

He cupped the back of her head, his thumb soothing the delicate skin below it. His other hand followed her buttons down her back to her bottom. "I'm not a good man any longer."

Olivia gasped at his boldness, then rocked her hips to meet his. This embrace was nothing like the sweet fumbles they'd exchanged as children. This was as dark and disillusioned as he'd become. "No, you are far better."

His growl sounded like both disagreement and longing. He wrenched himself away, and for the first time, she saw him. Not Clayton the cold-hearted spy, and not the innocent boy she'd once known, but some mixture of both. Wild. Aroused. Hurting. It was there in the defiant set of his shoulders. In the agony in his eyes. In the slight tremor of his hands.

Before she could inhale, he buried those emotions deep, leaving himself hardened and emotionless once again.

But his shield fell too late.

She surmised that his gaze was supposed to discomfit her now, but she met the steel in his eyes calmly. Or at least as calmly as her still pounding heart and tingling skin would allow.

She'd been wrong to think she could help him go back to the boy she'd known. That innocent, tender boy *had* been sacrificed by her foolishness all those years ago. But the man he'd been forced to become wasn't dreadful, as Clayton seemed to think. In fact, the things she'd admired most about the boy had survived, just reforged. Tempered. Strengthened.

And she'd do everything in her power to ensure he saw it, too.

Chapter Sixteen

Olivia nodded at the professor next to her at the imperial dining table. He taught chemistry at one of the universities, and surprisingly enough, they'd managed to find a topic of discussion: bleaches for paper manufacture. It was actually a topic she should have been able to pay more attention to; after all, it directly affected the mill. But as much as she focused, she couldn't keep her gaze from straying to where Clayton sat near the emperor and empress at the head of the impossibly long table, several hundred guests away.

He was watching her, his gaze dark and intense.

She knew she should be angry that he'd chosen to use her as bait, and part of her *was*. But most of her was stunned that he'd admitted to it.

And how had she never known her body could ignite like that? She'd assumed her expectations of lovemaking were nothing but fantasy. That her memories of what she'd shared with Clayton had become exaggerated with time.

There had been no exaggeration.

A footman reached past her, and Olivia let him take the plate even though she'd wanted to eat that last bit of meat. As soon as this course was removed, she could speak with the man on her left.

Golov.

He shouldn't be sitting by her. His rank was high and hers, nonexistent. A countess across the table cooed that it was an honor to have been singled out for attention by such a favored gentleman.

She'd spoken to him once during the soup remove. But that had been simple pleasantries. Why yes, she did like St. Petersburg. No, she hadn't had a chance to see any of the glorious churches. No, she hadn't heard about the fairs going on this week in celebration of some saint's day.

But this would be her chance. She had to ensure he believed the threat to the czar. "You must convince the czar to cancel the fete."

Golov shifted forward in his seat. "Is that so?"

The footman set another plate in front of her. She waited until he moved away before she spoke.

"Arshun is intent on this revolution."

"The count is an immature fool." He straightened the cuffs of his black coat.

"Yes, but he'll carry out this revolution. He's hungry for power." She took a risk. "A man in your position can't appear ignorant when the attack comes."

"Ah, perhaps you do interest me after all." A faint smile thinned his lips. "That is a bold gambit."

"We don't have time for anything else."

"Nice use of the word *we*. Now, perhaps, I shall seek to help you. The baron's an interesting man, is he not?" Golov ripped pieces of the pastry in front of him into small, precisely sized bits. She hadn't seen him eat once during the entire meal.

"Of course." But she didn't want to talk about Clayton. She wanted him to agree to do more to protect the czar. "The emperor will hold you responsible if anyone is killed."

"So you say. How did you meet the baron again?"

"We met as children."

"Ah, then you may not know that the baron's a hard man. He has many enemies." Golov set his open hands on the table. "I would help you protect him."

"Would you?"

"Of course. We may not agree on everything, but I *have* promised to keep him safe. So I want to do my best." He ripped each piece of bread in half again, the yellowed tips of his fingers paler than the pastry.

He thought she'd spy on Clayton. Olivia lifted the glass of wine to her lips, but didn't drink. "What would you want me to do?"

"Only inform me of his activities."

"Don't you already have a spy in the princess's household?"

Golov crushed a bit of the pastry between his fingers. "I'm always in need of more information. The baron might be too stubborn to know when he is in danger."

"Why do you think I would help you?"

"The woman who tried to convince me to save the czar over dessert? I think you know how to turn a situation to your advantage. If you help me, I can ensure you're not harmed in the coming battle between us."

"I thought you needed my help to protect him."

"Only until the fete. After that, we have no agreement. So I imagine you can see the benefit to having friends on both sides. This is nothing more than an old political struggle between the two of us. I would hate for you to get caught in the center. If he's managed to convince you he's anything but a hardened assassin, then perhaps you're not the woman I thought."

He didn't have to convince her. She'd seen it for herself.

"The baron killed a man in his bed while his wife and children slept only a few feet away," Golov said. "I wouldn't believe his claims to honor."

Clayton had never made those claims. His actions made them for him. If he'd killed that man, she'd no doubt it was necessary.

But she also began to understand what had caused the hurt she'd seen earlier. Death wouldn't have been a simple task for him. Not when he analyzed every little thing. When he remembered every moment. When he felt things so deeply. It would torment him.

She also began to understand the shield he'd erected a touch better.

"I could make you wealthy again."

This time she took a long sip of her wine.

"I have heard mention of a mill that is of particular value to you."

She set down her glass of wine. But despite the frantic beat of her heart, he'd made a very poor choice with his threat. "It is."

"Perhaps more so than the baron."

She longed to throw her wine in his face and

toss his plate of massacred dessert across the table. Instead, she said, "Perhaps."

Golov smiled, the grotesque expression contorting his skeletal face. "Sensible. I like a woman who is sensible."

The emperor and his wife stood, and everyone else rose to his feet. Golov inclined his head. "I will speak with you later." He trailed the royal couple from the room.

As soon as the emperor left, a woman shoved her aside and grabbed a hothouse flower from the center of the table.

"What—" Then she spotted the professor pocketing a handful of forks.

"A gift." Clayton appeared at her side and held out a spoon. There was a hint of mischief in his gaze, a playfulness that made her chest feel fuller and yet lighter at the same time.

She eyed the offering. "Is your gift a night in Golov's prison?"

Clayton stepped out of the way as two elderly women battled over a salt cellar. "The royal family never uses settings from official events again. So people vie to bring home tokens to their family as a sign of imperial favor." He held out the spoon once more.

"I think you're more in need of imperial favor than I."

"True enough." The spoon disappeared into his pocket.

Kate joined their group. "I believe this signals the end of the evening. Unless you desire to linger."

"*No.*"

Kate's lips curved at the perfect unison of their

response. "I'll find a footman to send for our sleigh." She disappeared into the crowd.

A beefy man in a green and red military uniform with a colonel's braids and a chest full of medals jostled past her in his haste to reach the head of the table. Her breath caught. "We need to find Golov." Although she shuddered at the thought of more time in his company. "I recognize that man from the count's estate."

Clayton followed the direction of her gaze. "No."

"He arrived the same afternoon as Count Arshun. He's one of Arshun's associates. He wasn't in uniform then, but I'm certain it's him. We can't let him freely roam the palace."

"We can when he's Golov's brother."

When the colonel didn't stop at the head of the table but slunk out the doors into the corridor, Clayton's interest was piqued.

"We should follow him," Olivia said.

Indeed. If the man was one of Arshun's associates, then Clayton would definitely be following him.

And it would be advantageous to have something else to occupy his thoughts.

He trusted Olivia. Now what the devil was he supposed to do about her? It had been difficult to keep his distance when he'd thought her a criminal, what was he supposed to do with her now?

And how would he ever make reparations for what she had suffered? *He* was the reason she'd been kidnapped. *He* was the reason she had scars on her wrists.

It was much easier to focus on trailing the colonel instead. Olivia's hand on his arm, they slipped out of the supper room behind the colonel. He walked down the corridor back toward the ballroom, then ducked into a room on his right.

Clayton knew from the layout of the palace that the room was only a small parlor. It would hold nothing of interest. Was he meeting someone, then? Clayton pressed his finger to his lips and motioned for Olivia to remain where she was. After several moments, no one else had joined the colonel.

Clayton crept to the door.

It was completely silent inside at first, but then came the faint scrape of someone lighting a candle.

Soon the sweet, acrid scent of a burning cheroot drifted from the room. Not an assignation. The man had secreted himself away for a smoke rather than braving the cold.

At least, that's how he wanted it to appear.

Clayton caught Olivia's hand and pulled her behind him. It would be obvious he wasn't alone, but the colonel couldn't see Olivia's face. Clayton swung open the door with a flourish.

The colonel leaned idly on the wall near the stove. The window was open next to him, letting most of the smoke waft out.

"Oh, pardon," Clayton said. "We'll find an unoccupied room."

The colonel crushed the cheroot against the windowsill, then tossed it outside. He had the same sunken eyes as his brother but they looked even sicklier in the colonel's fleshy face. "I was just leaving."

"No need to leave on our account. My lady just needs to . . . fix her hem." He paused and let confusion wash over his face. "I say, aren't you a friend of Count Arshun?"

The colonel's eyes flickered past Clayton, trying to see behind him. "No. I cannot say I know the man."

"Ah, too bad. I owe the count a rather large sum at cards. But I can't seem to locate him."

The colonel ran a hand down the medals adorning his chest. "I cannot help you." He skirted past them and returned to the ballroom.

Clayton shut the door to the parlor once he disappeared. And counted to thirty. "Now we will watch who he contacts." He ushered her back into the corridor.

"You think he will?"

"Either that or it will make him edgy. Nervous men make mistakes."

She glanced back over her shoulder. "You are good at this."

It wasn't something to boast of. "I was a spy for over a decade."

"How did you become a spy? I know you don't believe me, but my father did tell me that you were dead."

"The hour before I was to hang, a man came to me and offered me a deal—I would dedicate my life to the service of the Crown in exchange for keeping it. I took his offer. We were sent on missions they wouldn't risk on a dog." But Clayton had gobbled up every minute of training. Every chance to harden his heart.

And those lessons couldn't be unlearned.

"I lied. I killed. I destroyed."

"But you survived."

"Yes."

She laid her hand over his when he would have opened the door to the ballroom. "No matter what you think of me, I'm glad of that."

The devil would mock him for a fool, but he was rather afraid he believed her.

The ballroom was a jumble of chaos. Men shouted at footmen to bring sleighs. Servants ran about with their arms loaded down with furs and jackets.

"Do you see him?" Olivia murmured.

Clayton relaxed his gaze, seeing the entire room rather than the individuals in it. Patterns and movement. Ignoring all the colors but green.

He spotted him. "By the door."

The colonel's stride was determined. A touch too fast to be casual.

Golov stepped directly in their path. "I look forward to our meeting tomorrow, Baron." His attention drifted to Olivia and a strange half smile stretched his lips. "I am eager to protect the czar."

"I'm eager to speak to your brother." Clayton moved to the right to see around him, but the colonel was already gone. *Damnation*. At least he'd likely be staying in his own home. Clayton could find him later.

"I didn't know you were acquainted."

"Not as well as we will be."

Golov drew back slightly, his eyes mere slashes. "What do you wish to speak to him about?"

"A mutual friend."

"My brother doesn't have friends."

Clayton flashed his teeth, not bothering to hide his dislike. "Neither do I."

Chapter Seventeen

Clayton lifted his hand and knocked lightly on the door that joined his room with Olivia's. He kept the sound quiet enough that if she'd already gone to bed, the noise wouldn't disturb her. In fact, if she was breathing too loudly, she probably wouldn't hear.

What was he even doing at the door? He should be out prowling the streets for Arshun or the colonel, and he was here. Ready to give up his entire night for Olivia.

Saving the czar mattered to her. And strangely, he found it now mattered to him, too.

He could work on the code alone. But chances were slim he'd be able to decipher it in time on his own. His room was buried in the stacks of books and crates of papers he'd requested from Kate. Especially his bed. Kate must have taken great pleasure in giving the servants *that* order. It was too much to sort through on his own in the time he had. It would go faster with two sets of eyes. And Olivia had always been observant.

Except, perhaps, when it had come to her father. But he was forced to agree with her. She'd been young and naive. It was likely she hadn't intended the consequences her actions had earned him.

But her father had. Nothing she could say would ever change that.

He lifted his hand away from the door. She'd likely come home and slipped into a soft night rail and into a blissfully unobstructed bed.

A vision of her spread out under the white sheets prompted him to take a half step from the door. He couldn't wake Olivia, just as he hadn't been able to use her as bait. Every instinct in him screamed to protect her.

He still wasn't sure what had come over him at the ball, and worse, he wasn't entirely sure he regretted it.

No, you are far better.

Those words taunted him. Jumbling around in his brain until he wanted to rip open his skull and pry them out.

He shouldn't care what she thought of him.

But when she'd said that, he'd wanted it to be true. It was an awkward feeling. One he was fairly certain pointed to some weakness in him. And yet that realization hadn't helped the feeling dissipate.

Clayton pressed his forehead against the wooden door, swearing when it collided with his nose. He stumbled back, allowing the door to open.

Olivia didn't look the least contrite as he clutched his nose like an utter fool.

"Is your goal to see me in all states of undress?" Her voice was heavy with sleep and she had on a thick woolen dressing gown. Her hair was rumpled on one side, wisps loose from the braid she wore.

The meager light from his candle caught in the golden strands, giving her a lopsided halo. But her face was set in aggrieved lines, giving her the appearance of a rather surly angel. He fought to keep a smile from his lips. "If Golov's brother is with Prazhdinyeh, then we must assume Golov is, too. We can't truly work on the code with him present. Or risk working on it without him while the servants can report back."

She paused in the middle of rubbing her eye. "You're going to help me? I thought you'd be chasing the colonel."

"After we work on this."

"And what if you break the code? Will you trust me with that?"

"Yes."

Her smile was quick and radiant, but disappeared quickly as if she feared he'd crush it. "Why?"

Clayton rubbed his knuckles along his jaw and shifted back. "I no longer think you are a revolutionary."

There was a pause, a silence that perhaps someone else would have filled with an apology; instead, he would give her something far more useful—information. He stepped aside so she could see into his room. "I have heard rumors about Vasin's codes. It's why I chose to come here in the first place."

Her eyes widened as she surveyed the crates and books piled to chest height. "Those are all papers from Vasin and the prince?"

"Kate claims they are."

She hurried back into the room and returned with the code. "So what rumors have you heard?"

"That he used books to code his messages."

"How would that work?"

"One way to encode messages is for both sides to have the same book or writing and an agreed-upon page."

"Then what?"

"Then to encode a message, the sender takes the first letter from that page and adds that letter's number to the first letter of the message. For instance, if the first letter on the agreed-upon page is B, they would add two to the first letter of the code. If it was C they would add three."

Her teeth nipped at her lower lip as she analyzed the process. "The results would appear random." Her lips parted softly as she stared at the paper in her hand. "Like this." She glanced up. "So what do we do?"

"The best way to proceed is for one of us to catalogue the prince's items while the other does the same for Vasin's."

Olivia lovingly trailed a finger down a row of books, a caress he felt down his spine. "What are we looking for?"

"The prince corresponded with Vasin. They would both need to be able to encode and read the messages. If my theory is correct, there will be a book in common between them."

"So how will we figure out if we are right?"

"We try it on the code."

"Couldn't Prince Sergey tell us?"

"He's in Wales."

A light sparked in her eyes, and he cursed his tongue.

"You cannot tell Kate."

"Why not? She loves him."

"The prince has been free to tell her where he is. If he hasn't, then I must assume he has his reasons."

She tapped a jar of ink before picking it up. "Where do you want me to start?"

"On the bed."

They both froze and then started talking at the same time.

"I believe those belong to—"

"Whose books—"

She motioned for him to continue.

"Those are Vasin's books. I believe there are far fewer of them."

"Are you trying to be kind?"

Was he? He shrugged. "I'm a faster writer."

But as she shifted a pile of books so she could sit on the edge of the bed, a slight smile still pulled at her lips.

And he found himself inordinately pleased to be the one who had put it there.

She tugged her dressing gown tighter around her neck. "Your room seems colder than mine."

"It is. I think it's Kate's way of welcoming me." He settled in the corner of the room, his back turned to the tempting picture she made on his bed, and began to create his own list. A crick in his neck finally forced him to look up.

Olivia now sat in the center of the bed, her knees tucked under her. The books she'd already listed sat in a neat pile on the floor. At some point during the past hour and a half, she'd smudged a line of ink on her chin. She'd always had the bad habit of tapping her chin while she worked.

He could have come back for her ten years ago.

The thought made him ache with a cloying bittersweetness. He'd come back to England many times.

But no. He straightened the books in his pile, then straightened them again until his thoughts followed suit.

What would he have done if he'd come back? Married her? The hurt would have been too fresh and he'd still had his duty to the Crown.

And the more time he spent with her now, the more he was certain he would never make any woman a good husband. He was too harsh, too quick to suspicion, too scarred inside and out.

Then there was the matter of the mill.

He suspected she held out some hope that she'd be able to change his mind. That his agreement to work with her on the code would mean he'd be willing to compromise on other things.

He would just have to let her see that would not happen. Ever.

Chapter Eighteen

Hands swept under her shoulders. Caressed behind Olivia's knees. "Clayton." The moan of her own voice jolted her awake.

Clayton loomed above, his face only inches from hers.

She squeaked and jerked away, colliding with a pile of books. She blinked as she put the pieces together. She was still in Clayton's room. From the pale gray washing over the ceiling, it looked to be early dawn.

Clayton pulled away and straightened, a somewhat pained grimace on his face. "I was about to move you to your room before the maids come to build up the fires."

The last time she'd looked at the clock it was three. She'd slept on his bed, but then where had he slept?

The slight crease running from his temple to his chin made it appear as if he'd fallen asleep on a book. There was a crumpled blanket nearby where he'd been working.

She felt a pang of guilt. "You should have woken me. I would have given you back your bed."

Somehow, the fact that he hadn't yet folded the blanket along neat, precise lines made everything more intimate. That blanket would still be warm from Clayton's body if she touched it. Or curled up in it.

What would he think if she snatched it up and wrapped it around her? If she breathed deep to capture his scent?

"You were exhausted." He smoothed back a lock of her hair, his fingers following it around the shell of her ear and down the side of her neck. Her shudder had nothing to do with the cold. He'd removed his jacket at some point during the night, as well as his boots and cravat. But strangely, not his gloves.

"But you must have been freezing on the floor."

"Once, near Paris, we had to ford a river to escape a French patrol. We ended up taking shelter in an old farmhouse. The French army had already stripped it of anything of use, so Madeline suggested . . ." His words trailed off and a frown darkened his face. "Go to your bed."

"Did you love her?" The words came out before she could stop them. She could only blame them on her exhaustion and on the strange ease she found in this early morning conversation.

"Madeline?"

Of course, Madeline. The woman who was so beautiful men lined up to spill their secrets in her bed. The woman so incredible she had managed to gain Clayton's trust despite how badly Olivia had broken him. The woman he was doing all of this to protect.

"Is that La Petit's name?" She knew as soon as she asked that it was too much. Clayton would freeze up. Accuse her of trying to steal information.

Instead, although he frowned slightly, he nodded.

Air rushed into her lungs. Cleansing. Free.

Strangely, Olivia wasn't jealous as she awaited his answer, at least not much. She was more . . . curious. Hopeful. She still didn't fool herself that she had any future with Clayton. There was too much heartache in the past and more still to come between them. But if he had loved—or still loved, she thought with a jolt—this Madeline, then she could prove to him that he might not be as empty as he believed.

If she could help him realize that, then maybe she'd be able to move on as well.

The thought drove all the other joy away. She wanted Clayton to be happy so *she* could be free of guilt?

Despite the thuds of her heart, she refused to give in to the panic. No. She wasn't that girl anymore. That *wasn't* why she wanted him happy. She wanted him happy because he deserved to be.

She'd broken the hold her past had on her, but there was still one more thing she had to do.

She spoke before she could change her mind. "I went to my father because I was afraid of what would happen to me if you were right about your accusations. I wasn't just foolish. I was spoiled and terrified of losing what I had. I never, never expected my father to accuse you of his crimes. Even in my darkest imaginings, I never—*never*— thought past him denying your charges. But I was

selfish. I *am* selfish. I like to have my own way far
too much. I think sometimes that I'll never be able
to escape it." She sucked in a breath and then exhaled it slowly.

After a moment of silence, she forced herself to
look up so she could see the disgust on Clayton's
face. She deserved it.

His expression was neutral, but his eyes caught
and held hers. She couldn't breathe. She couldn't
do anything but look into their depths and try not
to reel under their intensity.

He reached out and stroked a finger across the
crease on her forehead. His caress continued down
the bridge of her nose to that small divot above her
lip.

"Madeline is like my sister." He didn't need to
say that he loved the other woman. It was there in
the gravity of his words. He lifted his hand away
and tucked it behind him.

A small weight lifted off her chest. "Did she
truly do those things people claim?"

"She saved kings. Entire armies. Me."

"You miss her." Why did her heart ache?

But his small moment of candor was over.
"You'll want to try to sleep again. I suspect Golov
will arrive in a few hours to offer his *help.*"

"He thinks I'm working for him." She thought
it best to be honest. They had enough conflict still
between them.

"What?"

She recounted the conversation from the night
before. "I decided it was best if he thought I
agreed." It wouldn't help either of them if Golov
knew how much Clayton meant to her.

Clayton scrubbed his fingers along the stubble on his chin. "Why only feign acceptance?"

Because she loved him. Instead, she asked, "Would he actually pay?"

"Would that change your answer?"

"No."

"Not even if it meant saving the mill?" He held up a hand to silence her, then closed his eyes briefly. "Go to bed."

Golov arrived before Clayton had finished breakfast, which was a shame because he'd saved his bacon for last and now he wouldn't enjoy it.

"I see I have interrupted your meal. My apologies."

He'd no doubt planned it that way.

Clayton hadn't had time to work out which of the servants reported to Golov directly yet, but he'd narrowed it down to one of two footmen. And a blond upstairs maid, but she'd been so obvious in her attempts to spy that it hadn't even posed a challenge.

Clayton lifted a piece of bacon, determined not to show how Golov's papery, sallow face rendered all notion of eating unpalatable.

"Have you had any success with the code?"

"Baffled, I fear. You?" Clayton had a copy of the page delivered before the ball yesterday.

Golov inclined his head. But since he was here, Clayton had to assume he didn't know how to break the code yet, either.

Clayton also needed to discover where Golov's loyalty lay. The man must know something of the plot. He kept too close a watch on the city and his family not to know his brother was a revolutionary. Was he committed to the revolution? Willing to let it happen?

Or did he actually want to stop it?

"I'm honored by your personal attention to this matter. I never knew codes were your specialty," Clayton said.

"No, that is yours, I believe. And that of your friend."

Clayton took a sip of tea so the sudden dryness in his throat would betray nothing. Even Golov with his nearly unlimited resources shouldn't have had time to find out those types of details about Olivia yet.

"She did destroy the weapons cache."

No. She'd been safely sleeping. But Clayton wouldn't correct him.

"I suppose *you* could have broken that code, but I was under the impression you were assigned elsewhere when she retrieved those documents from Vasin."

Madeline. Golov was speaking of Madeline, not Olivia. Relief swept through him, but was quickly quashed. Golov knew far more about the Trio's actions than he should. And he was flaunting it. How did he know Clayton had been assigned to Moscow while Madeline and Ian had worked on Vasin?

Clayton examined his tea. Madeline had stolen a packet of papers from Vasin, but they'd never translated them. They'd turned them directly over to the Foreign Office as per their orders.

But in Vasin's boastings as he'd tried to bed

Madeline, he'd given away the location of a stock-pile of weapons, which they'd tracked down and destroyed.

It had been a rather marvelous explosion.

That location must have been one of the things revealed in those papers. That was why the revolutionaries thought Madeline could break the code.

He couldn't allow that misconception to linger. "I broke the code."

"If you were the one to break the code, I must question why you're unable to do so now?" Golov cracked the knuckles on his right hand, the sound more dry and brittle than it should have been.

"I must be losing my touch. As are you, if you don't know what Prazhdinyeh is planning for the fete."

"I know other things. For instance, I know Miss Swift is obviously not La Petit. The question is, does that make her more valuable to you or less?"

Clayton set down his fork. The clink of the silver against the plate rang just a touch too loud.

Golov smiled, his lips never parting. "Ah."

Clayton's mouth tasted bitter and metallic. "She told me about your offer of employment."

That seemed to please Golov more. "Did it make you trust her? She's clever."

"I already trust her."

"No, you don't. You and I don't trust anyone." Golov settled into a chair. "She's clever, that one. I'd be happy to take her from you."

Never. Not as long as there was a breath left in his body. Hell, even after. He'd claw his way out of a grave to keep Olivia from Golov.

Olivia strolled through the door in a frothy pink dress, her back straight. Her step was light. "Golov. I'm so pleased you were able to come this morning."

"I hear you've rejected my offer of employment."

Olivia's gaze darted between them, but she smiled. "For now. But I will tell you we've been unable to get anywhere with this code. I am thrilled you are here to help us."

Golov blinked twice. He wasn't a man to receive many smiles.

She allowed him to raise her hand to his lips, the man's gallantry oily and disturbing.

"I suspected as much, but I'm glad to have it confirmed. Why don't you retrieve the page, Baron? I'm sure Miss Swift and I can entertain ourselves for a few moments in your absence."

He wasn't about to leave Olivia alone with that monster. "I have it on me, of course."

Olivia spooned jam onto an oatcake and then helped herself to a large portion of eggs. Apparently, Golov didn't affect her appetite at all.

Over the next hour, Clayton realized he'd severely underestimated Olivia again. He didn't know much about her work with the society she'd mentioned, but watching her now, he was surprised they weren't ruling London.

As they worked, she maintained the same constant worry about the czar, but managed to bring the whole process to a near standstill. She forced them to explain every type of pattern they tried, earnest in her desire to understand the mechanics, yet easily befuddled at the same time.

If he wasn't certain she already knew half the

techniques they'd tried, he might have been fooled himself. She was the perfect imitation of an amateur eager to help.

"Have you caught Arshun yet?" she asked.

Golov stroked his chin, which pulled down the skin by his eyes and gave him the appearance of an old, sick hound. "Not yet."

"What about the other revolutionaries from his estate?"

Clayton didn't look up from the page. He kept the exact same expression on his face. Hoping, in fact almost praying, that her question would slip by unnoticed.

"What do you know of other revolutionaries? Did you see any others at the count's estate?" Golov leaned closer. His breath smelled of fish and vodka. "I thought you were incarcerated."

Too late.

He'd picked up on the slip Olivia had no idea she had made.

Until that moment.

Clayton had to give her credit for her instant awareness of the increased tension in the room. "I was. I couldn't see anything well," Olivia said.

"But you did see something."

"Not really. They had me locked in the attics. I could see very little."

"I will need you to tell me everything so I can protect the czar."

Clayton doubted the czar fit into the man's calculations at all. He wanted to protect his brother.

"Certainly. I'll tell you what I can." Olivia recounted her time there. She was vague on everyone but Arshun and a man named Nicolai that the count had murdered in front of her. The tremble in Olivia's voice as she described his death was genuine, as was the slight gagging she couldn't hide as she described the blood.

He would slit Arshun's throat when he found him.

And why hadn't *he* asked for more details of her capture before Maxim-bloody-Golov had?

Because he didn't want to know. Every wound, every terror, every discomfort would be his fault.

His stomach clenched.

Golov reached out a hand and placed it over Olivia's, stroking it gently. "We're doing our best to apprehend him." Golov's nostrils flared and his lips disappeared. "And you can be certain he'll feel the full wrath of the Russian empire for what he did to you." He actually sounded sincere.

But Clayton also didn't for a moment believe that Golov trusted Olivia's words. Not if he knew his brother had been there.

His next words confirmed it. "You play me well. But you would do well to trust me with everything you know, *koteek*."

Golov had just called Olivia a kitten. Clayton didn't try to keep the disgust off his face. He stood and moved closer to Olivia. "She's told you everything."

Golov shrugged. "I find hidden depths fascinating. You, I think, hate her for them."

Clayton didn't like that she was keeping things hidden from him, but he didn't hate her. He was farther from that than he'd ever admit.

Olivia watched him for his response, but when he gave none, she shifted away.

He'd hurt her. The knowledge was a kick to the gut.

But it would keep her safe. And somehow, that had become his only concern in this conversation.

"Heavens, are you all still huddled in here?" Kate strode into the room. Golov was forced to rise.

Kate continued brightly. "Lovely. I have company coming for tea. General Smirken and his young bride."

General Smirken was one of the few men in the government who held power similar to Golov's. And he and Golov detested each other.

Clayton hoped for Kate's sake she truly had arranged for him to come, because Golov would surely verify her claim.

Kate's eyes widened. "Miss Swift! You look terribly peaked. Whatever are these men tormenting you with? You must rest. You look quite ill."

Clayton tucked the paper away. "We can continue tomorrow."

Golov frowned. "Tomorrow is unacceptable."

"Surely, you can figure out the meaning without me?"

He'd backed Golov into a difficult spot. The minister of police wouldn't admit to incompetence in front of both Olivia and Kate. He'd find some way to punish Clayton later, but for now, it was worth it to be free of him.

"I apologize for distressing you, Miss Swift." Golov bowed. He lifted his rheumy gaze to Clayton, one of his hands stroking the other. "But do not fear, you and I shall soon have time to discuss things. Privately."

Kate shuddered as soon as he left the room. "Sorry if he was useful, but my servants were refusing to come into the room."

Clayton nodded. "They probably dislike cleaning up all the maggots and decaying flesh he leaves behind."

Olivia and Kate both stared at him, their mouths parted in matching O's. Olivia was the first to recover, clapping her hand over her mouth to hide her laughter. But her laughter slowly darkened to something far more serious.

"How much more dangerous did I make things this morning?"

Clayton didn't pretend to misunderstand or brush it off. He checked to ensure the door was shut and the servant was outside it. "Even if he doesn't know his brother was at Arshun's that day, he cannot chance you knowing. The scandal would ruin him if it's revealed his brother is a revolutionary."

"In other words, much more dangerous."

Clayton didn't contradict her.

"What do we do?" Olivia asked.

"Continue to be cautious. I don't think Golov will risk acting against us yet. We're still his best option for breaking the code. In fact, there is the chance the revolutionaries may think so, too. That will give us at least some safety until the fete. "And I do not hate you."

"I—" She stopped. That hadn't been what she expected him to say at all. "You don't?"

"I did kiss you yesterday."

Kate coughed and glanced at Olivia with a lifted eyebrow.

Olivia spoke quickly, her voice a touch too loud. "Who made those delicious pancakes?"

Kate frowned. "The blini? It was that hulking brute Clayton tossed into my kitchen. My cook has become quite taken with her new assistant."

"What hulking brute?" Olivia asked him.

"Blin."

Olivia jumped to her feet. "Blin! Blin is here?" She glanced quickly at Kate. "And you said he was helping the cook, not locked up, right?"

"I don't think I have enough rope to tie him, but yes. Clayton asked if I would accept him as a servant for a few days."

The door thudded open as Olivia bolted from the room.

Clayton moved into the corridor at a more sedate pace. By the time he reached the kitchen, Olivia had her arms as far as she could around the other man, a single glistening line curved down her cheeks. She praised him, laughing through her tears, about the pancakes.

The other kitchen servants had gathered around, some smiling, some confused. The cook watched from over by the oven, her flour-covered hands clasped to her breasts.

Blin's face was so red, it was almost purple. He patted her on the back with a couple of quick pats. "With a name like Blin, my *babushka* said it was better to earn the name than give people a reason to mock it."

Olivia finally let go of him and stepped back. She was bloody glowing.

"How did you come to be here?"

Blin scuffed his toe. "I didn't leave like you

asked. I stayed to protect you. I was watching when—the baron?" His eyes found Clayton in the doorway, and Clayton nodded. "When the baron found me in the snow, and found a place for me in the princess's house. Even one in the kitchen when I told him I was good at cooking."

Olivia slowly turned to face Clayton, her face suddenly serious. She studied him for one heart-beat. Then two.

Clayton shrugged.

She faced Blin again, her smile returning. "Why didn't you go home?"

Blin's hand flopped at his sides. He lowered his voice so she had to strain to hear him. "I can't."

Clayton interrupted before Olivia could unwit-tingly cause trouble for Blin. "We should let Blin return to his cooking."

Olivia seemed to notice the other curious servants for the first time. "Oh, I am so sorry to interrupt." With one final smile, she walked toward Clayton.

Once they were in the corridor she grabbed his arm, stopping them. "Why can't he go home?"

"He's a serf who left his master without permis-sion. If he's discovered, the punishment is harsh. For both him and his family."

Olivia took a small step back, her hand tighten-ing on him. "And he risked it to come after me." Her voice quavered. "He said you found him in the snow?"

He gave her an abbreviated account of the en-counter outside. Apparently, not abbreviated enough, because her grip loosened to caress down his arm. "Thank you."

Clayton licked his suddenly dry lips. What he'd

done was hardly deserving of praise. "I put him to work in the kitchens." He tugged her forward until they were walking again. "I pulled a knife on him, too. Did he tell you that part?"

"Then you decided to be kind."

"He watched over you. If I had access to it, I'd give him my entire damned fortune."

Her hand trembled on his arm, her fingers fluttering, then digging into him.

Hell, but he'd said way too much with that line. And every word of it was the truth. His head spun as if he'd been on a ship in a squall. And for a moment, he feared his knees might actually be shaking.

What had he just confessed?

He hurried them both inside her room, not even caring that the servants might see.

He knew he was panting as he shut the door, far more loudly than their simple walk would warrant.

Her hand rested on his cheek then she leaned in until her lips brushed his. "Why did you decide to trust him?"

"Because you did." He trapped her waist and crushed her to him. He could no longer remember why he didn't think this was a good idea. This was the best idea he'd ever had. He deepened the kiss, his tongue tangled with hers.

His heartbeat echoed in his ear in perfect unison with her panting breaths.

He kissed his way across the neckline of her pink gown; the thing was far too high for his tastes, but it did lead him to an intriguing tendon stretched tight along the side of her neck. He caressed it with a flick of his tongue, and she shuddered.

So he repeated the caress.

He was alive. Every nerve vibrated. Each breath felt like his first. And it wasn't just sexual, although he was stiffer than a ten-pound cannon. He wanted to throw the window open and laugh at the moon. He wanted to spin Olivia in his arms until neither of them could see straight.

A loud, braying laugh sounded below.

The sound brought with it a touch of sanity. Clayton stepped back, shaking his head although that did little to clear it. "That is Smirken." He retreated until he couldn't touch her again.

She stepped toward him. "Can we claim to not be at home?"

Clayton knew he should step back again but he held his ground, sucking in a deep breath when her hand rested on his chest. "You will hate me if I allow this to proceed."

"Why?"

"Because it would go no further than this. Or rather that bed over there."

"What if that's enough?"

"It shouldn't be enough for you."

She pressed her lips to the corner of his mouth.

His breathing stopped.

Slowly, she kissed him again.

His lids lowered until all he could see was the blur of colors around them. "You play with fire."

"Good."

With a growl, he caught her to him again. Clayton traced his thumb over her lips, the leather of his glove smooth and cool. "Your lips taste of raspberries and the finest French brandy."

She almost kissed his finger, but stopped. "You don't like brandy."

His finger traced along her jaw and down her neck. "It's an acquired taste."

He must be able to feel her fluttering pulse at her neck.

"Have you acquired it?"

He just cocked a brow.

She stood on tiptoe so her lips were inches from his. "Perhaps you need another taste."

Clayton stilled, his eyes lowering to her mouth. She flicked her tongue over his lips, loving the way his eyes darkened further.

There were footsteps on the stairs. Servants come to summon them, no doubt.

Clayton stepped back, but his hand cupped her face for an instant before he released her. "If you claim to be unwell, you should be able to escape tea and get through much of the Vasin's remaining items." He drew a paper from his jacket then, and held it out. Her list from last night. Ever so slowly, he tucked it in the neckline of her gown, the paper sliding under her shift to nestle between her breasts. "It's best to keep this somewhere on your person."

Olivia barely managed to nod. Each minute they'd wasted with Golov had seemed like a nail in the czar's coffin.

A footman knocked on her door and announced the general's arrival, then did the same to Clayton's. She hoped he didn't notice Clayton's response came from her room as well.

"How well do you know Smirken?" she asked after the servant left.

They hadn't met very many who were pleased to see Clayton.

He snorted softly. "*He* thinks quite well. The regiment I marched with when I saved Alexander's life was Smirken's. He claims to recall me from all sorts of battles he was too drunk to remember." He disappeared into his room and returned with the remaining books and stacks of writing. "Rather like the time you tried to explain to me how the mill made paper."

She grabbed some of the books from him. "You're a beast. You knew I didn't know how it was made."

"I know, yet that didn't stop you. However, I thought you had *some* idea." He grinned at her. "But paper from milk?"

She glared back, but she loved his teasing. "The liquid in the vat *was* white. And it makes as much sense as it coming from dissolved rags."

He ducked back into his room, and a few moments later, knocked on her main door.

"I do know where paper comes from now," she felt obligated to tell him as he escorted her. She attempted to push a bit further. "In fact, I can tell you the time it takes for each weave to break down into fibers."

Clayton ignored her for the rest of the walk to Kate's parlor. Inside, Kate waited with a ruddy-faced man with thick gray muttonchops and huge mustache, and a dark, shapely woman who must be his bride.

"Baron Komarov! So glad to see that someone made it out of Siberia." Smirken spoke in Russian, laughing at his own joke, the loud, honking sound she'd heard from above.

Clayton clasped hands briefly with the older man as Kate made introductions. The general's wife ran a slow, appreciative glance over Clayton, her gaze all but caressing his lean, muscular thighs and what was between them. When Clayton lifted her hand to his lips, she let out a throaty sigh. "I don't suppose you remember me."

"You two know each other already? It is always good to find an old friend!"

The general thought it was good? Did he truly not see proof they'd been lovers shimmering in the air between them?

And Olivia thought to impress him with her few kisses.

"I remember you," Clayton said. "We met at the Rigisky ball."

Of course, Clayton remembered. He'd no doubt be able to name everything about her that night down to the color of her slippers.

He'd also remember anything that passed between them afterward.

The general's wife rose up on tiptoe to kiss his cheek. Although Olivia had seen women at the ball acknowledge introductions that way, this woman's fat, wet lips practically devoured him. "Your hand wouldn't bother me now," she whispered.

His hand?

Clayton's right hand, the one he kept constantly gloved, twitched, but he didn't tuck it behind him as he was wont to do.

Olivia might not know why he kept it concealed, but if the woman let anything distract her from the perfection that was Clayton, then she was a fool.

Olivia stepped next to Clayton, forcing the other woman back. How dare she imply that Clayton was wanting in any way?

Mrs. Smirken pouted. "I cannot believe you haven't come for a visit. I have been . . . lonely."

Now she thought to proposition him?

The general patted his wife on the back. "Sorry I cannot attend you more, my cabbage. Things have been busy of late. Then today with the scandal about the archbishop metropolitan. The people are in an uproar. It's a good time to remind the czar not to place so much confidence in those black crows."

"What scandal?" Kate asked, stilling as she arranged the cups on the tea tray.

The general's wife smiled, her expression superior. "The metropolitan was arrested."

"On what charge?"

At Clayton's question, Mrs. Smirken's expression shifted to one of outraged concern. "He's been killing young girls. I feel quite frightened." She reached for Clayton.

Olivia tucked her hand around Clayton's arm, blocking the other woman. "Thank goodness you have your husband."

"Shall we sit?" Kate came to the rescue for the second time that morning.

Soon they were all seated. Olivia thought she'd won when she claimed the seat next to Clayton, forcing the other woman to sit across from them.

Until the general's wife leaned forward, her bosoms trembling on the edge of her bodice, and sent Olivia a triumphant sneer.

So Olivia put her hand on Clayton's knee. She refused to look at him to see where his loyalties lay in this skirmish, but at least he didn't remove her hand.

Kate poured the tea faster than anyone Olivia had ever seen. "So, General, you must tell me again about your victory at Vinkovo. I never grow tired of hearing of your glorious battle."

Smirken settled back into his chair, fingers smoothing his mustache. "It was indeed glorious. We captured the artillery from right under Murat's nose. It's said to be the reason Napoleon fled Russia. Baron, you, of course, were right in the thick of things. I can recall you charging into the battle on your horse."

Clayton nodded seriously. "You lent me your horse, I believe."

Smirken nodded. "Yes, that is right. A fine steed, he was."

Clayton shook his head slowly. "I'm not sure what would have happened if you hadn't. Especially considering the poor condition of my horse."

The general's wife inched forward further, her bosoms jiggling. "What happened to it?" There was a bloodthirsty hunger in her eyes.

"It's quite tragic."

Both the general and his wife leaned even further forward. Olivia could definitely see a nipple. The headache Olivia was supposed to feign felt far too real now. But she was not going to cede Clayton to this trollop.

She opened her mouth to tell the other woman of her wardrobe inadequacy, but Clayton's hand clamped over hers.

"It simply goes to show that a horse should never develop feelings for a pig," he said.

Olivia didn't say anything, but neither could she make her jaw close.

"A pig?" Kate asked, her voice strangled.

"Indeed, a fine warhorse. He insisted on following around one of the swine the regiment kept for food."

The general chuckled. "That was quite the sight."

He really *did* think he'd been there.

"Unfortunately, one of the male pigs took offense and attacked."

"The pig attacked your horse?" Olivia asked.

Clayton turned to her, the concern on his face so almost genuine she had to bite her knuckle in pretended horror to keep the laughter from escaping.

Kate gulped her tea.

"It was a cruel attack."

The general's wife stiffened, offended. "Surely, your warhorse was able to trounce him."

Clayton let out a long sigh. "The pig rallied several of his friends to his aid. Clooter fought valiantly, but by the time I was able to reach him, it was too late."

Olivia knew then that this story was entirely false and entirely for her benefit. Clooter had been one of the workers at her father's mill, a crotchety old man with the face of a horse. She sucked in slow breaths. Kate really should have asked Clayton before filling his time with visitors.

"They killed him?" the general's wife asked.

"No, but he was terrified of grunts after that, and on the battlefield—"

Olivia jumped to her feet. She couldn't hold in her laughter anymore; she knew her face must be flushed from trying not to giggle like an idiot.

"I'm sorry. This story is too much for me. Please, excuse me."

Mrs. Smirken shot her a smug look. "Do continue, Baron. I find your stories fascinating."

Clayton's gaze moved between them. He lifted an eyebrow. "And added to his previous fear of chickens, that made him quite unusable on the battlefield—as you quite wisely counseled me, General."

Olivia fled. She managed to make it to the stairs before collapsing in poorly muffled mirth. She wondered what Golov's spies would report about that.

After a few moments, she was able to calm to a less embarrassing chortle and resumed climbing the stairs. Clayton would deserve two points for that story if they were still playing their little game. She'd forgotten just how good he was at the absurd. For a man so smart, one would have thought he'd have a dry intellectual wit. And while Clayton had possessed that, he'd also found hilarity in the ridiculous. The street puppet shows she found inane had him laughing until his sides hurt. Until she couldn't help laughing because he was laughing so hard he snorted.

Olivia settled by the stack of books and papers in her room and wrote down the remaining titles. There really weren't very many more.

She should help Clayton with his portion. He might be rather exhausted after any more time in the general's company. She picked up her list and opened the adjoining door.

A rough hand clamped over her mouth and yanked her inside.

Chapter Nineteen

Clayton took the stairs two at a time. He still wasn't quite sure where that story had come from during the general's visit. He hadn't liked seeing Olivia embarrassed by Marya's blatant overtures. But he could have stopped her with a cutting remark.

Instead, he'd chosen the option that made Olivia's eyes sparkle and her lips twitch.

Marya apparently wanted to try for a repeat of their night together. But that wasn't going to happen. There'd never been anything more than a single mediocre night at her instigation. And she'd spent half the time flinching away from his hand. The other half, after he put his glove back on, she'd just lain there limp. Apparently, gracing him with her beauty was enough. Not precisely what he was looking for in a bedmate.

Unlike Olivia, who had met his kiss with—

He wasn't going to follow that line of thought.

Like hell he wasn't. He hadn't been able to stop thinking of the perfection of her kisses. He'd crafted and discarded a dozen compliments that couldn't quite capture the bliss. He hadn't told Olivia, but each barely repressed quiver, each swivel of her hips, each gasp of pleasure had severed some band deep within him. Liberating him. Freeing him of years of constant tension and suspicion. Reminding him what it felt like to be a man who cared for passion and pleasure and the feelings of the woman in his arms.

He hadn't thought he missed that. It had been a frivolous part of him that he hadn't needed to survive. But he felt as if his soul had opened to the sunshine for the first time in years.

He slowed as he neared their rooms. The prospect of working on the code the rest of the afternoon no longer loomed so—

Voices.

He stilled. Training clamped back down into place. He quieted his breathing so he could hear more clearly. It was possible that Olivia was speaking to her maid.

No. It was clearly a man's voice.

Perhaps a maid and one of the footmen—but no, that was definitely Olivia. He couldn't hear what she was saying. Her voice was too muffled.

Frightened.

He drew the knife he had hidden in his boot, trying to relax his hand around the hilt before he reached the door. He needed Olivia's attacker alive for questioning.

Olivia squeaked.

No, he'd have Olivia's attacker's entrails dripping on his knife.

Clayton slammed open the door.

A man's broad back was to Clayton. He held Olivia. Or was trying to. She struggled wildly. He muttered something to her. She screamed an out-raged reply into the hand covering her mouth.

Clayton threw the knife.

Just before the knife struck, the attacker released Olivia and spun around, knocking the knife aside with his arm.

Ian.

Clayton had nearly killed his friend.

But before that could fully register, Olivia was screaming loud and long, a scream determined to bring the entire house running.

Ian swore. "Remember how I told you not to scream when I released you?"

"I never agreed." Olivia blinked slowly, taking note that Clayton hadn't moved to attack again and Ian looked more annoyed than concerned.

"I cannot believe you never mentioned me, Clayton. The Trio. That means three of us. Not just you and La Petit." Ian rubbed at his palm, where Olivia must have bitten him. "And I admire your determination not to believe me."

"You actually *do* know each other?" Olivia asked, her face flushed red from where Ian's hand had been clamped over her mouth.

Clayton hoped she'd taken a good chunk out of his hand. "Quite well. As he mentioned, he's the third member of the Trio."

"Wraith?" Ian supplied, hopefully. "Ring any bells?"

But Olivia just shook her head.

"Or Ian Maddox, if you prefer," Clayton said.

Ian raised a brow. "I didn't realize we'd progressed to the revealing-our-true-identity part of our relationship."

Footsteps pounded in the hall.

"Those would be the servants I was attempting to avoid rousing. Perhaps I'll disappear and let you deal with them." He bowed to Olivia. "I shall demonstrate why I was awarded such an intriguing title."

Clayton and Olivia turned to the door as Kate, two footmen, and a maid entered. "What's wrong?" Kate asked.

Olivia glanced back over her shoulder and froze. Clayton knew she'd noticed Ian's favorite trick—vanishing mysteriously.

Clayton had seen Ian's act enough times to know it was less than fantastical. Despite being slightly shorter and broader than Clayton, Ian moved with the agility of a tumbler. He was most likely in the wardrobe.

Olivia still wore a look of stunned admiration on her face. Clayton didn't want to explain his sudden desire to demystify Ian's trick.

Olivia rubbed at her nose with the back of her hand, obscuring the redness around her mouth. "I saw a mouse."

"It was truly repulsive," Clayton added with satisfaction. "In fact, I think it ran under the wardrobe. The servants should check."

The footmen glanced at each other, then with a grunt shoved the heavy wooden bureau.

Nothing was underneath, of course. But hopefully it had caused Ian heart palpitations.

Kate's gaze narrowed. "Would you like to move to a less distressing room, Baron?"

Clayton shook his head. "No, I'll make do with this one."

Kate circled Olivia. And Clayton suspected she didn't miss the new wrinkles in the dress from Olivia's struggle with Ian. "Why don't we inspect your room as well?"

Olivia ducked her head low. "I really don't think—"

But Kate linked her arm through hers. "No, I insist. I wouldn't want there to be a problem with vermin."

Clayton would have followed but Kate held up her hand. "You should keep watch in your room in case your *mouse* returns. Or perhaps an angry pig?"

Kate escorted Olivia and the herd of servants into the other room and shut the door after them, but Clayton could hear her speaking. He stepped closer and pressed his ear to the door.

"Now are you going to tell me what really happened or—"

"I wasn't in the wardrobe, by the way." Ian reappeared next to him, his comment making it impossible to hear Olivia's response.

"Pity," Clayton said. "Under the bed?" Ian's hair *was* slightly mussed on one side.

"*I'm sorry I almost stabbed you, dear friend.*" Ian copied Clayton's voice perfectly, then switched to his own. "I thought I'd save you from feeling guilty for not apologizing."

"I don't."

"I know. That's why I saved you the trouble."

"No, I don't feel guilty."

"You wound me, old man." Ian leaned forward

and theatrically placed his ear on the door. "Why are we spying at her door?"

Clayton stepped back. "I wasn't spying."

"Ah, the floor was slanted making you lean toward it. I understand." Ian lifted an eyebrow. "I'm glad she had the sense to scream once I let go of her. She's brave. In all your descriptions of her, you didn't mention that."

For a man who prided himself on his memory, there were too many things Clayton was uncertain of now. The bravery, for instance. Had that always been there only to be forgotten in his hurt and anger? More and more, he was doubting his justifications for staying away from her. Now when he thought of her, it wasn't about the betrayal, but the wonderful, nearly giddy times they'd shared.

He didn't want to remember. The memories were too tempting. Too sweet. Like eating a sugar cube after months of starvation. "There's a lot I never mentioned."

Ian sighed. "Ah, yes, because you're an uncaring villain. Full of secrets and driven by revenge."

"I never claimed to be uncaring." Clayton picked up a paper from the floor and tucked it into his jacket. It was her copy of the list. She must have dropped it when Ian had mauled her.

Ian flipped through the papers on the end table. "Hmm . . . I seem to recall this conversation you had with Madeline a few months ago— 'You really don't care if you destroy all those lives?' To which you replied, and I think I can quote you with some confidence: 'No.'"

Clayton moved the stack of papers away from

Ian before he confused their order. "She's under my protection."

"The perfect time to ruin her—in a far different way than you plan to ruin her father. At least I hope."

"I don't plan to ruin her."

"You've already done it then?"

"*No*."

"Then why was she in your room?"

"She must have finished the books in her room."

"You're going to try to claim she came into your room looking for a *book*? You know, as she struggled against me, I couldn't help noticing what a fine—"

Clayton's fist connected with his friend's chin before he could finish.

Ian shifted his jaw back and forth before grinning. "Spirit. I was going to say she had a fine spirit."

Clayton flexed his hand. The woman was driving him mad. It was as simple as that. "Thank you for coming, by the way."

"As if I could resist that cryptic message you sent me in the middle of the night. I never miss an opportunity to partake in violence and subterfuge. So what's going on? No, wait." Ian lowered himself into the delicately embroidered chair in the far corner of the room. "I know better than to stand through one of your explanations. You'll probably feel the need to tell me the color of the villains' shoes and what type of shaving powder they use."

But then Ian's banter disappeared, replaced by an intense focus and keen intelligence Clayton often suspected was far greater than his own. "Now the details."

Clayton recounted everything that had happened so far.

"They were going after Madeline?" Ian finally asked.

The comment jarred Clayton. At some point over the past day, concern for Madeline had been overshadowed by fear for Olivia.

Which only went to show he needed to realign his priorities. Madeline was the one who'd stitched him back together after the French were done with him. He owed her everything.

Ian stood, his fluid grace absent. "This is the second time we've been compromised. First, Einhern was led to Madeline. Now someone has given *you* away to our enemies."

Clayton hadn't thought of it in that light. The Trio was being betrayed one by one.

Ian walked to the window and surveyed the ground below. "Have you broken the code?"

"Not yet."

"Then the odds are slim that Prazhdinyeh can?"

He hoped his friend's confidence wasn't misplaced. "I don't know. But if they can find one of Vasin's exiled generals, they won't have to. We can't take that chance. And Vasin's agent might decide to act even if he doesn't receive a signal. He's been awaiting this moment for a long time, after all."

Olivia's door opened again. "I believe being manhandled entitles me to be part of this conversation." Her back was straight, and her eyes dared Clayton to contradict her.

Ian bowed. "I do apologize for my less than gentlemanly introduction."

"You could have *tried* introducing yourself," Olivia said.

"I did."

"Yes. Calling yourself the Wraith should have calmed me immediately."

Ian smiled that rugged, admiring grin that usually had women dropping at his feet. Then he turned to Clayton. "What are my orders, oh wise leader?"

Clayton often thought Ian would make the better leader, but he'd always refused the role. "I need you to find Arshun."

Ian yawned. "What will I do with the other twenty-three hours of my day?"

Clayton couldn't help grinning. It was good to have Ian at his side again. "The plan was set into motion about three years ago. Perhaps see if you can find anyone who's made a rapid rise in the ranks surrounding the czar. Someone who will be in the position to do what Vasin planned." He explained about the weapons he'd destroyed.

"That doesn't sound much like Vasin's type of plan."

Clayton nodded. "I think Arshun is feeling inventive. And I suspect I only blew up a portion of his weapons."

Ian slid open the window, dropping the room temperature by several more chilling degrees. "I'll see what I can—"

Boom!

Walls and floors shuddered.

A hot blast of air.

Olivia hurtled forward, lifted by the explosion behind her. Clayton threw himself on top of her as bits of plaster showered his back.

Breaking glass. Paintings crashing to the floor. Neck burning. Heat. Too much heat.

Then silence but for the faint, high-pitched ringing in his ears.

Olivia coughed in the murky air, wracking sounds that shook her body under him. How much of the blast had caught her? He'd seen men whose insides had been turned to liquid by blasts like this. Men who—

Terror hollowed Clayton's gut as he waited for her to pull her hand away from her mouth.

She lifted her hand. No blood.

The next choked exhale was his.

He rolled off her and gently flipped her onto her back. He wiped a finger through the pale dust coating her face, leaving a pink stripe down her cheek. "Are you all right?"

Ian leaped past them, running into the cloud of smoke and heat that was once Olivia's rooms. Clayton gave thanks again that Ian had come. It meant he could see to Olivia and not worry about the house burning down around them. He ran his hands down her arms. Her torso. Searching for any injuries.

Olivia coughed again and sucked in a wincing breath. "I'm uninjured. It simply knocked me to the floor and then an enormous man fell on top of me." She reached up and ran a hand through his hair, dislodging dust and bits of plaster. "You."

He'd thought destroying the mill would bring him the satisfaction he'd been missing. But now he feared it wouldn't compare to this. The awe on her face. The tenderness.

Stomping came from the other room—Ian obliterating any smoldering wreckage. There was a sharp crack, and Ian swore. "The floor's compromised in places. Nearly just plunged to my death, thanks for asking. But no fire," he called out. "Black powder, most likely."

Ian reappeared. He bent over, rearranging the leg of his trousers. "Blast originated by the stove. It wasn't the stove itself, although that's undoubtedly what we're supposed to think. Lucky for us, the mahogany wardrobe on her wall redirected most of the force away from us. Otherwise, your wall would have been blown out, too."

Clayton glanced through the door. Olivia's far wall had been demolished.

Servants shouted as they ran up the hall.

"Miss Swift!" Blin's shout was anguished; his boots echoed on the floor as he ran down the corridor.

"If that man's as big as he sounds, he'll go straight through the floor in that room."

"*Blin*," Olivia yelled. "I'm all right."

But his pace didn't change as he passed Clayton's room.

Olivia started to run to Clayton's door. "Blin, don't go into my room!" But she'd never make it before the other man had thrown himself into her room.

The adjoining door.

"Ian, can that floor hold me?"

Ian paused halfway out the window. "Most likely—"

Clayton darted through it.

Window glass was gone. Chairs were splintered. The books and papers had been reduced to scraps and tiny flakes that dotted the floor. He kept his feet to one of the structural beams that had been revealed by the missing boards in the floor.

The door crashed open.

Clayton leaped, throwing his entire weight at the man coming inside.

It was like hitting a wall, but Blin *did* stop. He grunted and stepped back and Clayton fell rather awkwardly onto one knee.

The other man was shaking, his mouth opening and closing. "Miss Swift? Where is she?"

Clayton rearranged his aching muscles until he was standing again.

"Blin. Don't go in there!" Olivia scrambled to their side. Her hair hung lopsided off her head. She jerked back, and her eyes widened when she saw Clayton.

"You went through my room." What little color she still had disappeared. "You could have . . ." She bit her lip and reached for him, and he knew that even if the floor had been nothing but a gaping hole, he still would have flung himself across it.

"Miss Swift?" Blin patted her cheek, his fingers stiff and slow. "What—"

The rest of the servants arrived. A dozen footmen and maids carried buckets of water. Others came simply to stare.

"Olivia!" Kate cried as she pushed her way through the servants. She wrapped Olivia in a fierce embrace.

Clayton turned back to the destroyed room. He

gripped the doorway to keep his hands from trembling at the utter devastation.

More servants crowded behind him, exclaiming as they glimpsed the damage.

The ceramic stove was simply gone. None of the remaining shards were bigger than his finger. The rest of the debris was scattered in a circular pattern around where the stove had been. Ian was correct. The blast *had* originated by the stove.

Clayton glanced back to Olivia, only to catch Kate's angry glare. "You" was all she said.

And she was right. Everything Olivia had suffered had been his fault. She'd been kidnapped because of him. Bound. Cut. Bruised.

The room. He needed to focus on the blast. He bent and picked up a small metal gear from the floor near his boot. From a clock, perhaps? Then why was it in this part of the room?

"He protected me," Olivia said. "I was in his room."

Kate sighed. "At least you're alive. Who could have—"

"—designed such a poor stove?" Clayton said. The person responsible needed to think them none the wiser. It would make him easier to spot. He pocketed a small brass screw.

"Perhaps the mouse tampered with it," Kate muttered. She let go of Olivia, allowing Olivia's maid to reach her. The young woman brushed dust from Olivia's gown, exclaiming about overheated stoves and how her aunt had been killed by one last winter and how the stoves killed hundreds every winter.

Clayton ran a hand down the door frame. He worked loose a flattened chunk of metal that had lodged deep within. A flattened lead disk. A rifle ball. The bomb had been made to mutilate. If Olivia had been in the room, she'd have been torn to shreds.

Clayton leaned his back against the door frame to remain upright. The buzz of the servants' voices echoed in his ears. The dust was dry and chalky in his mouth.

If he'd lost her—

He rubbed his fingers back and forth over the metal fragment, faster and faster. Until a hand clasped over his.

Olivia.

"How are *you*?" she asked.

The rest of the servants were hovering around her, wanting to see to her every wish. And she'd come up with the daft notion to worry about *him*. She wiped the dust from his gloves with the tips of her fingers.

Hell, but he'd missed her all these years. Why not be honest with himself now? He didn't want to lose her again.

So where did that leave him? He didn't do second chances.

Did he?

"You don't love me. You don't want me here. I can tell." His mother sobbed, her dark hair clinging to her cheeks.

"She is your mother, boy," his father said.

Clayton felt the mulish line of his lips weakening. His own eyes burned. He didn't want to see her cry.

Clayton placed his other hand over the top of Olivia's, needing the heat of her fingers to free him of the memories. The memories of how his mother had left two weeks after that episode. "I'm well. Just surveying the damage."

"The room actually looks better than I expected." But she edged away from it. With the dust still on her face, she looked rather like a frightened marble angel.

But she was right. The room remained more or less intact. Why not use a bigger bomb?

Clayton straightened from the door frame, focusing on the voices behind him until he could hear each one distinctly. "Someone didn't want to bring the house down around their *own* ears."

Chapter Twenty

"*My* maid," Olivia whispered. Her maid had brought in a dress box and set it next to the stove after the mouse scare. Now that Olivia's blind panic had ebbed, she could remember it clearly. She'd paid no attention at the time, thinking it was more borrowed clothing to add to her ill-fitting wardrobe.

Clayton's posture didn't change. "What?"

"My maid planted the bomb."

Iryna was standing at the edge of the crowd. She'd dusted off Olivia's skirts and now she continued to linger.

"We need to separate her from the others. I don't know who in this household answers to Prazhdinyeh. We can't risk someone coming to her aid."

Aid? "What precisely are you planning?"

"To question her."

That didn't sound too horrible, and yet the grimness deepened in his eyes. "Lean against me."

"Why—"

Clayton wrapped his arm around her shoulder

and pulled her close, and for a moment, everything faded but the hard-muscled chest pressed against her cheek.

"You there!" Clayton called to Iryna. "Your mistress is overset. She needs to be put to bed. Preferably in the other wing of the house."

After conferring with the butler, Olivia's maid came forward. "I can show you to your new rooms."

Rather than letting her walk, Clayton swung Olivia up into his arms and followed the maid.

For a moment, she worried her weight would be too much, but Clayton held her so effortlessly, her fear ebbed. She rested her cheek against him, enjoying the smoothness of his gait. The strength in the arms cradling her as if she was precious.

Until she remembered he was carrying her so they could interrogate the woman who'd tried to kill them.

She suddenly felt as ill as Clayton claimed her to be.

The maid led them into a small, graceful room decorated in pale yellow and cream. The stoves hadn't been lit so the room remained icy cold. "I'll see to the stove."

Clayton set Olivia on her feet and shut the door. "I'd prefer you didn't."

Iryna hesitated. "Just seeing to my mistress."

He locked the door with a sharp click. "As you already saw to her?"

She swallowed twice and inched closer to the door. "I didn't know what was in the box, I swear. He just told me to put it in her room. It was just a box."

"It would have taken at least five pounds of gun-powder for a blast that size. What did you think it was? A bonnet? Who gave it to you?"

Iryna crumpled to the floor with a keening sob. "I don't know. A man gave me a few rubles to deliver it."

"Who gave it to you?" he repeated.

Iryna curled up even tighter, rubbing her arms like she was cold. "I swear I do not know."

Clayton's lips thinned, his face colder than the air in the room. Olivia fought the urge to step back. She'd thought he'd been cruel when he'd come to the mill. She'd been wrong. This was pure ruthless-ness. This was who he'd been in his years as a spy.

For the first time, she could see the man Golov said had slain a man in his own bed.

Yet she didn't fear him. What she feared was losing him again to this darkness. Losing the teas-ing and banter she'd just found in him again.

Olivia tried to soften his interrogation. "If you know anything—" She took a step toward Iryna, but Clayton drew her back to his side.

"I don't know. I don't know anything. I swear." Iryna scooted on her backside toward the door.

Clayton blocked her escape.

"The truth, Iryna. I need a name."

"I don't know his name."

"You will tell me." Clayton pulled a knife from his boot. "Or I will have to carve it out of you."

Iryna squealed. "Please don't hurt me."

The darkness was there again, beckoning to Clayton. The emptiness he chose so he could do tasks like this. It would be an easy transition. He knew how to turn off the extraneous noise of his emotions and his thoughts. To slip behind his shields and let duty guide him.

Yet as they closed around him, he found himself struggling against them. The darkness was suffocating. He didn't want to lose himself to it.

Olivia was watching him. Her eyes were wide, worried. He didn't know why that bothered him. He'd intended to be frightening. And somehow, he knew he couldn't allow her to witness Cipher as the scum of Europe knew him. Brutal. Vicious. That gave him the strength to keep his shields at bay.

"Clayton—"

Olivia's distress worked in his favor. The maid sobbed louder. "He was dressed as a peasant. Gray hair. Full beard."

But without the darkness, he had to bear the brunt of the distastefulness of this situation. Deal with the maid's cries. Hear his father's voice reminding him to be a gentleman no matter the woman. Remain unflinching under Olivia's concern.

"What was he wearing?" Clayton asked. He'd find his answers even with his blasted emotions interfering.

"A heavy coat. Fur cap. Felt boots. But I don't know his name." She lifted her head before ducking it.

Her face was red and splotchy, but no tears. None at all.

His guilt dissolved. And he knew how to get his results. "You can continue to sob fake tears or you can tell me the truth and *perhaps* survive this."

Iryna looked up, suddenly silent. Clayton hauled her to her feet, pushed her against the wall, and put the knife to her throat.

Olivia inhaled sharply.

"Tell me the truth, and I'll give you a head start before I tell Golov."

Iryna paled, her nostrils flaring as she breathed. But her face twisted. "You won't live long enough to tell him anything. Everyone in Prazhdinyeh has orders to kill you. From the leaders to the lowliest recruits. And the reward is big. Do you know how many people in this household alone sympathize with the revolutionaries?"

Considering the prince had been one of the key generals in Prazhdinyeh before he'd been persuaded to change sides, probably far too many.

He pressed the knife to Iryna's throat. "How much did they tell you about me?"

"That you're an English spy who works for the *emperor.*" The word was filled with loathing.

He kept his tone conversational. Calm terrified people far more than all the anger and bluster he could try. "Did they tell you how many men and women I have killed? How I'm quite well-known for being able to slit a throat so cleanly that the person is drenched in their own blood before they feel the bite of my knife?"

She'd break soon. He saw it in the wildness of her eyes and the sway of her body. "How do they give orders?"

Iryna's throat worked nervously against the knife. "Everyone has two people they pass along news to."

If the orders were passed by word of mouth,

there'd be no help for the code there. "Who are your contacts?"

Iryna reluctantly gave the names.

"And which one gave you the bomb?"

"Barndyk."

He stepped away from her. "You have five minutes before I inform the police."

She started for the door, but he spoke before she could flee. "Before you think of joining your revolutionaries, know that I'll be quite truthful with your friends about who betrayed them."

She gripped the door frame to keep upright. "You've killed me."

"Perhaps. But I've given you a chance, which is far more than you intended for Miss Swift."

Iryna fled.

He locked the door again, keeping his gaze on the small brass key in the lock rather than looking at Olivia. "I do what I must to get answers."

"I know," she answered quietly.

"It got us results."

"Are you going to vomit?" she asked.

"No." She shouldn't be able to read him that well. He focused on calming the nausea churning in his gut. He'd thought such reactions banished long ago. He could hardly strike fear into the hearts of his enemies if they knew he'd cast up his accounts for two days after his first kill.

This was what came of allowing Olivia to weaken him.

Yet when she cupped his cheek, he leaned into her touch. The shared moment didn't feel like weakness. It felt like . . . completion.

He wanted more than a simple touch. He wanted

to lose himself in her lips again. He wanted to explore the delicate texture of her skin. Savor it.

But he couldn't be the kind of man to savor things. He needed to be the kind of man to keep her alive. "We'll finish cataloguing the books and papers. Then we'll find a new place to stay." There were too many dangers surrounding them here. Without knowing who else answered to Prazhdinyeh, they wouldn't be safe. There'd be far too many opportunities to be poisoned, stabbed, shot, tossed down the stairs. The list was nearly endless.

He wouldn't allow Olivia to remain here.

"What we need now is speed," he said.

Olivia straightened. "Then let's gather the books and get to work."

Nearly finished. Her hand had long ago cramped as they sat side by side at a table in the icy room. A servant came to light the stove, but Clayton refused to let him enter.

Instead, he'd wrapped a blanket from the bed around them both, which meant since Clayton was writing with his left hand, their elbows constantly collided. Olivia supposed she should offer to switch sides, but every now and again his arm would brush against the side of her breast. The accidental caresses stole her breath.

He didn't notice. He was so focused on scribbling down the titles in front of him.

With a sigh, she wrote the final title from Vasin's writings.

She rolled her wrist to regain blood flow and

tilted her head slightly, unable to resist watching Clayton as he wrote.

She'd never studied his chin from this angle. A tiny white scar highlighted one edge of his jaw, so small it might have resulted from shaving. She smiled at the idea of Clayton being human enough to nick himself.

The scar was in the exact place he'd held the knife on Iryna.

Olivia raised a finger to his chin, brushing the line there. "Who held a knife to your throat?"

"How did—"

She tapped the same spot. "You have a scar."

"I was cornered by a Spanish guerrilla who wanted information." He could have been discussing the weather.

"What happened?"

"I killed him with his own knife."

So blunt.

"Horrified?" he asked.

She should be, but she wasn't. "No. I'm glad you survived."

Although his expression didn't change, his exhale was long, as if he'd been holding his breath.

Knowing she was being far too bold, Olivia drew her finger farther up his jaw until she reached the hollow under his ear. She kept waiting for him to bat her hand away, but when he remained motionless, she ran her finger along his throat, relishing the small vibration as he swallowed. She then trailed down his shoulder until she reached his right hand that awkwardly held the blanket. "What happened to your hand?"

"The French. I waited at a meeting point to warn Madeline we'd been betrayed."

"But if you'd been betrayed—"

"I knew I'd be captured, but she was spared."

The more time she spent in his company the more flawed and selfish she felt by comparison. She was holding so many lies, concealing so many truths.

And she didn't want to any longer. She wanted to be able to lay her mistakes at Clayton's feet. To have nothing keeping her from speaking of her feelings.

"They broke my fingers one at a time to force me to tell them what they wanted. When I wouldn't, they cut my hand open to examine the mess they'd made. I didn't talk, but I did scream. I screamed until my voice was so hoarse no sound would come out."

The whole time he spoke, his quill never once stilled, as if the conversation meant little. But he was daring her to judge him. It was there in the set of his jaw and the taunt in his voice.

"By the time Ian and Madeline got me out, it was too late to reset some of the bones. They never healed correctly." He released the blanket long enough to clench his hand. It couldn't curl tighter than a loose fist. "Still not horrified?"

At her own bloodthirstiness, perhaps. Olivia longed to make each of his tormentors suffer for what they'd done.

But to be horrified at marks that proved his loyalty and bravery? Never.

She caught his gloved hand and lifted it to her lips, pressing a kiss on the back of each knuckle.

His quill froze.

Slowly, she peeled off his glove. White lines bisected his palm. Uneven, dark scars covered his fingertips. His index finger curved slightly inward.

It *was* shocking. But only because of the brutality that caused it. Not because the damaged skin itself was distressing.

She drew his hand to her lips again, pressing her mouth to the tip of one finger before laving the rough skin with her tongue. When his breath hissed through his teeth, she knew she had to give him more. She drew the end of his finger gently into her mouth.

With a curse, he tucked his damaged hand behind her head and kissed her.

His lips were smooth. Hot against her cool flesh. His left hand trailed up her spine, coaxing her closer. When his tongue brushed the seam of her lips, she opened for him, gasping as he pleasured her mouth.

The blanket slid to the floor, but neither of them bothered to collect it. He skimmed his hand up her arm, across her collarbone, and then down to the swell of her breasts.

She arched her back, pressing against him. *Yes.* She was still throbbing from his accidental caresses. She wanted this. Needed to have his fingers firm and purposeful on her. It was the only thing that would soothe the ache.

"Please . . ."

Clayton's lips lifted from hers and curled into a lazy smile. "You always did have such fancy manners. What do you need?"

Heat rushed up the back of her neck, but she

knew she'd answer. Something had changed in her since that kiss at the ball. She was more daring, more wild.

More in love.

"Please, touch my breasts."

After a slight pause, he lifted his good hand to her breast in reward, lightly cupping and kneading through the wool of her dress.

She moaned. The bliss was overwhelming but not enough. "More."

Clayton lifted his scarred hand slowly as though waiting for her to flinch away.

"Yes." The idea of both of his hands on her made her heart nearly explode.

Yet Clayton still hesitated a moment before giving it to her.

She leaned forward to complete the caress. She didn't care a jot what his hand looked like as long as it was on her.

He skimmed down her throat to the valley between her breasts before dipping into her bodice and cupping her, his bare flesh finally on her breast.

They both shuddered at the contact.

A knock sounded on the door.

Clayton had withdrawn and moved away from the desk before she'd even registered what the noise was.

"Why have you been sending my servants away?" Kate spoke through the closed door. "Olivia, are you well?"

"I'm well," she called out. She ran a hand over her hair, dusting white speckles across the desk. Heavens, she was still covered in plaster. A rather disheartening discovery when she'd thought herself seductive and alluring.

After ensuring Kate was alone, Clayton allowed her to enter. He tucked his damaged hand behind him. How many times had he done the same thing to Olivia without her even noticing?

No longer. She would never let him hide away his hand like it was something to be ashamed of.

"Your maid Iryna planted the bomb," Clayton said.

Kate paled. "I thought it was one of *your* associates."

"Not this time. Prazhdinyeh ordered it. How many people in your household are loyal to the revolutionaries?"

She shook her head. "I don't know. Some perhaps. They're serfs from my husband's estates. Many of them were here while he worked with the revolutionaries. I never thought to ask." Her hands clenched. "They set a bomb? In my house? Will they try it again?"

"We won't be staying," Clayton said.

Kate frowned at that. "Did you finish your investigation?"

"No."

"Then where will you be going?"

Clayton remained silent. Olivia wasn't sure if he wanted their destination to remain a secret or if he didn't yet know.

Kate ran her hands down the front of her trousers. "I think—" But then she stopped and sighed. "Do what you must. Do you need anything?"

"We'll be less conspicuous if we aren't covered

in plaster. Do you personally trust enough servants to bring up water to fill a bath?"

Kate thought a moment, then nodded. "And I'll see if I can arrange for a few things to be gathered for you to take—"

"No. I don't want it known we're leaving. It might make any potential attackers act rashly. And I will need you to keep Blin as one of your servants for now. There is no need for him to endanger himself."

"I think my cook would gut me if I did not."

After Kate had left, Clayton returned to his chair. He tugged his glove back on, grimacing slightly as he pulled it tight.

"Does it still hurt?"

"Always." He picked up his quill and dipped it in the ink. His lips quirked upward. "Except while it was caressing you."

How could a woman resist that? She lowered the neckline of her gown. "Well, if it helped . . ."

He dripped ink across the table but mopped it up with a blotting paper before it stained. "What precisely are you offering?"

"Everything." While her deceptions might keep her from casting her heart at his feet, they wouldn't keep her from casting her body into his bed.

Except they did.

She couldn't give herself to him without his knowing her part in the danger he faced today. "I asked you to take me to St. Petersburg because it would give the mill time to earn enough money to pay off the debts you hold."

"I suspected something of the sort."

Not precisely the reaction she'd expected. She'd

expected him to be appalled. She expected to have to tearfully explain all her reasoning, show how determined she was to protect the mill.

Had she hoped for it? Had this reveal been nothing more than an emotional trump card in her game to keep the mill?

Clayton held up his paper. "My list is complete. Since yours is shorter, read it to me and I'll mark off any we have in common."

He wasn't even going to respond to her confession?

"Clayton—"

"My plans for the mill will proceed with or without me. Nothing has changed."

"What? How?"

But he straightened his paper. "The list?"

She read the list slowly, waiting for him to call out a match, but also waiting for him to react to her confession. He couldn't truly be as uncaring about it as he seemed. But by the time she'd finished, he hadn't stopped her once. And not once had he looked at her with shock. Betrayal. Anything but focused concentration. "Nothing," she said.

"There was little chance of this working. After all, either one of them might have burned the book they used for the code. Or it might have been misplaced. Stolen by a servant. Given away." He stood and with a harsh exhale sent a pile of books crashing to the floor.

They both stared at the mess, shocked by his reaction. He strode to the window and braced his hands on either side of the frame. "What am I supposed to think about you?" His words almost desperate. "Tell me. Can I trust you?"

"I'm not a revolution—"

"I know you're not. But what am I supposed to do with this information you gave me? How did you think I would respond? How the devil should I?"

Olivia straightened the paper on the table, making it even with the edge, needing something to look at besides his face. Her throat felt dry, but Clayton hadn't allowed the servants to leave anything to drink.

She didn't know what to tell him. She couldn't tell him to trust her. Not when the truth about her father and the money she'd used for the mill was still unspoken. "I want to know if I can trust *you*."

He spun to face her. "What?"

Her answer surprised her as much as him. But it was too painful to be anything but the truth. "I need to know if I can trust you with my mistakes. I've made them, you know, big ones. And I know you don't like second chances. Or apologies."

"I saw my mother a year ago."

It might have seemed like a change in topic, but Olivia knew exactly why his thoughts returned to her. "Where?"

"She was at the theater. She's married to a butcher now."

Olivia picked the blanket up off the floor. "She must be doing well if they could afford to—"

"I saw her backstage with one of the actors."

Olivia stood and went to wrap the blanket around Clayton. He refused her with a sharp shake of his head. "Despite all the chances she had, she never changed."

The mill.

She clung to the thought to keep from exposing the rest of her deceptions. Those people deserved their second chance just as much as she did.

She couldn't take it from them.

And if she revealed her secrets, that's what would happen.

There was a knock. Clayton opened the door again and checked each footman before allowing them to enter with a large copper tub and steaming buckets of water.

Neither Clayton nor Olivia looked at each other. Neither of them wanted to finish the conversation they'd begun.

But even with the tension between them, he stood sentinel between her and the servants the entire time. When one of the footmen tried to bring in a tray of food, Clayton ordered him to return it to the kitchen.

Unfortunately for her stomach, the heavenly scents of pork dumplings with melted butter lingered.

"We'll require fresh clothing and a screen," Clayton said.

A screen? Did he intend— But of course, he did. He hadn't precisely let her state of undress stop him before.

Neither had she.

"And soap and oil for the bath. Jasmine, if you have it," Clayton added after a pause.

The soap made sense. "Why the oil?"

He paced the room checking the locks, watching out the window. "I thought that was the scent you preferred."

"It is." He'd done it for her. "That was . . .

sweet." And unexpected. And blast it all, why were her eyes stinging?

He wouldn't look at her. He was pulling away and she didn't know what to do to stop it. Her deceptions were a barrier for her. Her truths were a barrier for him.

When the footman bearing a large Oriental screen and the other requested items left, Olivia stood. If this didn't affect him, she wouldn't let it affect her. She'd slip around the screen and strip as if he hadn't just been stealing moans from her lips. As if she hadn't bared herself far more completely with words.

Clayton opened the bottle of oil and sniffed. "Rose. Will that work?"

"Do you expect me to protest?"

"You might have at one time, but not anymore." He poured some of the oil into the bath. "I'll leave you in privacy behind the screen."

She nodded as if this were a perfectly normal arrangement, as if—she was ashamed to admit—her breasts weren't still throbbing from his touch.

She lifted her chin and strode toward the black lacquered divider and the steaming water behind it.

"Will you need help with your buttons?"

Botheration. So much for her dramatic exit. "Yes."

He stepped behind her and made quick work of the buttons down her back. She wanted to look to see how he managed so easily with his injured hand, but she found she didn't want to know anything more about him. She didn't dare find more to admire.

Clayton cleared his throat twice. When he spoke, his voice was hoarse. "Will you need help with anything else?"

"No."

His boots were nearly silent on the carpet. "I'll recheck our lists and see if there's something I missed."

Even though she knew he hadn't missed anything, it was far preferable to think of him poring over lists rather than staring at the screen.

Had he ever seen the incomparable Madeline naked?

Olivia was suddenly quite grateful for the screen to cover her too long legs and less than abundant bosom.

And bruises. They covered her now. Her wrists. Her arms. Her stomach. It gave her an eerie resemblance to the cheetah she'd once seen at a menagerie.

As she slipped into the water, she couldn't suppress a moan. She hadn't spared a moment to think about her exhaustion and aching muscles until that instant.

But Clayton undoubtedly would appreciate use of the water for himself. So after scrubbing herself as thoroughly as she could, she stepped out and dried off, her skin pebbling instantly in the cold.

When she had a clean dress on, she moved from behind the screen and allowed Clayton to fasten her, trying to keep her teeth from chattering. As soon as he was done, Clayton took the blanket from his shoulders and tucked it around her.

Several minutes later, she wondered how Clayton had sat here without going mad. She stared at the same list he had, but each splash of water drew her eyes to the screen and her mind to what lay behind it. She picked up the prince's ring that Clayton had brought into the room with the stacks of books and papers. As she slipped it on and off her thumb, she looked at the heavy scrollwork that encircled the ruby. It wasn't decoration. It was artfully crafted Cyrillic.

Was that— "Clayton!"

Water sloshed, and he appeared from behind the screen with nothing but a dagger in his hand. Water dribbled down the hard, corded muscles on his shoulders, down the tight planes of his stomach, past his— She knew she should look away. But that was impossible. He was magnificent. A perfectly sculpted gladiator. A very *large* gladiator.

Her mouth was suddenly dry. Her body suddenly sensitive to everything. The scent of camphor on the blanket. The dampness of her hair.

The ache between her legs.

Clayton's eyes swept the room.

Blast. Speaking. Surely, she was capable of it. "There was no danger. I just— I had an idea," she finished rather lamely. She still couldn't take her eyes from him. A few silvery scars decorated his chest. On his muscular left thigh was the puckered reminder of a gunshot. She wanted to trail her lips over each scar, since she hadn't been there to tend him when he was injured.

Suddenly, the fact that he hadn't been swayed by her efforts on behalf of the mill seemed all too understandable. He'd given more than she could ever imagine.

Clayton lowered the dagger. "An idea?" Color darkened his cheeks, but his eyes met hers, then watched her traitorous gaze as it surveyed his body. He quickly turned away, revealing a tight, well-muscled backside. It was so intriguing, it took her a moment to notice the mass of scars crisscrossing his back. She pressed her lips together until she could feel her teeth imprinted on the back of them. He'd been flayed. There had to be at least fifty different lines.

"An idea about the code," she managed.

"Perhaps this conversation would be more appropriate clothed?" Clayton suggested.

"If you feel the need." Heat rushed to her face. That wasn't supposed to be uttered aloud.

He paused for a brief second before continuing to walk away. "What did you find?" His clothing rustled behind the screen.

"The prince's ring. It has an inscription."

"What does it say?"

She focused on getting the translation correct. "*From the ashes . . . reborn.*"

Clayton stepped back out. He'd pulled on his breeches but was still in the process of tugging on his shirt as he approached. "You're a bloody genius."

"Vasin had a pamphlet with that title," Olivia said.

"More than that." Clayton leaned over her, placing a warm, heavy hand on her shoulder. "He wrote it. It was considered one of the founding documents of the movement."

"Then his associates would have it?"

"Precisely."

She clenched the ring in her fist. "Then can we break the code?"

"If we can locate a copy."

"But we have—" No, they didn't have a copy. It had been in her room during the explosion. It was reduced to bits and ashes.

Clayton tugged back on his gloves. "I, unfortunately, know who does."

Chapter Twenty-one

"*H*ave a seat in the parlor. I'll join you in a moment," Professor Mir called out as they passed by the open library door. The stacks of paper that obscured the gray-haired scholar were even deeper than the last time Clayton was here.

The maid led them into a slightly less cluttered room. A few minutes later, the well-fed, gouty professor entered.

"Ah, Professor Lishpin! It has been ages. What brings you back to St. Petersburg?" He shoved aside a pile of books so he could sit; the chair creaked under the assault.

"More studies as always," Clayton said. "Professor Mir, may I introduce my assistant, Miss Britta Loenhiemer?"

Olivia nodded and remained silent. Clayton had warned her who Mir thought Clayton was—an Austrian philosophy professor.

"Is she as useful as she is lovely?"

Mir had always been something of a rutting goat. And unfortunately, when Clayton had visited him last, he'd given Mir the impression that he was the same. But Mir had the most comprehensive collection of Russian writings in the country. Partly because he never threw anything away, and partly because he had enough important friends that the police hadn't disturbed him when they purged the country of unpatriotic literature.

When a maid came in carrying tea, Mir gave her a swift pinch on the bottom.

Always a challenge to speak Russian with a German accent, Clayton found it even more difficult to do so through gritted teeth. "Miss Loenhiemer is indeed talented."

"I'll wager she is." Mir shifted his breeches.

"She has one of the brightest minds I've ever seen." He should be asking for the pamphlet, not defending his fictional assistant's honor.

"I like them clever." Mir chuckled. "Especially with their tongues."

Perhaps Clayton would pummel him senseless and find the writing himself.

"If you help my professor, perhaps I could show you just how clever I am."

The growl in Clayton's throat froze at Olivia's seductive murmur.

Mir's German was worse than Olivia's, so he had to puzzle through what she said, but there was no mistaking her tone. Or the way she placed her hand on Clayton's thigh and slowly massaged it. Clayton could hardly protest on her behalf while she did that.

He couldn't do much of anything while she did that.

Mir sucked in his stomach. "What was it you were looking for again, Professor?"

"An old pamphlet written by Vasin. *From the Ashes Reborn.*"

"A popular writing," Mir said.

"Has someone else inquired about it?" His chest slowly filled with dread. The inescapable dread that came from knowing the answer to his own question.

If someone else had come for the writing, then someone else knew how to break the code.

"Two days ago, some men from the academy came by and requested a copy."

If they'd come two days ago, it couldn't have been Golov.

Prazhdinyeh had broken the code first.

Olivia's nails were digging into Clayton's leg even through his thick woolen trousers. She'd made the connection as well. "And you gave it to them?" Olivia asked.

Mir motioned for Clayton and Olivia to take a cup of tea, then selected one himself, taking a large, noisy sip. "Of course. I always support academics."

Or revolutionaries, in this case.

"Why all the interest?" Mir's eyes glinted with the intelligence he so often neglected when there was a woman about.

Before Clayton could think of a lie, Olivia flicked her tongue over her lower lip. "Do you have another copy?"

Mir's eyes glazed over slightly. "I might. Let me go see."

Olivia sighed once he left and picked up a cup of tea. "They broke the code, didn't they?"

"Most likely."

"At least it means we were correct in our guess about the code." Olivia dropped two lumps of sugar and a dash of cream into her tea and stirred quickly.

Clayton lifted his cup to his lips and took a sip. Bitter. Cloying.

He spat out the tea and lunged toward Olivia, knocking her cup from her hand as she raised it to her mouth, sending the liquid splattering across the carpet.

She stared at the rocking cup, lips still pursed to take a sip.

"Poison." He set down his own cup, then jumped to his feet. "The professor."

She scrambled up from her chair. "Did he try to kill us?"

Clayton picked up the teapot and sniffed. "No. The entire thing is poisoned. And he drank some."

They ran to the study. The professor lay in a crumpled heap, his face purple, eyes bulging. Clayton knelt and checked the body for a heartbeat, then closed the eyes. "He's dead."

Pale crescents deepened on either side of Olivia's mouth, but she surveyed the piles of books, papers, and writings scattered around the room. "Do you know anyone else who might have Vasin's pamphlet?"

He understood her concern. There had to be thousands of books and papers. He could see no system of organization. They might search for days and never find the pamphlet.

"Wait." He stepped around the body. "This pile was twice as tall when we passed by originally."

He pointed to a stack in front of the bookcase a few feet from where the professor had fallen.

"You noticed?"

He'd always remembered small details, but the Foreign Office trained him to recognize the significance in them.

He sorted through the papers. There it was. Three pages down.

From the Ashes Reborn.

Clayton tucked the paper in his waistcoat, then pulled Olivia after him until they were safe in the dim twilight of the snowy evening.

Perhaps not so safe.

The sleigh that was supposed to wait for them was gone. Not a promising sign. He couldn't risk taking her back into the house, so he started walking.

They'd gone only a few hundred feet when a footman left Mir's house and started in their direction. He could be heading out on some perfectly valid errand, but Clayton wasn't taking that chance. He quickened their pace.

Olivia fell slightly behind him so she could walk in his footsteps in the knee-deep snow.

A stoop-shouldered laborer stepped from behind white-capped bushes ahead of them, deliberately blocking that path.

Clayton grabbed his knife from his boot, then spun Olivia around to head in the other direction. Two heavy men had joined the footman with a purposefully casual stroll.

Damnation. He should have anticipated an ambush.

Where could he send Olivia so she'd be safe?
The neighborhood had cleared of people as the
temperature dropped with the sun. Across from
the street lay the granite-lined bank of the Neva,
but it offered no cover. The thick snow made it difficult to walk, let alone run.

He'd take out the laborer with a dagger to the
throat, then send Olivia to safety while he delayed
the footman and the other two. "When I give the
word, I want you to run ahead. There's a bridge
a half mile up. There will be a policeman nearby
to monitor it. Don't stop until you reach him."
He handed his first dagger to Olivia, before un-
sheathing another. "Don't hesitate to use that if
cornered."

Another two men joined the laborer.

Hellfire. He had only three knives. He'd planned
on throwing the dagger, retrieving it, and throwing it at the party behind him to even the numbers
somewhat. But with two more so close, the thrown
dagger would be lost. It was still his best option,
but he'd be left with five to fight hand to hand.

Clayton waited until he and Olivia were a dozen
feet from the laborer. The man pulled a gun.

He'd just volunteered for death.

The dagger flew from Clayton's fingers, and the
man dropped to his knees with a wet gurgle.

"Now!" Clayton shoved Olivia to the right while
he lunged to intercept the other two. He stabbed
the short one in the gut, but the bulky fellow in
a gray scarf attacked in the same moment. Clayton blocked a cudgel inches before it slammed into
his skull. When Clayton tried to reattack, the man
deflected easily. Gray Scarf wasn't a simple thug;

most likely a former soldier, which made him far more dangerous.

The wounded man on the ground shrieked, making it difficult to hear the other attackers approaching from behind. Clayton backed toward the river and risked a glance over his shoulder. Ten feet.

The cudgel slammed into his side. Clayton would have dropped to his knees if the snow wasn't bracing his legs upright. His next block protected his head, but succeeded in driving his knees into the snow.

He couldn't let them go after Olivia. This thought brought him back to his feet and gave him the speed to slice Gray Scarf's hand as the man prepared to swing.

Gray Scarf merely grunted and switched hands.

Clayton flinched out of the reach of a new knife flashing toward him. The other attackers had reached him.

He stabbed one in the throat while kicking out to keep the other men back, but pain exploded as someone landed a punch to the side of his face.

Three remained. Including Gray Scarf, who was biding his time until he could land a clear blow.

Hell. If he wanted to survive this— Clayton leaped up over the embankment and onto the icy river six feet below. The ice creaked beneath him.

They all stilled until the noise ceased. When it held Clayton's weight, one of the men followed, leaping onto the ice nearby.

But Clayton could handle one man, even if he was armed. And with a single feint and thrust, his opponent fell.

With a shout, the footman jumped onto the ice. Clayton dispatched him as well, retreating from the crimson snow now encircling him.

Gray Scarf was wise enough to keep his vulnerable throat hidden beyond the edge of the embankment. Only his eyes were visible.

"Do you wish to join your friends?" Clayton asked, adjusting his weight so he'd be able to move quickly on the ice.

Then Gray Scarf's head disappeared completely from the edge of the embankment. But he wasn't the type to simply give up. Not a seasoned campaigner like him.

A huge chunk of paving stone landed on the ice next to Clayton.

The sharp, brittle sound of ice cracking echoed along the granite walls.

Another rock smashed clean through the ice, leaving a few remnants bobbing in the black space. Sharp white slashes splintered toward him.

Clayton scrambled back to the embankment, but he could gain little purchase on the smooth, frozen stone of the embankment. Water seeped up through the cracks, spreading around his feet.

Now Gray Scarf's entire head appeared. His scarf still covered his mouth, but Clayton didn't need to see it to know he must be grinning evilly as he held another huge rock over Clayton's head. Even if Clayton managed to dodge it, the rock would put him through the ice.

"Step away from him!"

Olivia.

What was she doing? She should be with the policeman by now. Cursing the weakness in his right hand, Clayton wedged his dagger in the seam between two of the granite blocks and pulled himself upward, ignoring the fact that his rib cage had been replaced with hot coals.

She stood no chance against the soldier.

Hell. What was she thinking?

Olivia spoke again. "I said step away."

"You will not pull the trigger, little girl." It was the first time Gray Scarf had spoken, his voice both higher and softer than Clayton had expected.

She must have picked up the dead man's pistol.

Clayton threw one elbow over the top of the embankment.

Olivia stood a dozen feet away, a pistol clutched in her hands. Her bonnet had gotten lost somewhere and her golden hair whipped around her face. She was a Valkyrie. Defending him.

"I always finish my fights," she warned.

Gray Scarf chuckled and lifted the rock.

She fired.

Gray Scarf fell, the rock landing with a near silent thump into the snow.

Clayton forced his body to obey once more and hefted himself fully onto the street.

Olivia took a step toward him before she collapsed, her whole body trembling.

He had to get to her.

It hurt to breathe. His vision blurred from the punch to his head. Air refused to fill his aching lungs. But he dragged himself toward her in the snow.

He'd gone only a foot when she stood, her face pale where it wasn't reddened from the cold. She wavered, but then set her chin and walked to him, keeping her gaze pinned on him rather than the carnage surrounding her.

"He's not dead," Clayton said.

As if on cue, Gray Scarf groaned. Olivia flinched away.

The gunshot had roused the curiosity of the surrounding neighborhood. People peeked out of windows and cracked open doors.

"We need to get out of sight before he recovers or the police arrive." Clayton forced his legs to stand under him. As long as he moved slowly, he could tolerate the pain in his side.

As they passed, he tugged the gray scarf off the man and passed it to Olivia to tie around her head so she didn't lose her ears to frostbite.

Clayton's toes had gone numb in the full leather boots, and Olivia had only those impractical half boots females were forced to wear. Her feet must be frozen. And that wasn't a term he used lightly. He needed to get her up and out of this snow completely.

She stumbled against his bad side, and they both fell to their knees.

"People . . . don't freeze to . . . death in the streets, do they?" Her chattering teeth made her difficult to understand.

He wished he could lie. "All the time." Clayton's pants and jacket were soaked through with melted snow, as was the hem of Olivia's skirt. The damp fabric robbed what little warmth their bodies would have created walking.

"Lovely."

A sleigh hissed across the snow behind them. *Let it be one for hire* . . . Clayton dropped his hand to the hilt of his last remaining dagger as the horse slowed beside them.

"I said to myself, who could have left such a fine body count along the streets of St. Petersburg?"

Ian.

Despite his agony, Clayton lifted Olivia into the sleigh before it had come to a stop.

"We need to get her inside and warm." He grabbed Olivia's red hands and rubbed them vigorously to get the circulation going again.

After her fingers had pinkened, he unbuttoned his greatcoat and pulled her hands against his chest. "I intend to buy you a dozen pairs of gloves. Which you'll wear."

"At the same time?" he thought she tried to ask.

"Bloody right. In the summer, too." Then he'd feed her chocolate, and biscuits, and the most exotic sweets he'd encountered, and he'd bury her under a dozen furs next to a roaring fire. "Give me one of your blankets, Ian."

Ian tossed one off his shoulders, making him a slightly smaller mountain. Clayton tucked it around Olivia.

Her hand traced down his side. "Are your ribs broken?"

Clayton shifted to test them. "Perhaps cracked. Not broken."

"You let someone land a blow on your ribs?"

He was glad Ian's mockery gave him something to think about other than Olivia's hands on his body.

Olivia frowned, blinking through the snow-flakes that settled on her eyelashes. "There *were* six of them."

Ian snorted. "Getting soft, old man. Did he ever tell you about the time he took out an entire regiment of French cavalry?"

"I did have a cannon."

"Judging from the gunshot, you at least had a pistol this time."

"No. That was Olivia's shot," Clayton said.

Ian glanced back, his eyes searching Clayton's. "I must say it is lovely to have a team again."

"Yes, it is," Clayton said. He'd give her a second chance. Despite her confession this afternoon, he owed it to her. Besides, didn't the fact that she'd told him the truth speak in her favor? The decision wasn't nearly as unsettling as he thought it would be. After all, Olivia was only one person. He wasn't being too permissive or allowing everyone to trample over him.

Besides, it felt right. Like he'd finally found the piece he'd been missing for a puzzle.

The sleigh slowed in front of a modest building. Ian hopped down, then returned a minute later, eyes twinkling. He gestured with a proud sweep of his arm. "Go warm yourselves and get naked."

Chapter Twenty-two

"*P*ardon?" Olivia's cold-slowed brain must have misheard.

But Clayton was already lifting her out of the sleigh. "A private room?"

"The finest," Ian replied as he flicked the reins on the horse. "Such as it is. I asked them for ink and paper for you, as well. You can thank me later."

The building had a small sign hanging out front but a heavy dusting of snow made it impossible to read. Two bull-shouldered men greeted them at the door, lightly dressed in white linen shirts and trousers tied around their waists. They bowed low and led them inside, casting only a single curious glance at Clayton's swollen cheek and the blood that dripped from the cut above his eye.

The air was heavy and overly moist as they walked down a corridor. The low rumble of voices was occasionally interrupted by the sounds of flesh pounding flesh.

The men stopped at a door and opened it. Smoke—no, steam—billowed in thick, white strands into the corridor. A man stalked out, glaring at them, skin raw, pink, and glistening. Only a towel was wrapped around his pudgy hips. Red stripes covered his back.

"A bath?" Olivia asked, although it felt more like a statement.

"Ian thinks himself quite humorous. But it will give us a private place to keep warm while he finds us a room for the night."

After convincing the attendants they didn't need any further personal ministrations, Clayton tipped them a few kopecks for a bowl of water and a fresh towel.

Olivia stepped through the curtain of steam.

The air in the room was on fire. There was no other explanation for how each breath seared her nose. She was reduced to taking small pants of air; deep breaths smoldered too painfully within her chest. The molten air smelled faintly of pine from the rough planks that covered the walls and the heavy, wide benches that ringed the room. Two small candles cast patches of light in one far corner.

They both stood still a moment, letting the heat from the glowing red rocks in the brazier seep into their bones.

Melting ice dripped from Clayton's hat across the dried blood of his cut, trailing streaks to his chin.

Olivia took the towel from him and dipped it in the water. "We should clean your wound."

The corner of his mouth inched upward. "It hardly qualifies as a *wound*."

The cut *wasn't* bad, only an inch long, and the

bleeding had already stopped. But she had to do something that involved touching him.

He'd been incredible. And terrifying. She'd never seen a man move with such grace and precision. "Can all spies fight like that?"

He didn't flinch as she dabbed the cut. "Most of the useful tricks I know came from Ian. But all spies have some training."

"You were amazing."

"The Trio had more practice than most." He tilted his head after he finished speaking. "I expected that to come out with more bitterness. See what you do to me?"

"What *do* I do to you?"

Clayton stripped off his greatcoat, then his gloves. She loved that he didn't hesitate before removing them this time. "Get out of your wet things, and I'll show you."

But he apparently didn't think she was quick enough at following his directions, because his hands were suddenly on her shoulders, lifting her sodden pelisse away. With the callused pad of his thumb, he brushed the powder burn on the back of her hand. "Next time I tell you to run, you don't come back."

"Your death didn't work so well for me before."

Clayton laid her wet cloak over one of the benches that lined the walls of the room. "If both of us had died, no one would translate the code."

Ah, the one time she thought she'd actually been selfless, she'd been selfish after all.

She barely registered what he was doing before her dress was draped over the bench, followed by her petticoats and stays. She kicked off her shoes, leaving her clad only in her shift and stockings. She should be shocked, but anticipation was flowing too swiftly for that. "What was this you had to show me?"

He lifted the cool rag to trace across her forehead, down her cheek, and under her jaw. "The Russians claim these baths have great restorative powers."

She swallowed. "Is that so?" The cloth was cheap and coarse. It shouldn't feel like paradise on her skin.

And from Clayton's heavy gaze, he knew it did, too.

"From the steam?" she managed to ask.

"The steam's only a small part of the tradition." Clayton dipped the cloth in the bowl behind him, then trailed it down the other side of her face. "After relaxing in the steam, most Russians would run outside and roll in the snow."

She longed to quench her heated flesh in the icy powder. The shock. The clarity. How could she have dreaded the cold seconds ago? Anything would be preferable to this inferno in her blood. "Naked? Like you aren't?"

She couldn't help it. Clayton inspired pure wickedness in her.

"Ah, but I must see to you first."

"You always do."

Clayton's hand slowed for an instant where he dabbed along her throat.

Perhaps she'd said too much. "So they are naked, writhing in the snow. Then what happens?"

He resumed his ministrations. "Then they return to the steam and throw more water on the coals, raising the temperature even higher."

Why did they need water to do that? The room was growing hotter all on its own.

She needed to move far, far away from this. But she said, "What next?"

"The attendants would rub their bodies, releasing any tightness. Soothing sore muscles." He moved behind her, his hands lifting to her shoulders. His fingers, still cool from the water, dug into her neck and she leaned into them. How could she not?

He kneaded his way down her back. "Then more steam and more cold."

More, more, more was the only thing her fevered brain understood.

She jerked as water replaced his hands, the sopping cloth leaving small strokes of comfort on her neck. The liquid dripped from the cloth, under her shift, down the length of her body.

"I never thought to be jealous of water." He traced a finger down one of the paths onto her collarbone, then followed its descent to the neckline of her shift. He paused.

He was holding his breath, awaiting her decision. She knew with certainty that if she remained still he'd stop. But if she arched, driving his finger lower . . .

She arched.

His finger slipped beneath the neckline. With a groan, Clayton cupped her breast fully, pulling her back flush against her chest.

"I've never had such trouble focusing on a code in my life. Do you know how these tight nubs taunted me? How long I've imagined how they'd look bare to my gaze? I've dreamed about that for ten years." He drew on the drawstring gathering the shift at her neck and tugged it loose. The garment slid off her shoulder, held up only by her back pressed against him and the swell of her breasts.

With a brush of his palm, the linen slid from one breast, baring it to him.

His chin rested on her shoulder and she knew he was studying her. She couldn't help looking down, too. His hand was dark as it cupped the pale skin of her breast.

The contrast sent a stab of pure desire straight to her core.

He teased the tip with his thumb. His exhale was harsh. "It was worth the wait."

When she shifted restlessly against him, the proof of his arousal pressed against her. When he groaned, she rubbed him again.

His hand tightened on her breast.

Apparently, he enjoyed that.

His other hand moved across her stomach, then dipped lower. She needed him to stop the ache. She twisted her hips. But rather than touch where she longed for him, his hand caressed down the front of her thigh.

She couldn't help her small moan of disappointment.

"Did you want my hand somewhere else?"

"Yes!"

"No 'please' this time?"

She was past politeness. Past anything but needing him. "Touch me."

His hand dipped between her legs. Her head dropped back onto his shoulder as the pleasure robbed her muscles of strength. He nipped her ear. "Whatever you desire."

"You." While her body hummed with the perfection of his caresses, her heart sang with the rightness of the man touching her. Slow circles. Bliss.

A new pressure began to build, radiating through her body from the sensitive flesh Clayton caressed.

She shifted against him, suddenly needing more than slow. She needed this moment of pleasure to remember when they both hated each other again.

But he seemed to know, increasing the pressure of his hand. More. She needed him. But she needed her hands on him, too. It wasn't enough just to feel pleasure. She wanted to give it.

She twisted until her hands were on him, slipping under his shirt, exploring the smooth, hot skin of his chest.

It still wasn't enough. She wanted him as wild as she was. She wanted him to be as mindless with pleasure as she was.

She leaned forward and touched her lips to his throat. Then, feeling bold, she flicked her tongue across the skin there.

His breath caught, then released in a shudder.

A wicked, contented smile stretched his lips. His face was relaxed, the glint in his eye almost devilish. He looked . . . happy.

She couldn't let him open his heart to her like this.

She tried to banish the thought. *Focus on his hands. On the fire in your blood.* But it was too late.

It had been one thing to kiss and provoke him while he hated her. She'd been able to convince herself that there was nothing wrong with the small tastes of passion between them. That it wouldn't mean anything to him even if it meant everything to her.

But he trusted her.

And he shouldn't. And once he discovered the truth about the lies she'd told to hide her father's condition and the money she'd found, he wouldn't.

If she allowed this to progress between them, she'd hurt him.

She'd been naive enough to let that happen once, but now she'd do anything to stop it from happening again. She loved him too much.

He cupped her breast and brought her nipple to his mouth. The small flick of his tongue made everything blur. Her heart ceased beating and raced at the same moment. She couldn't help herself. She closed her eyes against the sharp pleasure coursing through her.

Perhaps if she kept her eyes closed, she could pretend his trust wouldn't complicate things between them. That she could make love to him, and they could somehow overcome her lies.

But she couldn't.

"Now about that birthday gift you owe me. The one I'd never forget?"

She'd tried to forget about that. His birthday would have come one week after he'd been arrested. She'd planned to make wild and passionate love to him. At least, as passionate as her innocent brain at the time could fathom. She'd interrogated the maids for weeks to figure out all the details. Why couldn't he have reminded her of this yesterday, before her crisis of conscience? When she

could have showed him exactly what she'd planned
for him so long ago?

She wanted to rail at his poor timing. Instead,
she lifted her brow. "It was an appointment book."

"I almost wish that *had* been your gift. My
younger self might never have recovered from his
dashed hopes."

She wished she'd thought of it then, too.

Except, inside the book she'd have written something utterly scandalous.

"We should see if the pamphlet will break the
code." Her voice was raspy and low in her throat.
"Do you still have it?"

Clayton's hand ceased its magic, and she cursed
herself for the barest hint of uncertainty that
crossed his features as he drew back from her.
"Would you prefer I put my glove back on?"

She spun to face him so he couldn't doubt her
response. She caught his hand, raising it to her lips
so she could kiss his knuckles. "*No.* It is not your
hand."

He frowned. "Then did I misread your permis-
sion earlier? Or your interest?"

"Neither of those things."

"Then what the devil did I miss?"

"That I love you too much to make love while
I'm hiding things from you."

He stared at her. His mouth opened. Then
closed. Then opened. "What are you hiding?"

"Things about the mill. And I cannot tell you
my secrets if you'll use them to destroy it."

His face darkened. "If your secrets would destroy the mill, perhaps it's simply a sign that it
should be destroyed."

"I refuse to accept that. Surely, there's some compromise—"

"You tell me there are dark secrets about the mill and then expect me to work to safeguard it?"

She wanted to protest that the secrets weren't dark. But they were. They were truths she'd hidden in order to restore the mill, and now there was no way to escape them. Not without hurting far too many families.

They were both silent for a moment.

"So shall we work on the code?" she finally asked.

"Perhaps that would be for the best."

He pulled the pamphlet and the paper containing the code from inside his waistcoat pocket. Both were crinkled from moisture along the top edge, but it hadn't touched the ink.

He handed them to her. "If you'll allow me to see to my clothing, I'll assist you in a moment."

So formal. Her chest ached as she retied the strings of her shift.

Clayton shrugged out of his jacket, then began unfastening the buttons on his waistcoat. Olivia flashed her gaze to the walls of the room, not wanting to know if his breeches were going to follow. Not when she knew all too clearly what lay under them.

Had she truly just given up the opportunity to undo those buttons herself? To have his naked body pressed against hers? His fevered skin under her tongue?

I won't listen for the rustle of fabric. I will not.

Bunches of slender branches were tied together and piled in the corner. Were they used for cleaning somehow? But then she remembered the welts on the back of the previous occupant. Apparently, they had other uses.

Perhaps a solid flogging would distract her from thoughts of Clayton naked only a few feet behind her. But she wasn't quite mad enough to try it. Olivia turned to another form of self-punishment. The code. She laid out the pages next to each other on the bench.

"So how do I do this?" she asked as she compared the two pages.

"Determine the numerical equivalent of the first letter in the pamphlet and subtract it from the numerical equivalent of the first letter on the coded page. You need to reverse how they coded it."

But it wasn't as simple as he made it sound. The Russian alphabet had thirty-three letters. And she had to stop and think out each one. She went through the process on a dozen letters, but Clayton still didn't join her.

Against her better judgment she turned to check on him. He sat across from her, struggling to remove a boot, face contorted with pain.

The blow to his ribs.

She hurried to him and grabbed the heel of his boot. "You could have asked for help."

"I can manage."

Obviously, he couldn't. But he was too stubborn to admit that.

"I think I saw a bit more than your bare feet earlier."

She expected Clayton to laugh, but while his lips tilted slightly, his eyes grew hooded. "If you're willing to let go of the mill, you can see it again."

The oxygen ceased to exist. There was only heat. In the room. And in his gaze.

A bead of sweat slipped down her neck, then between her breasts.

Clayton followed it with his gaze.

She exhaled. "If *you're* willing to abandon *your* plan."

Clayton's lips resumed their familiar stern line. "Your father needs to be brought to justice."

She hadn't expected his desire for her to be greater than his desire for revenge. So it shouldn't sting so much that it wasn't. "My father's sick—"

"There is no other option."

"Then you know why we cannot act on this." She peeled down the top half of his boot, but it still refused to budge. "What in the blazes is wrong with your boot?"

That did return a slight smile to his face. "I feel better. I was quite appalled at my lack of progress."

Glaring at his boot, she grabbed the heel by both hands and yanked hard. The boot popped free. The other, luckily, required only a small amount of coaxing.

"I think I can manage my stockings." He rubbed the back of his neck, and his voice softened slightly. "Thank you for your help."

It should be criminal the way he could make his voice low and rumbling like that. She wanted him to whisper like that all over her naked flesh.

Olivia retreated to the safety of the papers.

"Any progress?" Clayton asked from behind her.

Was he taking off his pants yet? Why was that the question of most importance to her brain to-night? She removed the cloth from the bowl of water and wiped the sweat from her face and arms, claiming any distraction she could. "Not yet."

A few seconds later when Clayton stood beside her—still wearing his shirt and breeches—she'd finished the first line.

But it was gibberish. None of the letters combined into words that she recognized. In fact, they weren't even words at all. No vowels.

Clayton brushed at the corner of her scowl with his thumb. "Then we try the next page and the next until we find the right one. If that doesn't work then we go line by line. Then backwards."

"But I was hoping for something. At least a sign we had the right pamphlet. This is nothing."

Clayton frowned, then reached out and lifted her translation. "Too much of nothing."

His brow furrowed as he rechecked her work, not needing to write things down as she had. After a moment, he rocked on his heels. "Out of all these letters, statistically, there should have been at least one vowel. There are none. You did break the code." He picked up the quill. "We just were almost fooled by a second one." With a few slashes of ink, he divided her line into grouped consonants. He read the line phonetically.

Vasin had taken out the vowels before he encoded it.

Olivia jumped to her feet and kissed Clayton on the cheek. "We've done it!" Or perhaps even better—they *could* do it. They might actually be able to stop the revolutionaries. She scooted aside as Clayton went through the rest of the paper with much greater efficiency.

She loved the way his quill scratched across the

paper. The occasional grin he lifted in her direction that she couldn't help returning. The flush to his cheeks, half heat, half excitement.

She leaned closer to his shoulder. She didn't speak Russian well enough to divide the rows of letters into words on her own.

But Clayton seemed confident. Finally, he set down the quill.

"What does it say?"

He held out the paper and translated the words into English. "*To my fellow lover of freedom: Three flags will free Russia from its shackles of corruption: A flag in the window of the Nevsky Monastery will bring the unrighteous to his knees. A flag by the westernmost cannon at St. Peter and Paul's fortress will fell the mighty. A flag on the cupola at St. Igor's will vanquish a crown. Then you will know the time is ready to light the fire of freedom.*" He reread the page. "It's a little more poetic in Russian."

"I was rather hoping for a name." She wiped at the sweat itching on her cheeks.

Clayton lifted the cloth from the bowl and scrubbed it over his face, then rinsed it before offering it to her. "This is a list of signs to be given to Vasin's agents."

"Agents?"

"Four of them, I suspect. One to coincide with each signal. And one to do the final act. This paper must have belonged to the man who is supposed to kill the czar."

Olivia sat down with a thump on the bench. He didn't seem surprised, but it had never occurred to her. She'd thought they would need to locate a single gunman and stop him. But four? "So what now?"

"We prevent the revolutionaries from giving the signals."

"Will that prevent them from acting?"

"It's our best option."

Then that's what they would do. "How far away is the monastery?"

"Not far. Perhaps twenty minutes."

Her soaked dress hadn't dried at all in the steamy room. It still dangled limp and heavy over the bench across from her. How long would it take it to refreeze once they returned outside? Longer than twenty minutes?

Clayton must have followed her gaze. "We'll wait until Ian returns with supplies and a vehicle."

"And what do we do until then?" she asked.

"We rest." He sat on the bench next to her and pulled her against him.

"Clayton—"

"There is no mill here now, is there? Rest."

Slowly, she allowed her head to press against his shoulder. His linen shirt was soft and smelled of him. She inhaled deeply, the warmth melting her bones and her resolve.

For a moment, Clayton's head rested on hers.

"Can we just stay here?" she whispered.

"I am fairly certain you would die from the heat before too long."

She turned her head and bit him lightly.

His exhale was half laugh.

"I need you to be clever for me," she whispered. "I need you to find a way for us to both be satisfied with what happens to the mill."

His lips brushed her hair. "You always were demanding."

"I don't want to hurt you again."

"Why are you so certain you will? I'm not precisely fragile." His muscles tightened under her cheek.

"Did you just tense to show off your muscles?"

His shoulder tensed again, even tighter this time.

A knock sounded on the door. Clayton was on his feet before it could open.

"I've returned victorious." Ian sounded quite pleased with himself.

"That was fast even for you," Clayton said.

"Did I interrupt?"

Clayton must have scowled because Ian laughed.

"I *did* interrupt. Madeline owes me a quid when I return. But now for the news—I know where to find Arshun."

The sledge jostled over the uneven snow. They'd emerged into one of the older parts of St. Petersburg. Most of the buildings were wood and only a single story. Not a neighborhood Clayton associated with Arshun.

Ian pointed to a squat house a short distance down. Its windows had been papered to keep out the cold. And also, no doubt, so the police couldn't see what was going on inside it.

"How did you find it?" Clayton asked.

"I'd like to claim something impressive, but as it turns out, your favorite lovable giant helped the count deliver boxes to several houses around the city. This was one of them. Why didn't you ask him?"

"He said he didn't know where Arshun was. I suppose I didn't ask the right questions."

"Blin knew?" Although she was finally dressed properly for the cold, with a fur hat, mittens, and coat, Olivia could barely keep her eyes open. And she had to be starving. They hadn't eaten all day.

Ian was far too well trained to give in to his exhaustion, but the horses he drove had clumps of ice around their nostrils and his good cheer was a bit more forced than normal. "Indeed. And can I just say that man has pastries running through his veins? His tortes are divine."

Secrets or no, Olivia was Clayton's to protect. To watch after. He supposed many might think that obligation a burden, but he relished the right to claim the responsibility even as it terrified him. He cradled her against him, offering what little added warmth he could.

But Olivia had been correct earlier. No matter how irresistible and undeniable their attraction was, he couldn't pursue her while he planned to ruin something she held dear.

Was there a way they could both be satisfied with what happened to the mill? What if he forced her father to sell the mill privately? He could punish her father but keep her safe. He could even arrange for the mill to be bought by a fair businessman so the townspeople she cared about could be safe. He could have his justice, but it wouldn't affect those who didn't deserve it.

Ian continued past Arshun's house. Smoke wafted from the chimney, and the snow on the walk leading to the house had been packed down by many feet. Arshun wasn't alone in there.

When Ian was a good distance past, he slowed the sleigh to a stop.

"How many revolutionaries are there?" Olivia asked.

Clayton leaped down. "That's what I'm about to find out."

Without Clayton's warmth at her back, Olivia shivered. She knew she shouldn't stare after him but she couldn't help it. "He isn't going into the house, is he?"

Ian shrugged. "He better be. Otherwise, next time *he* can stay with the horses." Ian clicked his tongue and coaxed the horse into maneuvering the sleigh to face the way they'd come. "Don't worry. There probably won't be more than six or seven."

Six or— "You are jesting, right?"

Ian frowned and tapped his chin. "Not this time." He climbed down and threw one of his blankets over the back of the horse. "You're wasting a perfectly good opportunity." He wiped the frozen sweat from the beast.

"What?" She tried to banish all thoughts of Clayton fighting half a dozen men.

"I'm a fount of information about Clayton, and you've yet to ask me anything."

That distracted her. "You'd tell me?"

"A woman who doesn't shoot Clayton when given the chance is a rare woman indeed. Madeline did, you know."

"What?" she found herself repeating.

"Shoot him. In the thigh. She claims it was an

accident, that he moved into her line of fire, but I think we all know the truth."

Olivia's head was spinning a bit, but not enough that she didn't realize that was probably the effect he wanted.

"Isn't this information secret?"

"Private—maybe. Secret—no. But I figure if I leave Clay to his own devices, he'll be all dark and mysterious long after you've given up on him and it's too late." Ian hopped back into the sleigh and pulled the rest of his blankets over him. Then his hand reemerged holding half of a smashed pastry.

She took the piece he offered. "Too late for what?"

"For him to realize he still loves you."

"Wha—" She just barely stopped herself from repeating her confusion for a third time. "He doesn't love me. Not anymore." He might trust her. He might desire her. But he didn't love her.

"Then why didn't he look into your history when he researched the mill?"

The answer seemed rather obvious. "Because he didn't care."

"Wrong! You know Clayton better than that. He is entirely methodical and meticulous. Yet he refused to look into your life over the past ten years. Odd, is it not? Almost like he was trying to prove something to himself?"

"If you think he came after the mill just so he could interact with me—"

Ian laughed. "No. No. He will destroy everything." The grin faded on his face. "He will just hate himself afterward."

"I'm trying to stop him."

"No, you're trying to save the mill."

Why hadn't Clayton mentioned the man was mad? "They are the same thing."

"Wrong again. There's information you could give Clayton that would stop him."

There was no way he could know—

Ian tapped his temple. "All-knowing. It's a curse, really."

She ripped the pastry. "Then I'd be the one who destroyed the mill. I'd be no different from my father."

"Are you now? Trying to reach your goals no matter the means?"

Father's daughter. "If I've had to lie, it was for the greater good—"

"If you keep to your lies, you'll destroy Clayton all over again. He trusts you. You know Clayton. He cannot do anything by half. So you have to choose: the mill or the man."

"If I tell him about my lies, I'll lose him *and* the mill."

"Probably." He plucked the bits of food he'd given her out of her hand and popped them into his mouth.

Did he think she'd just give in and lose both? She was done losing the things she cared about. "Then I can't."

Ian shrugged as he chewed. "Feel free to disregard the advice of the all-knowing."

"Who's all-knowing?" Clayton asked from the side of the sleigh.

He was safe. She jumped down and threw her arms around him.

"Madeline and I chose to call him all-gloating instead."

Olivia tried to smile, but Ian's observations had been too close to the mark. The mill or the man. Surely, the mill was the better option; after all, it would improve dozens of families.

"There are nine of them plus Arshun," Clayton reported.

Ian landed in the snow next to them.

Clayton grabbed her by the waist and deposited her on the driver's bench. Ian handed her the reins.

"What are you doing?" She tried to climb down but Clayton stopped her.

"If we do not signal you in ten minutes, you drive away and do not come back."

They thought she would wait out here while they fought nine men?

Ian clapped his hands together. "Your lover won't say it so I will. You're not trained. You'll make things more dangerous for us if you come."

She knew he was right, but she still scowled at him. "If you're not out in seven minutes, I'm following you inside."

Clayton took Ian's remaining blanket and tucked it around her. "Is that a threat?"

She glared at him, hoping it masked some of her fear. "Yes."

Ian rolled his shoulders, then twisted from side to side. "Seven minutes . . . I've always liked a challenge. We'll do it in five."

The two men approached the house, then disappeared.

Silence.

No matter how she strained, she couldn't hear any sounds of a struggle.

The horse whickered in complaint and Olivia loosened her hold on the reins. She began counting in her head. It was better that than think about what was going on inside. She'd counted to sixty five times when the front door swung open. Ian stepped out and waved.

She urged the horse toward the house. Once she'd secured the reins to a tree, she ran up the steps to the house.

"Is Clayton all right?"

Ian led her past where three unconscious young men were tied. "Of course. Sorry I took so long, I was trying to keep Clayton from killing the count with his bare hands. Well, not his bare hands, they're gloved as always, of course."

Olivia didn't wait to hear the rest of Ian's commentary. The corridor into the back of the house was impossibly dark. Twice she tripped over crates and bound revolutionaries.

She heard Clayton's voice ahead followed by the thud of flesh hitting flesh. She picked up her skirts and ran toward the noise.

In the middle of a back room amid a jumbled pile of spilled crates, Clayton stood over a bruised and bloody Arshun. The count's nose looked to be broken and his eye had already swollen shut. The sleeve of his lemon-colored jacket had been nearly torn off and he'd somehow lost a shoe.

Next to Clayton, Arshun was tiny and cowering. Not just physically.

Clayton's voice was little more than a growl.

"And perhaps then you'll think again before hurting—"

"Can I take over before you kill him?" Ian asked from behind her.

"No."

Arshun tried to stand, and Clayton leveled him again with a single punch.

"You're going to get blood on Olivia's skirts."

Only then did Clayton's gaze lock with hers. He stepped away.

"Now if you want answers," Ian said. "Wait outside."

She wouldn't mind seeing Arshun get hit again. "Why?"

Ian slowly advanced on Arshun, his steps slow and measured. He removed one glove, then the other. "My methods are my own."

For the first time, no humor lit Ian's gaze. She didn't argue when Clayton took her arm and escorted her out and shut the door behind him.

"What are Ian's methods?" she asked.

Clayton shook his head. "He'd have to tell you."

"Would he?"

"When I discovered by accident, he stabbed me twice and left me for dead."

Olivia stared at the closed door. "So that's a no."

Clayton grimaced. "I don't recommend asking."

She followed Clayton as he checked the house. He stooped and gagged each revolutionary they passed. By the time they returned, Ian poked his head out of the door. "You can come in now."

Arshun was curled on the floor, his knees tucked to his chest, shaking and pale, but there were no additional marks on him.

Ian stood over him. A hint of something ugly and dark lingered in his eyes. His coat had been removed and his sleeves rolled to his elbows. "Who told you about Cipher and La Petit?"

Arshun's terrified eyes darted to Olivia, then quickly away. "I don't know. The information came in the note. I assumed it was from one of Vasin's former associates, but I don't know."

"How did you find out about Vasin's plan? You weren't one of his confidants."

Arshun rocked side to side. "It was in the same note. It told me where to find the code and what it contained."

Ian crouched down next to Arshun. "What are you planning for the night of the gala?"

"My revolutionaries will collect the weapons, then march in the streets at midnight, inspiring the populace to revolt." He coughed. "That was *my* plan. Vasin's signals were put in place this morning. The plan is in motion."

His small spurt of arrogance disappeared when Ian spoke again. "How did you break the code?"

"I received instructions on that as well. Two days ago. But I don't know from whom."

Arshun hadn't broken the code. Someone else had broken it for him. Someone else had been pulling the strings from the beginning.

Ian unrolled his shirtsleeves. "You know I warned you about lying." Blackness still clouded his eyes.

She thought, perhaps, he might enjoy carrying out his threats.

Arshun shook his head frantically from side to side. "Lying about what?"

Ian's smile was far colder than any Clayton had ever given. "Who's been sending you information? You're not quite fool enough to take orders from nowhere."

"The man with his match to the fuse."

"Who?"

A smug look settled on Arshun's battered face. "I truly don't know. And since I don't know, neither can you."

Chapter Twenty-three

The stillness of the sleigh woke Olivia. Clayton's shoulder was a bit too hard and flat to be truly comfortable, but the warmth of his body as they'd traveled had been too lulling to resist. He'd tucked his arm around her, too, keeping her steady in the uncertain motion of the sleigh.

"We're here?" she asked.

"St. Igor's." Clayton lifted his arm from around her and swore softly as he surveyed the church.

Olivia lifted her head and blinked to focus her eyes. St. Igor's was a small, sky blue church, nestled under five golden cupolas. The first rays of dawn glinted off the domes and illuminated a small red flag.

She'd held out some small hope that Arshun had been lying.

He hadn't been.

St. Igor's was the third location they'd checked. All three signs had been given. She shivered.

Ian strolled up to the woman selling small white candles by the front of the church. After only a few seconds, the elderly woman's wrinkles had rearranged in cheery bursts around her eyes and mouth. His Russian was a little fast for Olivia to follow all of it, but he was asking about any regular patrons who frequented the church.

But what were the odds the woman would know the revolutionary?

But Olivia refused to give in to despair. "We need to warn the czar again."

"If Golov is part of the plan, it will do us no good."

"Then going to the czar will give us a way to know if he *is* part of the plan. If he confirms our claims to the czar and helps us, then we know he isn't."

Clayton's brows lifted slightly. "It's a solid plan."

She thought at first he might be teasing her, but his gaze was sincere. Almost proud.

A wide grin slowly swept his face. "And when we're finally alone I'll tell you my new plan. For the mill."

Her heart skipped in her chest. "What is it?"

Ian returned and tossed her a squat white candle. "Wait inside where it's warm. Or at least less cold. We'll examine the area briefly. Again, easier if you aren't tagging along."

She desperately wanted to know what Clayton had decided. Yet again, she realized she'd only slow the two men down.

Besides, it was chilly without Clayton's extra warmth, so she nodded.

Clayton handed Olivia a knife. "Use this if you need to." Then the two men were gone.

As she stepped inside, she copied the elderly man

who'd entered the church just before her, kneeling to cross herself. The walls of the church were hidden behind gilded, bejeweled icons, and the haze of hundreds of small, flickering candles.

An old man knelt a few feet in front of her in the empty center of the church, his forehead resting on the stone ground. His simple dedication was a perfect contrast to the riches around him. A few other worshippers huddled by various icons, either silently bowed or whispering quiet supplications between kisses to the stylized saints.

Her vicar would no doubt have palpitations at such blatant idolatry, but Olivia sensed a certain enviable sincerity in all of it.

She made her way to a section of wall that was unoccupied by other worshippers. The small engraving under the icon said St. Eulalia. Olivia didn't know what she was a saint of, but the woman was lying nearly dead under a blanket of snow.

The stern-eyed saint watched her reproachfully.

Olivia glared back. The candles before her sputtered in a gust of cold from the opening doors. Two priests entered, their long robes damp at the hem from the snow.

"I've heard General Smirken is already speaking to the czar about removing three of the priests from his council," one of them said.

"The people will never stand for it."

"Yesterday. But after the revelations about Metropolitan Stanislav killing those girls, things aren't so certain. People are angry that—" But their conversation was silenced after they passed through the richly decorated screen that concealed the altar, leaving Olivia straining to hear that last bit of gossip.

Olivia dipped the wick of her candle into the dwindling flame of the only candle by St. Eulalia, the candle little more than a puddle of wax.

She looked up when someone else entered the church. It wasn't Clayton but a well-dressed woman heavily cloaked in furs. A few wisps of the woman's red hair curled around her face.

Red hair?

"Kate?"

Kate whirled, relief crossing her expression. "You're here. But where's Clayton?"

Olivia frowned. "How did you know we were here?" They hadn't seen her since they'd left her home yesterday.

"Because I knew the flag was here. It was meant for me."

Dread twisted down Olivia's back. She pulled out the dagger. "You're one of the agents." The words seemed to emerge from her mouth too slowly.

The other woman nodded, holding out her hands to show they were empty. "I'm not armed. I came here to confess."

Olivia tightened her grip on the knife.

"I knew if you broke the code, you'd go to the places where the signals were given. I hoped I could find you." The other woman's face was drawn and tired. "If I was still working for them, why would I give myself away?"

"You could be planning to kill us."

"Again, why would I have told you who I was first?"

Olivia suspected Clayton would have been able to think of a reason, but she couldn't. She slowly lowered the dagger.

Kate exhaled. "I need your help. Well, as loath as I am to admit it, I need *Clayton's* help."

"With what?" Olivia tensed when Kate's hands disappeared into her reticule, but she only emerged with a candle of her own.

Kate lit her candle. The flame wavered in her shaking hand.

"You have to understand." Kate set her candle on the ground, letting her hands hover over it for a moment as if to warm them. "I saw so many horrors on my travels that never made it into my book. Children with their stomachs bloated from starvation while fields heavy with the czar's grain mocked a few dozen yards away. Serfs tortured by their masters until they were barely recognizable as human." Kate flinched at some remembered horror. "Whole towns without men because they dared rebel against the emperor. Other towns stripped bare by the war. Filth, disease."

Olivia had seen hints of that in Kate's writing. "So you chose Vasin?"

Kate glanced around the small church. "I forget you only know of Vasin through Clayton and that fool Arshun. Vasin was"—Kate shook her head slowly, her face serious—"so many things. Charismatic. Brilliant. Yes, he was ruthless, but that was because he had such a pure vision of what Russia could become. A soft man could never free Russia." Kate's eyes gleamed when she spoke, a zeal that Olivia never suspected she harbored.

"Then why are you here?"

"I didn't agree to help Arshun."

"What were you supposed to do when you saw the flag?" Olivia asked.

"Vasin had me gathering information on the empress these past few years. Nothing as damaging as what they had on the metropolitan—"

"Wait, what metropolitan?"

"The archbishop who was just arrested for killing those girls. Vasin placed one of his revolutionaries in that household as well. A clerk, I believe."

"And you were assigned to the empress?"

Some of Olivia's shock must have come through in her voice because Kate's jaw worked for several seconds before she spoke. "There are things going on in this empire that are wrong. The people need a voice in their own government. My opinion of that hasn't changed."

"Then why not reveal the information you have? You think it is a noble goal. How can you give up on it?"

Candlelight flickered over Kate's pale face, making her resemble one of the icons surrounding her. "I thought the results would justify the evils I had to do."

Didn't they? Why did it sound so wrong when someone else uttered those words?

Kate rubbed her eyes, then closed them for a minute. "Empress Elizabeth isn't at all like I expected. She's shy and kind. I can't betray her trust. And I don't want her killed."

"Surely, the good of many is more important than one woman."

Kate's gaze sharpened. "Are you trying to convince me to change my mind?"

Olivia's cheeks heated. "No."

"Then what are we discussing?" Some of Kate's

pluck returned as she studied Olivia. "Is this about you and Clayton? Your mill?"

But Olivia wasn't ready to discuss her quandary with anyone.

Kate sighed. "Never mind. I suppose you have no desire to share those things with me anymore. But I can tell you what helped me decide. I'll have many opportunities to change Russia. But this will be the only chance I have to save the empress. There is no going back from that."

Could this apply to Olivia? What if Clayton followed through with his plans to destroy the mill? Could she rebuild it?

No.

Not once Clayton knew the truth.

This was her only chance with Clayton *and* her only chance with the mill.

Olivia supposed she should feel betrayed by Kate's lies, but she didn't. They were far too similar to her own. In fact, she admired the woman's courage. She could have remained silent and no one would ever have known. "Clayton won't take this news lightly. He'll never tell you your husband's location." She knew all too well how ruthless Clayton could be.

"I still have to tell him." Kate rubbed her brow.

Olivia would have given anything for an ounce of the princess's courage. To not be trapped by the lives of the other people at the mill.

But when it came down to it, she was as much of a coward as her father had been. And she'd continue torturing herself with what-ifs for the rest of her life.

It was what she did best, after all.

A hand latched on to Olivia's shoulder.

It was bony, almost skeletal despite heavy gloves. "Thank you, Princess, for making sure we didn't miss our meeting this morning. Now where's the baron?"

"Have you figured out how the devil they got the flag up there?" Clayton asked.

Ian peered down from the tree he'd climbed at the back of the church. "It actually wouldn't be that hard. They'd just have to scale the wall. Jump to that windowsill. Then grab the ledge."

Not hard was a relative term for Ian. The distance between the window and the ledge had to be a solid ten feet. But if Ian said it was doable, then it was.

"Any idea who the sign would have been meant for?"

Ian glanced around from his perch. He was nearly as high as the flag. "None. You can see half the city from here. Which means half the city could see the flag if they happened to be watching for it."

"Baron!" Heavy steps crashed through the snow.

Clayton whirled around to find Blin barreling toward him. His hair and beard streamed behind him in a wild tangle.

"He took them." Blin grabbed Clayton's arm and began to pull Clayton toward the church.

"Who?"

"Golov. He took the princess and Miss Swift. When the princess left her house this morning, Golov followed her. Then I followed them so I could warn her. Golov's not a nice man."

Clayton nearly stumbled. His hands suddenly

felt clammy inside his gloves. Golov had Olivia. The man who'd ordered Madeline's torture. Who'd personally planned it out. Who'd watched her writhe and beg. Madeline said he'd smiled.

Panic was like a chain on Clayton's thoughts, tangling them and weighing them down. But in less time than it took to exhale, he'd freed himself link by link as he'd been taught to do.

Or tried. He couldn't seem to escape it as he had in the past. How could he when Olivia's life was the one at stake?

He needed to focus. He needed more details for this to make sense.

"Kate came here?"

Blin nodded, his fingers gripping and tugging his beard. "But then Golov and his policemen took the princess and Miss Swift from the church."

Why would Kate have come here? A slow suspicion grew in his chest. Kate had known Vasin quite well. She'd been married to his nephew.

Clayton shouted over his shoulder, "Ian, can you see Kate's house from the flag?"

Ian was already halfway down the tree, but he stopped and glanced around. "Yes. Quite clearly, in fact."

Clayton increased his speed until they reached the main door of the church. The candle seller was gone, no doubt frightened away by the police.

Clayton ran inside and swore. Olivia was gone just as Blin had said.

"You have a bad habit of losing your women." Ian's voice echoed in the empty church.

Ian always jested no matter the situation. Normally, it helped defuse tension.

But Clayton had no tolerance for it now. "She won't be lost for long."

Ian didn't take the hint. "If you weren't so busy pissing your trousers with panic, you'd remember we do have a sleigh just outside."

"I'm coming, too," Blin said. "And I'm not walking this time. I'm too tired to go fast."

They needed all the muscle they could muster to deal with Golov. "It will be dangerous."

Blin's whole body moved with his nod. "I want Miss Swift safe. And the princess. Cook will be mad at me if something happens to her."

Ian opened the door and motioned for them to leave. "You heard the man, Clay. No one risks a cook's ire."

But Clayton stopped him before the big man climbed into the sleigh. "Do you have any experience fighting?"

A touch of disbelief crossed Blin's face. "I have *five* brothers at home."

"You realize this whole rescue could end with our deaths."

Blin's massive shoulders lifted, then fell in a shrug. "Yes."

Clayton stepped aside so Blin could squeeze into the sleigh. Clayton claimed the small space left and gave Ian the address.

Ian's eyes narrowed at the location. "Do you think Golov would have taken her there?"

"She's there. This is a taunt." Clayton's jaw tightened. "I even know which room the bastard has her in."

Chapter Twenty-four

Olivia glared at the minister of police across from her in the coach and tried to avoid the frantic looks Kate had been casting her.

"You promised the emperor we'd be safe in St. Petersburg," Olivia said, hands clenched in her lap. Perhaps Kate was right and she shouldn't be yelling at the man who could order their deaths.

But Olivia found she was done with being abducted. And threatened. And separated from Clayton.

Golov still held the knife he'd taken from her at the church. He rolled the hilt in his hand. Back and forth. Back and forth. Until Olivia had to force herself to look away. "I haven't harmed you, have I? I merely ensured you remembered our appointment. Which I feared you would have forgotten otherwise."

"Why kidnap us?" Olivia asked.

"I couldn't risk the baron deciding to avoid me further. There are questions I require answered. Kate was kind enough to lead me to you."

Kate's hand locked on Olivia's. "You followed me?"

"Of course. I trusted you'd have a way to contact Olivia and I was right."

Kate sank back against the seat, her brows together. "You weren't seeking *me* out?"

"Why would I seek you out? You're nothing but an annoyance."

Kate exhaled slowly, her expression heavy with relief.

Relief?

Ah, she must have feared Golov had followed her because he knew of her part in the conspiracy. But Golov had no idea Kate had been working for the revolutionaries. He thought the church nothing more than a meeting place. He hadn't broken the code.

Some of the color returned to Kate's cheeks. "I object to being taken off the street at the point of a rifle. I'm a princess. You have no right—"

"You *do* think that, don't you? Sergey is dead."

Kate stared down her nose at him. "I know."

"No. Sergey was dead years before you met him. The real Sergey's death wasn't an accident like the British thought to take advantage of. I killed the prince personally. Although I must admit even I was momentarily struck by the resemblance of the man the British found to take his place."

"No, Sergey was—"

"You never knew Sergey. I have let you live as a princess because I haven't yet seen a reason to bother changing things."

Kate swayed against Olivia.

Olivia placed her hand over Kate's, trying to

offer what little comfort she could. "And because you were saving this information for a time when you needed something to hold over her." Like a dagger he could slip between her ribs in the dark.

Golov seemed to find Olivia's accusation amusing. "Precisely. Don't make me change my mind." He leaned forward, offering his hand to Olivia. "Now I believe you and I have an arrangement to firm up."

She wasn't about to move to his side of the sleigh. "I don't particularly want to work with you."

"You don't particularly have a choice. But if it makes you feel better, we're both trying to save the czar."

"Are you?" Olivia asked.

He withdrew his hand. "It is a good thing I am fond of you, Miss Swift. Men have died for far less."

The carriage stopped in front of a gleaming white building. "We'll wait for the baron to join us."

Rather than leading them up the marble stairs and past the Grecian columns to the front door, he prodded them down the stairs on the side of the building into the basements.

It wasn't until the doors locked tight behind them that Olivia heard the screams.

Chapter Twenty-five

Manacles hung from the walls. A pile of moldy straw rotted in the corner. Scratches on the back of the door bore testament to some poor soul who'd been trapped down here. In the summer, water must seep through that crack in the wall, but for now, it was sealed with an uneven bubble of pale green ice.

Yet Golov ordered the room set with a table covered in white linen and fine silver. Soon an array of soldiers tromped in carrying covered dishes.

"Join me." Golov gestured to the two chairs across from him, then sat without waiting for the women. He opened a lid, revealing a savory red soup. "Hardly captivity, is it?"

"We *are* in a prison." Kate might not be a princess, but she'd never looked more like one than in that moment. She'd march in front of a firing squad before she gave Golov the satisfaction of cowing her.

Olivia, too, was determined not to play mouse to his cat. She needed to discover what Golov had planned for Clayton when he arrived. So she sat and helped herself to a large portion of food. Golov wouldn't be the only one to eat, picking his teeth with satisfaction and spite.

Golov studied her as she lifted a bite of braised carrots to her mouth. "I think we're much alike, you and I."

Olivia moved her jaw with careful deliberation, the well-cooked vegetable now tasting of dirt. "In what way?"

"I can see it in you. Always the focus on your goal. The search for a way to arrange things to your benefit."

Perhaps he'd be more willing to talk if he thought she agreed. So she nodded.

Golov smiled. "You're doing it now."

She had been. "It is a flaw I'm trying to over-come."

Golov laughed, the sound so eerie that the cries in the neighboring cells silenced.

"You cannot overcome it. It is a part of your nature. Most have the will to survive. But you and I have the will to thrive." He rested one bony finger on his chin. "Have you convinced yourself it is a bad thing? You fear being selfish? Manipulative? Every good deed doesn't count if you benefited, too?"

She stabbed a bite of chicken too hard.

"She has too much of a soul to be anything like you," Kate said.

Olivia appreciated the defense but feared Kate was mistaken.

He sipped from his goblet, the wine staining his upper lip bloodred. "I think you know, Olivia, that I am correct. I will help you along with a key realization. Necessary things must be done. If those things also benefit you, so much the better. If you were the passenger in a cart headed for a cliff, would you hesitate to stop it because *your* life would be spared? It makes no sense, does it?"

No, it didn't. "But there *is* a difference between us, Golov." And a difference between her and her father. "I wouldn't have been the one to whip the horses toward the cliff just so I could stop them."

"Wouldn't you? Not even to let the others in the cart see you stop it?" He dabbed at his mouth with a linen. "Not even to save your mill?"

She sipped the soup, fearing she'd be unable to choke down something more solid. Was that true? She didn't want anything from this horrible man to be accurate. But his words resonated deep in her thoughts.

Had she been so focused on doing good with the mill that she'd lost sight of actually *being* good?

The lies she'd told to rebuild the mill seemed to say so.

What had seemed like a necessary evil before now appeared as vile and dishonest as she knew Clayton would see it.

When she told him.

She *would* tell him. Her remaining hesitance vanished completely. Why had she clung to it for so long? She was finished being a coward.

She'd spent her whole life trying to avoid outcomes she didn't like.

No longer.

It was time she accepted the consequences she was due.

He wouldn't forgive her. Ian was generous when he said she could choose between Clayton and the mill. There was no outcome where she'd be able to keep Clayton. She'd lose the mill *and* she'd lose him.

There'd be no benefit to her for telling the truth.

Yet she'd do it anyway. The people of the mill deserved stability, not a teetering fabrication that could come crashing down around their ears at any moment.

And Clayton . . . He needed someone honest and open, who had no dark places hidden away.

She would do everything in her power to keep from hurting him ever again.

The realization gave her hope even as the pain from losing Clayton carved a hole in her chest. But now she knew what she had to do to protect him. "Shall I offer you a tidbit of wisdom in return for the one you gave me?"

"Feel free." For the first time, Golov took a bite of food. He loved this. The game of it all.

"There are things going on in your city that you didn't expect. Things you cannot explain. They will make you look foolish."

"Olivia—" Kate started to warn her, but Golov silenced her with an upheld finger.

"Go on."

"They're connected. Prazhdinyeh has broken the code. They want to see the empire crumble around your ears. It's already crumbling. You may wish to battle wits and trade threats with the baron, but Russia's chances of survival are much greater if you stay out of his way. He's the one who can stop this cart from tumbling off the cliff. The only one."

Before Golov responded, the door of the cell clanged open and Clayton was ushered inside, flanked by two guards carrying rifles. His hands were bound in front of him, and his eyes were shadowed.

His gaze locked on hers. It held relief. Regret. Concern. Determination. More was said in that one look than he might ever have said in words.

He'd come for her.

Again.

But soon he'd walk away from her and not look back.

"Ah, Baron, so good of you to join us."

"Did you think bringing me back to La Petit's cell would discomfit me? All it means is that you're far too predictable." He stepped behind Olivia, and for an instant his hands brushed the nape of her neck.

The touch sent warmth and comfort flooding through her veins. And she straightened in her chair. She had no idea what Clayton's plan was, but she had no doubt that he had one.

Golov set his fork on the table. "So are you. You came here just as I knew you would."

"Because I have a present for you. Count Arshun."

"You found him?"

"Perhaps if you focused on finding criminals rather than kidnapping innocent women, you wouldn't have to ask."

It was time to try her plan. She would have preferred to tell the czar as well, but this would have to suffice for now. "The revolutionaries' plan is real. Arshun has already given the signals. Someone is going to try to kill the czar tomorrow."

Golov hesitated. "Where is Arshun?"

Clayton shrugged. "Let us go, and I'll tell you."

"Speaks the man who is bound in my prison. You *will* tell me."

"You think to torture it out of us?"

Golov's tongue slid along his lip. "No, just out of you."

Clayton lifted his bound hands and examined them. "Haven't you ever wondered how we freed La Petit from this cell the first time?"

Golov's thin nostrils flared and he leaned forward. "I know."

Clayton's lips curved in a satisfied grin. "No, you don't."

There was a sudden crash. Bricks collapsed into the room, revealing a man-sized hole in the wall. Ian and Blin stood in the center of the dusty opening.

Olivia scrambled to her feet with a gasp. Had they just pushed down a brick wall?

"If you had known, you would have replaced the dirt behind those bricks," Clayton said.

"And we bloody aren't going to bother hiding our exit this time," Ian added.

The guards rushed to raise their rifles, but Blin stopped one with a single blow of his massive fist. Even with hands tied, Clayton stripped the rifle from the other man. Then Ian cut the rope at Clayton's wrists with a flick of his knife.

Clayton leveled the rifle at Golov. "I wouldn't recommend moving. Is Kate working with Golov?"

Olivia shook her head. "No."

Clayton nodded and Blin grabbed Kate, tossed her over his shoulder, and walked through the hole in the wall. Clayton handed off the rifle to Ian, then pulled Olivia into the tunnel.

"Run," he ordered.

She stumbled behind him, the ground of the tunnel rocky and uneven.

An explosion boomed behind them.

Clayton turned and threw himself on top of her as a blast of air and rubble roared past them.

His breath was hot on her neck. But he'd rested most of his weight on his forearms to keep from crushing her. Part of her wished he hadn't. Part of her wished to be pressed into the rocky ground by him so she could memorize the weight and heat of his body. She wished to be pressed down until there was no space between them at all. She wanted to be cut off from the future and exist only in this filthy piece of tunnel.

After the dirt and dust clogging the air had settled somewhat, Clayton helped her to her feet and dusted her off. They started walking. Before they'd gone a dozen feet, Clayton caught her arm, slowing her. Ian passed, hurrying ahead in the tunnel.

Clayton spun her slightly and pressed her back against the rock. "You seem to have a talent for surviving danger."

His mouth fell hot and hungry on hers. Desire clenched tight within her. The darkness in the tunnel was absolute. She couldn't see Clayton. She could only feel him. Smell him. Taste him. The rasp of stubble on his chin abrading her neck. The scent of wax and incense from the church. The tiny flicks of his tongue in between kisses. The brush of his eyelashes against her cheek as he kissed her chin. The sweet, honeyed taste of his mouth.

She had no idea where his hands and lips were going to caress next and she didn't want to. She wanted to be lost in this glorious frenzy. She wanted this, too.

More than she'd ever wanted anything.

Soon she discovered if she cupped his face in her hands, she could coax him to linger where she needed his mouth the most. Then the slightest pressure of her hand would bring his lips to her throat. Her breasts.

Some rational part of her warned that she had to stop.

But she needed one last touch before she lost him. She needed to know the corner of his jaw. The thickness of his hair. The planes of his shoulders.

Suddenly, there were too many things she might forget when he left. Not enough time to memorize each of his fingers. And why had she never paid attention to the shell of his ear? To the lobe she wished she'd have more chances to catch in her teeth?

Enough.

Never enough.

No. She wouldn't be like Golov, snatching benefits for herself without caring for the repercussions.

What she'd done to save the mill had been wrong. She needed to set things right. "Clayton—"

She could feel his cheeks widen into a smile. "Shall I tell you of my plan for the mill now?"

"First, I need to tell—"

"I don't know how you got lost. The tunnel goes in a straight line." Ian's voice echoed around them.

Clayton lifted away from her with a curse. But then he laced his fingers through hers and spoke, his voice a velvet whisper. "I won't let you go again."

Chapter Twenty-six

The five of them barely fit in the small basement room Ian had found for them. And yet Clayton hadn't been able to get close to Olivia.

After that kiss in the tunnel, he'd thought she would have stayed by his side. He'd expected her to be eager to hear his new plan for the mill.

For them.

But although she was tending Blin's wound, Clayton was no fool. He knew when he was being avoided. His mother had been an expert at that. Even when she lived with them, she was always too busy to see to Clayton. Most of his memories of her were of lingering around the edge of her dressing table, trying to stand straight and tall so she'd notice him.

Clayton fought the urge to throw everyone else from the room, yank Olivia to him, and kiss her until she could think of nothing but him.

"You're mooning," Ian whispered in a quiet, singsong voice as Clayton handed him a cup of melted snow to soak the thumb he'd burned while lighting the explosives.

Clayton glowered at him. "I am not."

"I expect you to start spouting couplets about her golden locks any moment."

Clayton's attention drifted to the tendrils of Olivia's hair that had come loose during their escape.

He couldn't look away from the gentle pressure of her hand or the slight lift on her lips as she spoke to Blin, her words soft, comforting, admiring as she tended a cut on his head. The big man puffed with pride at her words. No wonder he followed her blindly around.

Clayton gritted his teeth against the urge to step closer so she'd glance at him. Damnation, he wasn't a child. He'd ask why she was avoiding him as soon as they were alone.

"*Olivia with hair of soft gold. Let's escape Golov and cavort in the mold.* Hmm . . . perhaps not one of my best," Ian mused.

"Shut it, Ian."

Ian shrugged. "If you want her to stop avoiding you, you might try to stop scowling. Just a thought. What did you do to gain her indifference? Maddie and I always suspected you'd be a terrible kisser, but—"

"*Enough!*" His voice was loud enough that Olivia finally glanced over, but then jerked her gaze back to Blin.

But Ian never shut his mouth. "You might also ask yourself if there's a reason she might want distance from you."

"Damned mill."

"Is it worth losing her over?"

"I won't lose her over it."

Ian shut his mouth, but his astonishment lasted for only a moment. "You're letting it go?"

"No. I'm simply altering my plan."

"Does it still involve destroying her mill?"

"Only partially."

"Sounds like it will work brilliantly."

It had to. "She's stubborn, but she knows why I have to do it."

"Who's the stubborn one?"

Could he let the mill go completely? In exchange for Olivia? He'd have given up anything to get her back safe from Golov, but this?

Olivia was only on the other side of the small room, and he despised the distance between them. He wanted her by his side.

If he married her, he'd have the right to keep her there.

The decision seemed as natural as breathing. And yet his breathing no longer seemed to function properly, coming high and fast in his chest.

"Clayton, catch Kate!"

At Olivia's yell, Clayton lunged in time to grab Kate as she slumped toward ground.

Kate's gaze was unfocused as he helped her settle against the wall.

They were still unclear on just how much Kate knew. He knew she was a revolutionary. Olivia had told them that much as they climbed into the sleigh. He had started to question Kate, but Olivia had stopped him with a look he didn't understand but knew enough to obey.

But he couldn't give Kate any more time.

Since he still wasn't precisely clear what Golov

had done, he tried to be as gentle as he could. He rested a hand on her shoulder. "Kate?"

She either shook herself or shuddered, but then brushed off his grasp. "Who was he?"

"Who?"

Her hands fisted at her sides. "My husband. Who is he?"

He looked to Olivia for help.

"Golov told her the Sergey she knew wasn't the real Sergey."

That was what brought her to this? Kate had once helped a town in southern Siberia battle raiders while armed with only farming equipment, flaming cow dung, and a pistol. The village named itself after her.

But now he understood her devastation better than he ever could have before.

Empathy. Hell, he might start composing couplets after all.

"I knew nothing of this," Clayton said. Although it did explain why the Foreign Office was so insistent on faking Sergey's death and getting him out of there when things grew difficult. He was one of their own.

"I did," Ian said, lifting his thumb from the water and prodding the blister there.

"What?" Clayton found his question echoed by both Kate and Olivia.

"It may or may not have been my idea to use an impostor."

"Then who is he?" Kate asked.

Ian shrugged. "No idea. I just told Glaves my brilliant suggestion on how to get one of our men close to a man who trusted no one. I didn't handle the specifics."

When had Ian begun advising the Foreign Office on strategy?

Kate rested her head on her knees.

Olivia went to her side, the compassion on her face making Clayton ache with pride.

"You said you knew where he is now?" she asked Clayton.

Kate hadn't earned the information, but he'd tell her for Olivia's sake. "Llanfyr along the south coast of Wales."

Kate's eyes flashed for a moment, focusing again, as if that kernel of truth gave her the strength to continue. She shifted, lowered her knees, and tucked them under her. "Ask your questions about Vasin."

"Who are the other agents?" Olivia asked.

"One was a clerk for Metropolitan Stanislav, I believe."

"Evidence agrees," Ian seconded. "The timing of when the clerk was placed with him matches."

"The metropolitan deserved to be disgraced. What he did to those girls—" She cut herself off with a slow exhale. "The plan was to have all the major powers in Russia disgraced. The church. The royal family. The army. By the time the final agent moves at the fete . . ." She closed her eyes briefly. ". . . killing the entire royal family, there will be no clear favorite to fill the void. Vasin intended to be poised to move into place with his vision of equality and democracy, but now there will be nothing but chaos."

Clayton wasn't used to being beaten, especially by a dead man. The Trio had outwitted Vasin once; they'd do it again.

Of course, now he had Olivia instead of Madeline.

But Clayton found himself confident with the new arrangement.

Kate wiped her hands across her face. "I don't know who Vasin put in place to kill the emperor, but it would be someone whose dedication he didn't doubt. One of his inner circle. But then again, I imagine he'd choose someone no one would connect to him."

Olivia frowned. "Who was supposed to give the signals?"

Kate frowned. "I don't know."

Pieces were coming together in Clayton's mind. "We may not know who he is, but we know what he will do. Remember the final line of the code? *Then you will know the time is ready to light the fire of freedom.* The code must have belonged to the final agent."

Ian was lying in the center of the old wooden dining table. He waved his hand with the injured finger above him as if he was conducting music. "He's decided to have his own little revolution."

"But then why involve Arshun?" Kate asked.

Olivia cast a questioning glance at Clayton. "And why not choose someone who would have made a better leader afterward?"

"Because he never intended Arshun to rule. He needed Arshun to take the blame."

"Did anyone notice there haven't been any scandals about the military yet?" Ian sat up, swinging his legs off the table. "Church, yes. Royal family, almost. Military, no. They're the most powerful force in Russia. Vasin couldn't have planned to rise to power with them still unscathed. And there were three signs given in the code. Three agents that were supposed to do something."

"Could the agent have changed his mind like Kate?" Olivia asked.

"Or he could have missed the sign. We weren't told when we'd be called upon to act. I didn't know when Vasin's plan would be set in motion. I was supposed to simply always be at the ready. But to be honest, I had stopped looking for the sign after Vasin died. I only began watching for it after you both showed up with talk of revolutionaries."

It was possible the third agent had missed their sign, or was perhaps still waiting to act, but Clayton suspected the final agent would have been more careful than that.

"How did a weasel like Arshun get a war hero like Golov's brother, Colonel Pavlo Golov, to follow him? Olivia, when the count arrived at his house, you said there were two young men and the colonel with him?" Clayton asked.

Olivia nodded.

"And when we found Arshun yesterday, all the revolutionaries in the house were young, too. About the same age as the count. University age. Most likely his friends."

"Ah! Interesting fact— When did the colonel become a war hero?" Ian leaped to his feet. "Not after the battle like you'd expect. No, several months later, a few of his soldiers came to the czar to tell him about the unknown, unbelievable bravery of a certain colonel. Amazing humility for such a pompous arse, isn't it?"

Olivia's nose wrinkled as she considered. "If it *is* the colonel, what is he planning?"

Clayton tapped his fingers on the table. "He wouldn't be able to shoot the entire royal family. Not before being stopped. And people would know he was responsible. He wouldn't be able to take power after that. He must be using another method. A bomb. Small, portable. Timed fuse."

"Like the one they tried to use on us?" Olivia asked.

Clayton stared at her. How had he not seen it before? "*Exactly* like that one."

Ian pulled a coarse, dark roll from his pocket and broke off chunks for the others in the room, saving the largest piece for himself, of course. "What are the odds the revolutionaries happen to have two skilled bomb makers in St. Petersburg this time of year?"

"Very, very small."

"So how do we find this elusive maker of infernal devices?" Ian asked.

"I return to Kate's."

Chapter Twenty-seven

Olivia had no idea why Clayton thought she'd let him go on his own. "Prazhdinyeh still has orders to kill you. And Golov will know you're there within minutes. I'm coming."

Clayton glared. "You're not."

Ian sighed. "Didn't you learn your lesson with Madeline? Either you let her come or she'll find a far more dangerous way to come on her own."

Kate also protested. "If the final agent knows who I am, it will be best if I am where I'm supposed to be. Then he'll be less likely to improvise."

Blin stood, his shoulders as wide as the door frame behind him. "I'll go to protect the women."

Ian tugged on his hat. "I suppose this means I must follow you as well. But I'm not driving. I need a nap."

By the time they arrived at Kate's, the roads were already growing dark in the early dusk of winter.

Kate and Blin walked in her front door, but Clayton led Olivia and Ian through a side window. Clayton's hands lingered on her waist before he lifted Olivia inside, and just for the barest instant, his lips found a small, bare patch of skin on her neck.

Kate ordered her servants to leave her alone for the night, and their small party slipped into her room without having been seen.

None of the spies from either side knew they were there.

Soon Olivia and Kate sat in the bedroom staring at the closed door that led to Kate's dressing room. Olivia hadn't even remembered that the maid Iryna had named the revolutionary who had passed along the bomb, much less known who he was. But Clayton had. Now all she could do was wait outside while Clayton and Ian interrogated Kate's groom Barndyk.

Minutes passed.

Olivia removed her kerchief and her gloves, and as her body warmed, her coat followed.

The room was silent except for the murmurs in the dressing room.

Kate pulled a ruby ring off her finger and then on again, her motions jerky. Upset.

"I don't think they've hurt him." At least there hadn't been screams. And as much as Olivia strained to hear, she still had no idea what Ian's methods were.

Kate blinked, staring at the door as if she hadn't noticed it before. It was clear her worry hadn't been for the events inside.

"What are you going to do about Sergey?" Olivia asked, suspecting the real source of Kate's distraction.

Kate pulled the ring off again and set it on her knee. "I'm going after him."

"What are you going to do when you find him?"

"Get my answers. What are *you* going to do about Clayton?"

This time, Olivia's resolve matched Kate's. "I'll tell him the truth."

And lose him.

No.

She was finished with this fatalism. She'd worked incessantly to save the mill, and that wasn't even one tenth as important to her as Clayton.

She was done making a decision, then cringing and waiting for the repercussions.

Her life wasn't made of one choice. It was made up of dozens. Hundreds. Millions.

And she would use them to convince Clayton to forgive her.

She'd probably lose Clayton when she confessed her lies. But she would win him back. She might not deserve him, but she was working on it. She loved him. She wouldn't back down. Not even from Clayton himself.

The dressing room door opened.

Barndyk was tied to a chair, his skin ashen, much as Arshun's had been, but again, with no apparent signs of injury.

Ian was glaring at him. "Couldn't you have held out for a bit longer? Really, you need to speak to your superiors about your training. Quite unsatisfying."

"We have a name," Clayton said.

"Who?" Kate asked.

"A clockmaker on Nevsky Prospect. Only a few short blocks away."

Olivia was already retying her kerchief. But Clayton stopped her. "We go in the morning."

"But—"

"We know where he works, not where he lives. We won't find him until the morning."

"So we just wait?"

Ian yawned. "And sleep. Don't forget the sleeping part. Prone, eyes closed. In case you've forgotten what it is."

"What about my groom?" Kate asked.

Clayton glared at the other man. "We'll leave him tied. You said you have a few servants you trust?"

Kate nodded.

"Send the rest away. Tell them Barndyk is ill with some horribly contagious fever."

It was completely dark outside now. "Now?"

"It is not that late. Send them to an inn."

Soon, after a great commotion and dozens of vehicles, the house was empty. Her housekeeper, two footmen, and Blin were the only ones that remained.

"That will make Golov suspicious," Kate said.

"Yes, but it will keep us from getting our throats slit tonight. Once Ian secures the house."

Ian groaned and disappeared.

Kate echoed the groan as she stood. "I refuse to sleep in a room with a bound man a few feet away. I'll go find another bed."

Olivia looked around the now-empty room. "So what now?"

The intensity in Clayton's gaze shifted, centering on her. Devouring her. "Shall we sneak to the pantry and glut ourselves before Ian has a chance to empty it into his pockets?"

Olivia nodded.

After all, she did have something she needed to discuss.

It was time.

Chapter Twenty-eight

Blin was the only one in the kitchen when they entered. His back was to them as he worked on something, but then he swayed on his feet. Olivia darted to his side. She tucked herself under his arm. He was rather ashen about the lips. He'd lost a good deal of blood from the cut. "What are you doing down here? You should be resting."

Clayton moved to his other side.

"Cook will need this started for dinner tomorrow." Blin's hands still worked at the dough.

"You need to lie down."

"This is the only thing I am good at. Not protecting you. I should have been able to stop Golov from taking you. I should have stopped Nicolai, too." He punched the dough with a massive fist, rattling the table. "Sorry I didn't stop them. I am not much better than Nicolai, am I?"

Olivia swallowed, her throat suddenly thick. "You are far, far better. You are a good man."

"I kidnapped you."

"I forgave you while we were still on the boat."

Blin's motion slowed. "Do you think the princess will let me stay?"

"Yes." Olivia would make sure of it. "Now, where do you sleep?"

"On a pallet in the attic."

The man swayed again. The attics would be too far and too cold. Instead, with Clayton's help, she got him into one of the empty guest rooms. They removed the holland cover from the bed.

Blin grunted as he lay down. "Never slept on a mattress before. I'll have to tell my *babushka* about this. Don't know if I will tell her about kidnapping you, though."

"Why don't you tell her about rescuing me instead?"

Blin was softly snoring by the time Clayton had finished lighting the stove, and they crept out. He lit the stoves in two nearby bedrooms so they would have a warm place to sleep as well.

After he'd finished, Clayton caught her to him. "Enough of this waiting. Let's get some food and I'll tell you my plan."

This time the kitchen was empty when they passed through to the pantry.

Clayton lifted the cheesecloth to reveal half a loaf of bread. Fresh, too. He ripped off a large piece and handed it to Olivia.

She smiled at him, then took a large bite.

Clayton pulled down a jar. "Once in Brussels, Ian came to us ecstatic because he'd found a warehouse full of food."

She swallowed and brushed the crumbs from her

lips. "I notice a lot of your stories center around food."

"That's because we never had much. Unfortunately, once we got inside, it became clear that all those glistening cherries, pears, and pineapples were wax. Decorations for ladies' bonnets."

Olivia laughed, the sound echoing up to the gleaming copper pans hanging in the kitchen. She clapped her hand over her mouth, trying to quiet her mirth.

He didn't want her to. The servants were upstairs in the attic. There was no one to hear them on this level other than Ian. And Clayton would be more than pleased if Ian knew where they were so he'd stay away. "Madeline surprised Ian with a fine new hat covered with fruit the next week. I think he actually wore it twice."

"Surely, it was a man's hat."

"Oh no. Ian makes quite a fine-looking woman. Although finding a dress to fit his shoulders . . ."

That set Olivia laughing so hard she almost dropped the bread she held. Finally, she quieted. "Do you wish she was here with you in the larder instead? Madeline?"

Clayton froze. Madeline had been his constant companion. One of the only people he'd allowed himself to care about. But would he rather have her here with him now, debating what food to take upstairs for an impromptu late night repast? "No."

"What about on this mission?"

He didn't like the uncertainty in her voice. He needed Olivia to understand that she and Madeline weren't in competition. He cared for Madeline.

But he loved Olivia.

"Shall I tell you of my plan for the mill?" He selected a jar from the shelves in front of him and opened it, revealing a sticky dark substance. He smelled it. "Jam."

Olivia's eyes widened. "Take."

He'd known it would appeal to her sweet tooth.

She dipped her finger inside, then licked the jam off. The movement of her tongue was slow and deliberate. "Blackberry. Perfect."

She hadn't meant to be provocative, he was certain. Her enjoyment of the jam was too quick and simple. Still his body hardened.

And there was no reason to resist her anymore. He had a solution to the mill. And he was going to marry her.

He caught her hand before she wiped it on her skirts and brought it to his mouth, drawing her finger between his lips. It was still slightly sticky, slightly sweet. He sucked gently.

Her eyes fluttered closed and her breath hissed between her teeth.

But he slowly released her hand. When he made love to her, he wanted it to be in a room lit with glowing candles. The bed would be covered with the softest silk and he'd ensure there was no one around for miles, so they could give themselves entirely over to passion.

Even more than that, he wanted the perfect sunset over the cliffs so he could ask her to marry him.

But for now he'd settle for telling her of his plans for the mill.

And his feelings for her.

He set the jar down, then took the piece of bread out of her hands. "I haven't treated you well on this mission. I believe the term *coldhearted bastard* was rightfully applied." He exhaled. Hell, he was shaking like a drunk recruit. "But you reminded me that I haven't always been thus. You provoked me until I was forced to see you differently. I understand—"

Olivia's hand clamped over his mouth. It trembled. "No more. Please."

He twisted his head away so he could speak. She loved him. She'd told him earlier. But perhaps she needed more time to be willing to say the words again. He needed to woo her with soft words and gifts rather than bombs and stolen jam. "Olivia, I love you."

She pressed her fist to her mouth instead. "When my father came back from the courthouse that day, he told me you'd been hanged. The news shattered me. I told him I didn't want to live. I went to my room. When I wouldn't get up the next day, he ordered me out of bed. When I refused, he lost control again. I'd never really disobeyed him before, you see. I was his little pet he paraded in front of his friends. He'd have none of it. *You may be no better than a whore, but I'll be damned if I let anyone know it.*"

He'd gut the old man. Clayton's hand brushed her cheek, caught the tears. But she pulled away, her back colliding with the shelves of earthenware pots behind her.

"He grabbed me to pull me from the bed, and his face just went slack. He fell to the floor. The doctors said he'd suffered an apoplexy."

She said she had secrets. He'd readied himself for them. He loved her. He could look past them. "It's not your fault—"

"He didn't recover." Her voice had firmed and her eyes finally met his.

"Wait. What are you saying?" A wary chill slithered up his spine. What precisely had she hidden?

"Despite all the doctors who promised to cure him, he's never recovered the ability to speak or interact. He can swallow and breathe, but that is all."

"Where is he?"

"At my home by the mill."

"But I was there the night you were kidnapped. Your maid said he and the servants were out."

"I told my staff to lie about his condition. And there weren't any more servants than what you saw. I told them to lie about that, too."

Clayton stepped back now. His body rigid. His lungs solid blocks of iron. He couldn't draw air. Her revelations shattered inside him, fracturing and slicing deep as they rearranged into an ugly truth. He didn't care about her father, at least not as he had. It appeared the universe had dealt him its own form of justice. He cared what the revelation meant about Olivia. "What about the mill?" His voice was soft. It was the only way he could keep his true emotions—desperation, anguish—from showing.

"I told everyone my father had recovered enough to give orders. But it was only me. My father had nothing to do with the rebuilding of the mill."

"The Bank of England?" That was why he'd become involved. To keep England from being cheated again.

He never thought *she'd* be the one behind it.

"I hired a man to pretend to be my father when the representatives came." She clenched her hands tightly in front of her.

"Lies and manipulations, all of it?"

"Yes. I told myself I had to do what I must to save the mill. That saving the mill—that helping those people—would outweigh any lies I had to tell. But it didn't. I'm so sorry." She took a deep breath. Her lips had gone white around the edges, as had her knuckles.

His shock and his hurt crystallized, piercing his chest. He'd been a fool. He'd wanted her so much that he'd convinced himself that he could accept her secrets. But he couldn't. Not when his mother uttered those words. And his father had listened. *I'm sorry I abandoned you to tup the baker. The traveling actor meant nothing to me.*

He'd hated his father for taking her back even as he'd hated himself for believing her, too.

Now he was no better. He'd almost been willing to look past anything to have another chance with Olivia.

Olivia wasn't his mother. He knew this. Olivia probably *had* intended to help the people in her town. But this pain was too familiar. A pain he refused to suffer again.

"Why not sell the mill? Why the deception?"

"Our solicitor knows my father. I wouldn't be able to fool him with the actor. The mill and the house are both in my father's name. I can't sell them while my father still lives. I will just have to give the mill up."

The words were ones he'd hoped to hear. But now they meant little.

Yes, she might give up the mill, but how long until the next betrayal came?

Clayton had been willing to overlook her original betrayal of him to her father. He'd been ready to marry her. All the time she'd had this lying in wait for him. She'd warned him, yes, but he'd been wrong to think he could forgive.

Not when it would do nothing but weaken him.

"What other lies are you keeping from me? What other manipulations do you have in store?" His own breathing was loud in his ears, mingling with the pounding of his heart, until he could hear almost nothing at all.

"I—"

Hell, there *were* more. His stomach churned. And even though it made him look like a weak fool, he had to brace his hand on the shelves as any remaining hope shriveled.

"The money I used to buy the machinery for the mill." She pressed both her hands to her cheeks. "I found them in my father's things. They were all fifty-pound notes. Fresh. Never used."

"The banknotes he'd printed illegally?"

"I—I don't know." She wrapped her arms around her waist. "But they could have been."

Good. This was what he needed. More proof so he'd never be fool enough to open himself to her again.

Her tears deepened to sobs, horrible little sounds she tried to hide behind clenched lips.

Why is she telling you these things?

Because perhaps if he was a different man—a better man—he would have been able to move past these revelations. But with the past that already lay between them, it was simply too much.

For him, that would never be possible.

He clenched the hand that had already started to lift toward her and drew it away.

Clayton strode from the room.

Chapter Twenty-nine

"You really are a coldhearted bastard, aren't you?"

Clayton didn't turn away from the window in the empty bedroom. "Shut up, Ian." His breath obscured the glass with white. A person watching below would know someone was in this room, but he couldn't bring himself to care. He clenched the windowsill, digging his fingers against the wood. No new snow had fallen during the day, leaving the remaining snow scarred and muddy.

"Oh, wait, no. You're tender when a woman trusts you with her darkest secrets."

"I said, shut the hell up."

"She's crying in her room in case you can't hear her. She's crying into her pillow to try to muffle the sound. So considerate."

Clayton whirled around. Ian stood less than a foot away.

"Leave now."

Ian's eyes glittered with a genuine anger Clayton could only ever recall seeing twice. "She loves you."

"So I'm supposed to let her lie? Deceive everyone around her? Make a fool of me?"

"We lied all the time. Why do you hold it against her?"

Clayton clenched and unclenched his damaged hand, finding solace in the pain it caused. "I don't. But I cannot look past it. How could she expect that?"

"Oh, I don't know. Because you forgive those you love?"

"I was prepared to forget that she ran to her father all those years ago. I could look past her betrayal."

"Look past? How magnanimous. Look past until when? When she makes her next mistake? You're still protecting yourself."

"And I was bloody right to!"

"Why did she tell you about her lies in the first place?"

"Because she saw me as a mark. Sensed it the way sharps always spotted my father. Someone weak enough to take advantage of." But even as he said it, the words made no sense. What purpose *had* it served her?

"Or because she loves you. And couldn't stand to have it between you?"

I love you too much to make love while I'm hiding things from you.

Clayton swung at Ian rather than answering. But they'd trained too long together. He knew precisely what Ian would do. So when Ian blocked, Clayton locked his arm and drove him to the ground. But Ian kicked out, knocking Clayton on his back.

His breath whooshed out of him and with it,

his anger. "If I forgive her once, how will I know I won't have to do it again?"

"You don't. You forgive over and over again. Cruel, cruel love. Makes you fall in love with an imperfect person when you're so perfect yourself."

Clayton flinched, but then stood and offered Ian a hand up.

Ian accepted. "I think I'll go see what I can discover about our clockmaker before we meet him tomorrow. Maybe I'll take Olivia with me before she dries up like a prune."

Clayton knew Ian hoped for a reaction, but he wasn't getting one.

Ian paused by the door. "Have you ever really stopped to think what you'd lose if you forgave her for all of it?"

Clayton sat heavily on the bed. What would he lose?

Nothing.

Everything.

He'd been so in love with Olivia when they were young. When he found the proof that her father was printing extra banknotes, he hadn't thought twice about going to her. He'd needed to warn her, wanting her to know he would spare her the pain if he could. He hadn't suspected her of anything but complete loyalty until constables had knocked on his door.

When he saw her father in the courtroom, he'd begged to be allowed to speak to Olivia. Mr. Swift had laughed. *Don't be a fool, lad. She's the one who turned you in.* Clayton hadn't spoken again, ashamed that he'd still have done anything to go crawling back to Olivia despite what she'd done.

He'd vowed he'd never reveal vulnerability like that again. That he'd never *be* vulnerable like that.

Clayton buried his face in his hands. He'd always known this misery would come from allowing second chances.

My father was happy.

Clayton slowly lifted his head. Despite the money his father was never repaid. Despite the wife who left him and didn't even bother to move to a different town with her lover, his father had been happy.

Clayton had been embarrassed for his father, but his father had never been for himself.

What had his father lost by forgiving his wife in the end? Only years of pain and anger.

Had his father been more passive than was good for him? Yes. But perhaps it wasn't forgiveness that made him that way.

When Olivia had comforted Blin earlier, Clayton had ached with pride at her strength and determination as she forgave the man who had wronged her terribly.

There had been no weakness there.

Clayton returned to the window. His mouth felt dry, his throat tight.

Forgiveness hadn't given the others power over Olivia. Forgiveness had allowed her to take the power back.

Clayton swore. *Oh, Da.* Had he really been so bloody blind? No wonder his father had merely shaken his head when Clayton raged on his behalf. He should have slapped him along the side of the head instead.

What did he have to lose by forgiving Olivia?

Anger. Bitterness. Both of which had always rattled foreign and jagged in his thoughts about her.

He'd only lose if he *didn't* forgive her.

He'd lose *her* if he couldn't forgive her.

The thought gutted him far more efficiently than a French bayonet.

But was it even possible for him to forgive? It wasn't a skill he had much practice in.

He examined each shard of betrayal he'd kept so perfectly polished and was shocked to find them thin and brittle. Easily broken and tossed aside. Each betrayal, each action, he understood. She'd never meant to hurt him.

Olivia wasn't perfect. But neither was he. Perfection was static and sterile, with no room for growth. Or learning. Or laughter. He didn't want Olivia to be perfect. He loved her stubbornness. He loved her teasing. He loved that she refused to take him entirely seriously.

Now that he was over the shock, the spy part of him could even admire the work and skill that had gone into her deception. Not that lying had been the best option, but he was glad she was no longer the soft, naive creature she had been. Instead, she was brave. Clever.

Which was fortunate, otherwise, how could he ask her to accept a coldhearted bastard for a husband?

She was sobbing in her pillow. The woman who'd faced down killers to save him. Who'd dedicated her life to saving the people in her town. Who'd wanted him to know the truth before he confessed his feelings.

He forgave her.

A gasp befitting a drowning man expanded his lungs. But the world didn't come to an end. In fact, he felt lighter. Stronger.

Why had he refused to do this for so long?

He loved Olivia. Forgiving her didn't change that. It proved it.

As had her courage in confessing her deceptions to him.

Clayton stumbled over his own feet in his haste to get to his door. She would not shed a single tear more because of him.

He hoped to hell he'd be able to convince her to forgive him. His memory recalled every cruel word, every sneer. Every single bloody one.

He paused by her door, hesitating to enter. Surely, she'd forgive him. She forgave Blin. But then again, Blin hadn't ripped out her heart. No sounds came from within. Had she fallen asleep?

Clayton cracked the door open and stared at an empty bed.

He'd kill Ian for this.

Assuming a bomb didn't kill them first.

Chapter Thirty

Ian fiddled with the slim piece of metal in the window. "Many people think being omniscient is a gift. But it's actually hard work." Ian had the ability to speak in a soft voice that went no further than he wanted it to.

Despite the need for stealth, Ian had rambled on about this and that since he'd collected her. She recognized his words for the diversion they were, but they were still welcome. Especially after he'd taught her to curse Clayton in seventeen languages.

She'd lost him. She'd known it would happen. But she hadn't known every single breath would hurt after that.

She'd played the situation dozens of times already in her mind. His reaction would have been the same no matter what words she'd chosen.

She'd done the right thing. She'd just have to find a way to convince him she'd done it for the right reason, too.

The streetlamps had been poor to begin with, but now the light could do little but knock against the ice coating the glass. Luckily, Ian had brought his own. It was a strange lantern that allowed light to escape only from a single slit on the side.

"Ah, there." The window swung open. Ian lifted her through, then followed her inside.

Ian lifted a flap on the side of the lantern, allowing the room to come into focus. They were in some sort of workroom. Weights dangled from thin golden chains from a shelf. Ledgers sat in a straight line, pinned in by a clock weight on each side of the shelf. Along one wall, there were rows of drawers, each marked with a number. She pulled one open and found it filled with tiny brass gears. The one next to it held gears of a slightly larger size.

"What precisely are we looking for?"

"Any proof that he's been building bombs. Black powder. Fuses. Or any information on him personally. Tidbits. Knickknacks. Crumbs."

"This is how you're omniscient?"

"Bloody difficult."

Olivia continued her examination of the drawers. Screws. Springs of various sizes. All sorted into exact rows.

"Anything?"

Olivia spun around at Clayton's voice, in time to see him slip noiselessly through the window.

Ian lifted up a scrolled clock hand, then replaced it on the shelf. "Forty-two minutes to pull your head out of your arse. I thought you'd be quicker."

"Go search the front of the shop."

Ian snorted and disappeared through the door that led into the shop.

Clayton inhaled. "I—"

"Ian was searching those clocks over there." She

wasn't ready for him to speak. Not until she could school her hope that he'd come to do more than collect her and berate her for going with Ian.

But he chose not to take her hint. He moved next to her, his hand closing over hers when she would have opened the next drawer. "I'm sorry for the way I reacted."

"I'm giving up the mill because it is the right thing. I— Wait. What?"

"I'm sorry." He grimaced. "I feared if I forgave you, it would mean I was weak. That I would be letting you take advantage of me. You trusted me with the truth, and I failed that trust." His eyes were bleak in the near darkness.

But he'd hurt her. She wanted him back more than anything, but not if their future only lasted until she made another mistake. That would break her. "How do I know you won't cast me aside the next time I do something wrong? I swear I'd never knowingly hurt you. But I will make mistakes. Frequently, most likely."

"As will I. Tonight being an example of that. Learning how to not be a coldhearted bastard will likely take time. I'll understand if you don't want to deal with that. But you've reminded me what I lack in my life." He closed his eyes for a moment, pain etched on his face. "I can't go back to that emptiness. And I can give you my word I will never again hesitate to beg your forgiveness whenever you demand it."

Her heart skipped in her chest.

"Please, don't let me drive you away."

Never. If he could forgive her, she could do the same. "I wasn't going to let you." She lifted her hand to his cheek, and then her lips. "I don't chase away easily."

"I would have made him grovel longer," Ian called from the shop.

She couldn't help a choked breath of laughter. "I don't want him to grovel." She lowered her voice. "I want him to kiss me."

Clayton's lips obliged instantly. A dozen pulls from a dozen drawers dug into her back but she didn't care. He tasted of snow and exhaustion. Of blackberry jam and forgiveness. Wondrous, heady freedom. Happiness.

For the first time in ten years, she could kiss him with no regrets, no hidden secrets. She twined her fingers around his neck and pulled him closer. Wanting him to deepen the kiss, but also to just savor the feel of him. Pleasure sang through her body, tightening her muscles. Tingling over her skin.

She lowered her hands to his shoulders, exploring the ridges of muscles, the broad strength.

"You've been silent for two minutes. Stop whatever lovey mush you're up to and finish the job."

Clayton lifted his head but continued to trace her lips with his thumb. "You said Ian was looking at the clocks?"

"Yes, the ones on the workbench. He's currently—"
That was odd.

"What is it?" Clayton asked.

"At the mill, I always make sure my workers are close to their tools and supplies."

"Efficiency."

"Exactly. So why is his worktable over there when all his tools and pieces are on this side of the room?"

Ian scrambled through the door. "You are marrying a bloody genius, Clayton." He shook his head on the shock that must be on her face. "You haven't asked her yet? When were you bloody planning to? In another forty-two minutes?"

"Perhaps when we aren't standing in a bomb shop."

Her heart did a little leap in her chest. "You *were* going to ask?"

His voice was gruff. "Yes. But you deserve better than to be asked here. In front of that idiot."

"Too late. I accept."

Clayton pulled her into his arms, grinning. "Not until I ask you properly."

"The woman was foolish enough to say yes once," Ian said. "I wouldn't risk it again."

Clayton released her with a quick kiss on her lips. "Shut up, Ian, and help me move the table."

After both men lifted the enormous oak table, Ian bent over and examined the floorboards. "A trapdoor." Part of the floor dropped away, revealing a ladder.

Ian lowered his lantern into the hole. Olivia crowded next to them. The light glinted off a spool of thick twine. A bowl of black powder had been placed next to it. Another bowl held small, round metal balls.

Ian turned the lantern.

Two legs sprawled on the floor. A torso covered in blood.

A dead man.

She gasped and jerked back from the trapdoor. Clayton's arms wrapped around her, but she didn't let him pull her away.

The man had been shot. There was no mistaking the gaping hole.

"Well, it's a good thing we didn't waste all that time waiting around for him to show up in the morning."

"How long has he been dead?" Clayton asked, his voice rumbling under her ear.

Ian leaped down into the hidden room. "A day. Two at most." She could hear his footsteps. "One day. There's still a touch of warmth to the stove. What are the odds that our final agent picked up his explosive, then killed the witness?"

"Pretty good, considering our luck these past few days," Clayton said.

"The clockmaker's been a busy boy. There are several partially constructed bombs down here."

Olivia pushed away so she could see more clearly.

Ian shone his lantern on a row of boxes. "It appears our friend had a specialty. These all contain about seven pounds of powder. Clockwork interiors. Flint igniters. All small and portable. Easily concealed."

"How close would the agent have to be to the czar for this to be effective?" Olivia asked.

"Fifteen, perhaps twenty feet," Clayton said.

"Does he have any records down there?" The workshop she stood in had been neat to the point of obsession. The worktable held logs of every gear he used and when. That type of man would also track every ounce of gunpowder and every inch of fuse, too. She couldn't imagine his secret business would be different.

"What will they say? Deliver three bombs to— The devil! He did keep a ledger." Ian paused.

"He doesn't give anything useful like names. But he does the list size of the bombs and payment. Hmm . . . perhaps a trade worth looking into."

"What was his last entry?"

Ian swore. "It was for a bomb containing fifteen pounds of powder."

"How close would the killer have to be for that?" she asked.

Clayton's hand tightened on hers. "He would just need to be in the same ballroom."

"So now we—" She rubbed her temples, trying to clear her thoughts.

"Now we take you home to rest."

"But the bomb—"

He ran the back of his hand down her cheek. "You haven't slept in twenty-four hours. A spy quickly learns there are always more crises to solve, and you can't solve them if you've killed yourself from exhaustion."

"Take her to bed." Ian's grin was far too innocent. "Oh, I meant put her to bed, of course."

But the words couldn't be unsaid. The deliciously wicked thoughts unthought. The heat of Clayton's hand on hers was suddenly nearly unbearable as he led her to the window.

There was no regret to stop her now.

Finally.

"That sounds like a good idea," Olivia said. Her voice didn't sound like her own. It was throaty, her syllables heavy with desire.

Clayton froze, his hand resting on the windowsill. "Which idea?"

"Both."

Chapter Thirty-one

Clayton couldn't risk kissing Olivia on the walk back to Kate's. He needed to keep his eyes on their surroundings to ensure they weren't followed.

But Olivia wasn't making it easy.

And the devilish minx knew it. When she whispered in his ear, her lips caressed it as well. Her teeth worried her lower lip, leaving it rosy, and as soon as she saw him notice, she slowly licked it.

"Hell, woman, if you keep this up, I'm going to take you in a bank of snow and there will be a decided lack of silk sheets and candles."

"Silk sheets and candles?"

His ears heated. "I may have pictured it a time or two."

She lifted her brow, and it disappeared under the edge of her cap. "So have I."

"What did you picture?"

She just smiled at him and sashayed in front of him, letting her hips swing. "We never made it to the sheets."

Since they were only a block from the house,

Clayton scooped her into his arms and ran the remaining distance. "Before we get eliminated by a dozen revolutionaries I've been too befuddled to notice."

He loved the quivers in her chest as she laughed at him.

He hefted her through the window with enough force that she nearly stumbled. "Sorry."

But she'd regained her footing and had already grabbed his coat to help tug him inside. "Like your new word?"

"Yes, strangely enough."

They climbed the stairs so fast they were both out of breath as they skidded to a stop outside his door.

He loved that, too.

How could he have considered a life without this?

He opened his door and they fell inside.

"I've wanted you every day since I met you." Her hands already grappled with his buttons.

He swept off her hat and tried to trap her hands to remove her gloves. "There must have been some days these past few weeks when that wasn't true."

She grinned. "Always so precise. But no, there weren't."

"Even when I appeared like a damned ghost at your mill, threatening you?"

"I dreamed of kissing you until I found the boy I knew."

His body throbbed as her hand slipped inside his jacket. "Do you still hope to find him?" Despite the parts of him Olivia had restored, he'd never be that person again. Too much had happened to him.

She shook her head. "No, now I dream of kissing you until I know the man that boy became."

Clayton threw off his coat. "What precisely do you want to find out?"

Her lips curled with pure feminine satisfaction. "A good question. First, I'm desperate to find out how quick you've become at unfastening a lady's buttons."

"Desperate?" He nipped the side of her neck.

"Completely." She offered her back.

"I'm quite good at tests." He'd thought to impress her with his speed, but he found himself unwilling to resist the delicate curve where her shoulder met her neck. He pressed a kiss to it, then along the valley of her spine until he was stopped by the rest of her clothing. "Sorry. That was a bit slow."

He traced his thumb up and down where his finger had just been.

"It's— I'll let you try again sometime." She let the gown pool at her feet, then tipped her head back so it rested on his shoulder.

He laid small kisses along her hairline. Her ear. Her jaw.

"I have also been wondering how you'd react if I bared myself for you?" She pulled away and faced him. Her petticoat fell to the ground. Then she drew off her shoes and stockings.

She reached behind her for the ties to her stays. "Last time I didn't quite get to finish. And I didn't get to see your reaction. Would your eyes darken?" Her stays fell to the floor. "Would your hands clench? Would you be able to resist coming closer?"

He was already stepping toward her.

She tapped him on the chest, stopping him. "You asked me what I pictured when I fantasized about us making love. It was this." She slipped off her shift.

Clayton did not know if it was a growl or a groan he made at the sight of her. Probably some portion of both. She was perfection. The saucy tilt of her chin. The wild challenge in her eyes. The strands of her blond hair that had come loose to tease her breasts.

No wonder he'd never felt anything for the other women. They'd always been in competition with her. And nothing could compare to her.

"This is all you pictured?" he managed to ask.

She leaned toward him and brushed her nipples across the linen of his shirt. "Not even close."

"So you think my candlelight and silken sheets a paltry excuse for a fantasy?" Clayton stripped off his shirt, revealing those hard rows of muscle.

She couldn't resist reaching out to trace her finger down the line that bisected his abdomen and disappeared into his trousers. "Oh no. Not paltry. Sweet, perhaps?"

Clayton's hand snaked around her waist and pulled her to him. "Sweet? I thought you'd want to be wooed."

She nipped his chest. "Perhaps at some point. But right now I'd like you to toss me on that bed over there. Or if we can't make it that far, the floor right here will do."

His lips tangled with hers, his tongue promising wicked things to come.

She arched as his lips moved on to her breasts, then gasped, twining her fingers in his hair to keep him there. "I vote for right here. Now."

He pulled away and lifted her into his arms. "If I'm tossing you, it will have to be the bed. The floor would hurt."

Always so precise. She barely stifled a gasp as she tumbled from his arms and landed with an *oof* in the middle of the bed. "Did I mention in my fantasy you aren't wearing any trousers?"

He kicked off his boots, then stripped off his trousers, pausing at the edge of the bed.

Sweet heavens.

As lusty as she thought she was, this might never work. Yet she scrambled up on her elbows, desperate to touch him. She ran a fingertip down the thick length of his arousal. And he shuddered.

"How do you expect me to have tame, ladylike fantasies after seeing this?"

He groaned when she swirled her finger over the tip, then caught her hand, pinning it over her head.

"Despite the fact that my fantasy had you in bed, it wasn't tame." He climbed onto the bed beside her and his finger traced a slow line down her belly, only to stop at the curls at the tops of her thighs. "I planned to make you beg."

"Beg?" She rolled her hips, trying to urge that finger lower. But when that finger traced down the fronts of her thighs, she suddenly understood his devilishness.

Slowly, his finger inched back up, circling that most sensitive spot but not touching. Instead, he lowered his lips to her breasts, teasing the aching nipples.

Confound him. She clenched her legs together, alarmed at the wetness between them.

With each flick of his tongue, the throbbing need increased. "Please."

"We're back to politeness?"

She would say anything at this point. She'd been wanting this for too long. "I need—"

"You need this?" His hand finally cupped her aching core. But when one finger slowly parted the folds and brushed that most sensitive nub, once and then again, her body flew apart. She grabbed his shoulders in shock as waves of bliss radiated through her, her core clenching and throbbing, begging for more. She cried his name until he covered her mouth with his own, drinking of her passion. Driving her pleasure higher.

When she could manage opening her eyes, Clayton was watching her with a smile crooked on his lips. "I'd intended to make you beg a little more first."

"I'll let you try again sometime." She reached up to stroke him again and he flung his head back. This naughty side of her personality was proving quite insatiable. She caressed him again. The throbbing resumed between her legs, reminding her of what was yet to come.

This whole final portion of the lovemaking might not work, but her body was eager to try. She slowly positioned him at her slick entrance. "In fact, you can try again now."

Clayton had never known a man could die of pleasure. But he was certain of it now. He pressed slowly forward, giving her time to adjust to him. But her body was tight and inexperienced. He slowly stroked her until she relaxed around him.

Only then did he slowly begin to move.

He'd thought to call on every ounce of control he possessed to make her beg again, but he didn't need it. She was already growing wild beneath him.

When she began to writhe to meet his thrusts, all thought of control disappeared. He gave himself to her completely, hiding nothing, concealing not a single weakness. Not the way his body shuddered. Not his desperation to give her everything.

And she pressed kisses to his chest and reveled in it all. When her body clenched around him and she moaned his name again, he rode her pleasure to his own. Emotions long contained swirled, peaking, flooding every inch of his body with ecstasy. Blinding him to everything but the woman under him.

So beautiful. His diamond.

Mine.

His heart threatened to break through his rib cage long after his breathing slowed. He rolled to the side and clutched her to him.

Happiness. He was bloody elated for the first time in a decade.

After a moment, Olivia lifted her head; her brow was creased.

He stroked her side. "What's wrong?" Had he been too rough? He'd taken her virginity without much finesse.

But her look of concern was ruined by a single quirk in her lip. "How long would it take you to retrieve the jar of blackberry jam?"

Chapter Thirty-two

"*I* hate to interrupt your preconnubial bliss. But we have a very irate minister of the police downstairs who wishes to talk to you. And Olivia." Ian spoke from outside the door.

Light streamed in the windows. How long had she slept? It had been months since she'd slept more than a few hours. Always fearing her plans for the mill would come crashing down around her.

Clayton pulled her tighter against him, the hair on the back of his arm tickling the underside of her breast. But she was fully alert now, and a similar tension hummed through Clayton.

Apparently, Golov had decided not to take her advice.

"Is he armed?" she asked.

"A knife and two pistols, but he came alone."

Perhaps he *had* listened.

Clayton shifted behind her. "I will speak to him, but there's no need for Olivia to endure him again."

"He said, and I quote, 'Tell the baron I'll see him now. And tell Miss Swift she'd better come so I don't put a bullet between his eyes.' I think he must love her with all his entire heart, which is admittedly only the size of as a fig, but—"

"Tell him we will join him in twenty minutes," Olivia said. She placed a regretful kiss on the crook of Clayton's elbow, her tongue flicking out along the crease of soft skin.

He wiped a finger over her cheek, lifting his finger to reveal a smudge of purple jam. He grinned. "How fast can you get dressed?"

"Eight minutes."

He lowered his mouth to her right shoulder, nipping his way down it. "Then we don't have to get out of bed for twelve."

Twenty minutes later, Ian met them as they walked to the library. He scowled. "Sometimes I regret being all-knowing."

Olivia's cheeks heated, but Clayton returned Ian's glare. "That knowledge had better be theoretical."

Ian lifted a brow. "No skulking this time, I swear." His face grew serious. "Kate, Blin, and I have already been busy this morning. Try not to act surprised at anything Golov says."

When they entered, Golov looked even more emaciated than the last time they'd talked. She really needed to tell him to eat more.

"Here to give me thanks for delivering Arshun to you?" Ian asked as he pulled a piece of toast from his pocket. "I tied an especially nice bow on him just for you."

Golov glared. "He's worthless. He doesn't know a thing." He turned to Olivia. "I know you've broken the code. What does it say? Since I haven't killed the baron for what he did to my prison, I will expect recompense."

"It gave signs and where to leave them. Unfortunately, they've already been given. As I told you," Olivia said. "It said the killer would act. Did you call off the fete like I suggested?"

He stiffened. "No." Then he shifted in his chair. "But I did order an extra regiment of soldiers to guard the event. Nothing will happen to the czar."

"Why are you here, Golov?" Clayton asked.

"First, explain why I have dead men in my city. Two. Their throats slit. That was your specialty, wasn't it?"

"Yes," Clayton said. "But I haven't used it lately."

"Unfortunately, I think you might be telling the truth. The metropolitan's clerk was killed while you were destroying my jail."

Which reminded her of their discussion yesterday. "Who else was killed?"

Golov tugged on the cuffs of his jacket. "Some assistant to General Smirken. Not a man of importance. Again, it makes no sense why *you* would kill him. But someone wants me to think you're responsible, Baron. The question is why?"

"Or who," Ian muttered, smiling far too broadly.

Olivia knew Golov wasn't a good man, but she also suspected he wasn't purely evil, either. "We should tell him." She locked gazes with Clayton, begging him to trust her.

He frowned, but slowly nodded.

Ian tucked the rest of his toast in his pocket. "There have been stranger bedfellows. No. I take that back. But do what you will."

Olivia explained what they knew about the bomb and the final agent, leaving out only Kate's identity.

"You think my brother Pavlo is the assassin?" Golov seemed oddly bored.

"We know he is a revolutionary." She was taking a large risk, but they had few options at this point. And while she doubted she could trust her safety to him, she suspected she could trust Russia's. "The rest fits."

"I fear you must have been fooled. My brother is not in St. Petersburg. His regiment was ordered to the Crimea. They left yesterday with my brother leading them."

What?

But the pieces had fit so perfectly.

"We can verify that," Ian said.

"Do." Golov shook his head, rising to his feet. "Apparently, you know even less than I do."

Ian snapped his fingers as if something had just occurred to him. "And in case you're considering having us murdered to allow the plot to proceed, Kate paid a visit to her friend the empress this morning. She is quite adamant that we all attend the fete tomorrow. Of course, we reminded her that she had your promise we'd be safe."

Golov tapped the back of his chair with his yellowed nail. "Indeed."

"Don't worry. We'll make it up to you by doing your job," Ian said.

Golov paused by Olivia. "You see, *koteek*, I am a man of my word. Your baron is still alive." He patted her on the cheek. "For now."

Chapter Thirty-three

If the ball a few nights ago had inspired awe, this was one that demanded it. Hundreds of servants had been employed all morning, brushing snow from not only the exterior of the building, but from the individual leaves of plants outside.

Each crystal in the massive chandeliers had been polished by hand with satin and vodka.

Servants dressed in livery with buttons of pure gold.

The ball was a masquerade, which had worried her at first, until Kate had explained that no one wore masks, it simply meant that all the guests dressed in traditional Russian costume.

Kate had somehow arranged for Olivia to have another perfect dress, the heavy golden embroidery on the full sapphire blue skirt of the gown glittering like a thousand stars when she moved. A matching cloth-covered tiara rested on her head, from which flowed a white satin veil threaded with more gold.

And the best part was that Clayton hadn't left her side once this evening.

Not that she had much time to enjoy his attentiveness. Every glance from either of them scanned the crowd, searching for someone suspicious. Someone out of place.

They'd spent the day searching for the colonel, but they couldn't find him. His servants also claimed he'd left town two days ago with his regiment.

And they'd yet to see him tonight. None of the palace staff they'd questioned had, either.

But there were so many men in green uniforms that she wasn't sure they would see him even if he *was* there.

They strolled around the perimeter of the ballroom again, slowing by the veiled painting on the stage. It was enormous, easily twenty feet across, but it sat on a simple gilded easel that could conceal nothing. And nothing had changed since the last time they'd passed. Nothing looked unusual.

Kate joined them. "If I hear the description of one more glorious battle, I will scream." She lowered her voice. "But I have seen nothing unusual yet among the soldiers I spoke with. And no one in the ballroom is holding anything the correct size to be the bomb. Nor has anyone seen the colonel."

"The footman only let me have one joint of mutton. One. The gall of that man." Ian spoke from where he waited by a column as they passed.

They paused by him. They had less than twenty minutes until the unveiling.

"Nothing yet," he confirmed. "But there are so many bloody people. It's impossible to tell."

The final strains of a waltz ended. But rather

than a new one filling the silence, the guests began to mill toward the stage in preparation of the unveiling.

"Split up again," Clayton ordered. "Meet by the rear doors to the ballroom after you've searched your area of the room again. If we don't find something by then, we will clear out." His arm tensed under Olivia's. "I will not see you hurt."

Kate and Ian nodded and headed in opposite directions.

A feminine hand latched on to Clayton's other arm, stopping them. "Baron. I'm so pleased to see you this evening."

General Smirken's wife fluttered her eyelashes up at Clayton, and pressed a kiss on his cheek. Her husband was nowhere to be seen. "I've missed your company this week."

"Where is your husband?" Olivia asked. They didn't have time for her.

Annoyance flashed across the other woman's face. "He suffered a great tragedy. One of his lieutenants was viciously murdered." She leaned against Clayton, her face stretching in false sadness. "He and some of his friends have met to drink to the man's memory."

"They chose to meet at the same time as the imperial fete?" Disbelief was clear in Clayton's voice, and the other woman huffed.

"No, they're here. The czar was kind enough to grant them use of one of his parlors. Colonel Golov requested it as a personal favor for him."

Both Olivia and Clayton straightened.

"I thought the colonel was sent to the Crimea?" Clayton asked.

"His regiment was, but he isn't joining them until after the fete."

Olivia knew her fingers were digging into Clayton's arm, but she couldn't seem to loosen them.

The colonel had never left St. Petersburg.

"Where are the officers meeting?"

"I don't know." Her lips thinned. "Colonel Golov brought cigars from his own personal stock. I cannot abide the smoke. It gives one wrinkles. But the crates of French brandy did look rather fine."

"Colonel Golov brought crates?" Olivia and Clayton asked at the same time.

"Tonight?" Olivia clarified.

The other woman blinked. "Yes. Of the finest brandy."

Clayton asked, "How much brandy did he bring?"

"I don't know," she huffed. "Three, perhaps four crates."

"Where was the brandy placed?"

"I don't know. The parlor, I suppose. I'm not a footman."

Clayton disentangled her from his arm. "Thank you. You may go."

The woman's face flushed blotchy red before she flounced away.

Clayton didn't even notice. His eyes were already scanning the crowd. "We need to find Ian and Kate. We need to move our search."

If this was going to happen, it would happen soon. The entire imperial family was gathered like sheep in a pen.

Olivia spotted familiar red hair. "There's Kate."

Olivia caught her eye and Kate hurried back over. "What have you found?"

But then Golov approached. A group of six soldiers appeared behind him. "You'll come with me," he hissed.

"Your brother is here." Clayton tried to move around him, but the soldier surrounded them. "He brought in crates."

Golov's sunken eyes burned. "*You* are the one who brought in a crate."

The stern-faced soldiers all carried rifles. Their confrontation was over to the side. However, it would soon be noticed. Once that happened, Golov would lead them away. The time for discussion was over.

"We didn't," Olivia said. "And your brother *is* here. He didn't leave with his regiment. Who told you we brought in a crate?"

Golov's sparse brows lowered. He held up his hand, stopping his men from apprehending them. "I was given the information by a footman." Golov pointed at the middle soldier of the group behind him. "Bring that footman here. Someone will pay for lies tonight."

"Doesn't it seem odd to you that the two groups that should be stopping the colonel are fighting with each other instead?" Olivia asked.

Olivia had no idea the amount of power she held. Golov had actually paused to listen to her. Golov didn't even overly care for the opinions of the emperor.

Yet he'd held back his attack dogs while he listened to Olivia.

The soldier returned, escorting a young, pudgy

footman with a hawkish nose and thick mustache. The servant clicked his heels together and bowed to Golov.

"Did these people enter with a package?"

Biyul had the exaggerated posture of a man who wore a corset. "Yes. A large wooden crate." He rubbed his thumb across the fingers of his right hand like he was holding a deck of cards. The nervous tell of a gambler.

Clayton searched him until he found the telltale rectangular bulge under his uniform. "How much money do you owe at cards, Biyul?"

The man's face lost its color. "How does that relate?"

But Golov's career had been built on piecing together rumor and hearsay. He spotted the connection immediately. "How much would someone have to pay you to lie?"

"I would never lie."

"How much money do you owe?" Clayton asked.

"Nothing more than I can repay, of course." Biyul tried to back up but he was blocked by Golov's men.

"How much?" Golov asked.

"Five thousand rubles."

Clayton tried not to dwell on the fact that he was working alongside Golov on this. But they didn't have time to stand in the ballroom talking. The colonel was in the palace. He needed to be found. "And how long have you been a revolutionary?"

Biyul lunged, trying to get around the guards, but they grabbed him.

"Who told you to lie?"

"Freedom. Justice. Equality!" Biyul shouted, finally drawing attention. Some of the couples headed toward the stage turned. Conversation hushed.

"Who?" Clayton tried once more.

"Freedom. Justice. Equality!"

"I hate when they get like this," Golov said.

Had he just shared a look of commiseration with Golov? Clayton shuddered.

"Take this man away," Golov ordered.

The largest soldier clamped his hand over Biyul's mouth as they dragged him from the ballroom.

Golov pointed to the conductor of the orchestra with one long, yellowed finger. And they launched into an energetic reel despite the fact that there were no dancers on the floor.

"Your brother's going to kill the czar. He had at least three crates brought in," Olivia said.

If anyone else had said that, Golov would have ordered him flogged until he vomited his own blood. Instead, Golov's eyes widened a fraction of an inch. It was the most emotion Clayton had ever seen from him.

"You're telling the truth." His sentence sounded suspiciously like a question.

Olivia actually placed her hand on the man's arm. "You didn't know he was a revolutionary?"

Golov stared at her hand as if bewildered by her action. "If I had, he'd be dead."

Olivia told him about the gathering of officers, having to raise her voice to be heard over the servant announcing the unveiling.

"Pavlo will pay." Golov spun to his men. "Find the butler. Find where Smirken and his friends are gathered. Then place a man at each entrance to the ballroom. Pavlo will not enter." He turned away and stormed off into the crowd.

Olivia's heart beat loudly in her ears. "We should order everyone to leave."

But Clayton shook his head. "Colonel Golov is as vain and power hungry as his brother. He'll never abandon this without at least some benefit to himself. If he sees that people are starting to evacuate, he'll detonate the bomb."

The imperial family was invited to the stage to re-create the grouping shown in the portrait.

The crowd shifted as people began to mount the platform. The lesser members of the imperial family arranged themselves, jostling for the space nearest where the czar would stand.

If Olivia were the bomber, this was when she'd act. When else would the entire extended imperial family be grouped so close together? "Clayton—"

"I know. Lambs to the slaughter." His brows lowered. "He'd want to ensure the death of the imperial family, so he'd set the bomb as close to them as possible.

"You're looking frantic, Clayton. They did supply chamber pots. If you need—"

"The colonel is here. He's been spotted."

Ian disappeared into the crowd.

If she were the colonel, she'd try to get as close to the stage as she could. But she wouldn't be able to get too close. Golov's men had ringed the stage, creating a gap of about a dozen feet between the crowd and the platform.

The closest point the colonel could reach would probably be along the far side of the stage. The crowd had edged the policeman Golov just assigned there backward slightly. He was pressed so tightly against the door that he'd fall if it was opened.

The door.

"When we followed the colonel earlier this week, he slipped into a parlor. It was there, wasn't it? Right behind that wall." She pointed to where the royal family gathered. "Could a bomb that size blow through that wall?"

"He doesn't plan to be in the ballroom at all." Clayton's eyes narrowed as he made the calculations. "And he doesn't have to be. Get as far away from this ballroom as you can."

"No."

"The bomb could already be in place."

"Ian's advice still holds true. If you don't let me come, I'll find my own way." The emperor and the empress had begun to approach the stage, accompanied by the tiny, silver-haired dowager grand duchess. The final members of the portrait.

"You could die." His horror at the thought was clear; it was almost enough to make her change her mind. But not quite.

"So could you." She lifted her hand to his tense jaw. "Remember how I told you I wasn't perfect? This is one of those things. I'm not biddable."

"No, you're damned stubborn." He exhaled, shaking his head. "But hell if you aren't incredibly brave, too."

The crowd was thick around the platform, but Clayton moved past the people like they didn't exist. He seemed to know when a space would open up that they could move into. When a gentleman would lean to his left to speak to the lady at his side. Or when a woman was going to try to edge around for a slightly better view.

Finally, they were at the door.

The policeman straightened as they tried to get past.

"We don't want to get to the platform. The lady just needs some air."

The sweaty, red-faced policeman looked a little longing at the thought, but he inched as far over as he could so they could get into the corridor.

The corridor was wide and blessedly free of people. Olivia sucked in a calming breath, but it lodged in her throat as Clayton drew a pistol. "How did you get a gun past the servants?"

Clayton shrugged. "Ian did. I didn't want to ask."

He motioned for her to stay behind him as they approached the door.

Clayton eased it open.

The room was filled with men in uniform. Laughing faces flushed with drink. If the bomb was in this room, it would kill not only the imperial family but most of the leading military officers as well.

It took her a minute to find the colonel. He was bent over a crate at the far end of the room. He opened the lid.

"Clayton—"

"I see him."

But the colonel saw them in the same moment. "Smirken!" the colonel said, his jovial tone the complete opposite of the loathing Olivia could see on his face. "The baron was a friend of the lieutenant, wasn't he?"

"Baron! Yes, we all served together!" Smirken reached for Clayton and pounded him on the back. "Come to join us in a drink to our poor lieutenant. To Mikhail!"

Everyone lifted his glass.

Colonel Golov edged toward the door. Clayton was trapped in the middle of the huddle of soldiers.

But Olivia wasn't.

She ran past the knot of officers, reaching the door at the same time as the colonel. She slammed herself in front of it. He'd have to go through her to get out. Surely, he wouldn't want to die. He'd have to stop the bomb—

The colonel pulled a pistol from his jacket and pushed it against her stomach.

Clayton freed himself from the condoling slaps and proffered glasses. Didn't any of them notice he had a damned pistol in his hand? How much alcohol had the colonel given them? They'd be of no help stopping—

Clayton froze.

On the far side of the room, the colonel had a gun pressed against Olivia's stomach.

The colonel put his finger to his lips, then gestured for Clayton to clear the others from the room.

"The emperor wishes you all in the ballroom. He said he will take note of the ones who are absent," Clayton announced.

Bleary eyes focused on him, then everyone started speaking at once.

"*Now*," Clayton said.

Even drunk, they recognized the command in his voice and filed from the room.

"Leave her alone, Colonel." Clayton lifted his gun.

But the colonel didn't move away from Olivia.

"La Petit and Cipher." He still thought Olivia was La Petit. Perhaps he and his brother really didn't talk after all.

The colonel's lips thinned. "I thought my brother would detain you longer."

"Your brother knows what you are. He is looking for you, too," Olivia said, her voice steady.

The colonel shifted slightly, moving one foot closer to the door. "You'll do nothing to stop me from leaving."

Clayton inched forward. "Why is that?"

"Because I can tell you who's betraying your identities to your worst enemies. General Einhern. Count Arshun. Me." Einhern was the man who'd tried to have Madeline murdered last year.

Every muscle along Clayton's spine tensed. "Who?"

"I thought you might be interested. It's someone far more regal than you would have expected."

But Clayton wasn't going to play his game. He would do everything in his power to protect the Trio's identities, but his most important task was to protect Olivia. That meant removing the pistol held against her.

He stepped to the side so he'd have a clear shot at the general. "Put down the gun and stop the bomb, Colonel."

"I think I'm the one who holds the upper hand

here, spy." He jabbed the muzzle of the pistol harder into Olivia.

She gasped, her face tensing. But then she glared. "Don't put down the gun, Clayton. He only has one shot."

"Aimed at you," the colonel said.

"Then once you shoot me, Clayton will kill you and disarm the bomb."

"Do you want to die?" The colonel's finger tightened on the trigger.

"A bullet seems cleaner than a bomb blast."

Olivia claimed she didn't know when to back down. He hadn't appreciated just how much until this moment, when backing down should have been the glaringly obvious choice.

Yet she'd given up the mill for him. He'd examine his greater understanding of that gesture at some later moment.

The general glanced at the watch dangling from his waistcoat.

"Nervous? How much time did you give yourself?" Olivia asked.

"I'm ready to die for the cause."

"For Arshun?" The disgust coated with disdain in her voice was perfect.

A flicker of loathing crossed the general's face.

"I didn't think so."

"Arshun isn't the one who will rise to power."

"Ah, do you think it will be you?" Clayton asked. "That will be rather difficult if you're dead."

The colonel's cheek twitched. "I'm not going to die. The imperial family will. Then when I lead the troops to quell Arshun's little moband with the church in disgrace, I'll move into my rightful place."

"Arshun has been arrested. There is no uprising for you to fight."

The colonel hesitated, but only for a moment. "No matter. The plan will still work."

"Are you sure?" Olivia asked. "How much time until the bomb—"

A gun fired and a hole appeared in the center of the colonel's forehead.

His body fell back in an awkward slump.

Clayton spun, expecting Ian. Instead, Golov stepped into the room, a smoking pistol still in his hand. Was he human enough that killing his brother would affect him? But Clayton didn't have time to see.

He raced to the bomb, reaching it at the same time as Olivia.

Clayton removed the lid to the box. Shiny clockwork gears hummed and clicked. The gunpowder lay underneath them, impossible to get to.

"I think this would be a great time for you to evacuate the ballroom, Golov."

"My loyalty's to the emperor. Never question that again," he said behind them, his voice strained.

Olivia tensed as she glanced back at the body of the colonel. His head lay in a growing pool of red.

She pulled away and walked to the window. She yanked down the curtain with a big tug. Then returned to lay it over the general's body.

Golov's cheek twitched once, much as his brother's had done. "Thank you."

He turned and hurried from the room.

"You should leave, too," Clayton said.

"And you should stop the bomb and save us. You saw the bombs at the clockmaker's workshop, the ones partially built. What did he add last? Wouldn't that be the item that set the tension?"

In that instant, he could see the other bombs perfectly in his mind. But he still didn't know what to remove. There were far too many gears and moving parts. A flintlock from a pistol sat primed, ready to ignite the powder when sprung. He couldn't take out the wrong thing.

"If flint hits steel, the whole thing will explode, right?" Olivia asked. "Then—"

Then he'd just have to see it didn't.

He ripped off his glove and jammed it under the flint.

The flint swung.

Thud.

No spark.

The gears stopped spinning.

With the breath resuming motion in his lungs, he yanked the entire clockwork from the box and tossed it aside.

"Nice choice. I was about to do this."

He barely dodged the curtain of water that hit the box, flooding the powder.

"Brilliant girl." He scooped her in his arms and trailed his lips down her throat until he found the rapid flicker of her heartbeat. He placed a kiss there. Then another.

Ian stuck his head in the room. "The grand duchess wanted to know who ruined her birthday. I made sure to tell her it was Golov."

Kate was at his side. "And the empress is none too glad that the grand duchess is upset."

Golov would have some interesting things to contend with in the next few weeks then. The least of which would be his grief over his brother. Strange, strange world. "The colonel claimed to know who was betraying us. He said it was some-one *regal*," Clayton said.

Ian stilled. "Interesting. Very." Then he relaxed. He'd filed away the information wherever it fit in his endless stores of data.

"Can you two get home on your own?" Clayton asked.

"Why? What is wrong with my sledge?" Kate asked suspiciously.

Ian took her arm. "Trust me. You won't want to know the answer to that question."

Clayton caught Olivia's hand and pulled her out of the parlor and into the now-empty corridor.

For a moment, they just stood there. Hand in hand. Alive. Breathing.

The corridor was plain. Simple parquet floors. White walls.

Not romantic in the slightest. But he refused to risk never having this moment.

He dropped to one knee.

She stared at him, her lips parted. At least he could claim to have surprised her.

"Olivia, will you do me the honor of becoming my entirely too beautiful, brave, and good wife?"

She grinned at him, but she was also blinking furiously. "I already agreed. But I'll do it again. Yes." She tugged him to his feet and kissed the corner of his mouth. "And in case you decide you must ask me still another time—yes, again."

He whirled her around until they were both

dizzy and laughing. He kissed the wing of her eyebrow. The thin ridge of her nose. Then finally, her glorious lips. Then he had to kiss those again.

After a long moment, he lifted his lips again. "But promise me one thing."

"What?"

"Promise me you'll run if you're ever confronted with another bomb."

She grinned at him and cupped his cheek. "Sorry, but nothing will ever make me leave your side."

Epilogue

Olivia sorted through the mail the butler had delivered as she walked into the library. The first was a short, elegant card announcing the arrival of Princess Katya Petrovna to London. Penned at the bottom was a handwritten note from Kate with her plans to visit on her way to Wales.

Olivia's hand froze on the next envelope. The letter from her solicitor. This was it then. The official end of the mill. At least of it being her mill. When they'd returned to England, Clayton had helped her secure permission from the courts to act on her father's behalf. Then she'd ordered the mill sold. Someone else would take over the responsibility for the workers. With a portion of the money from the sale, she'd fund the Society for the Humane Treatment of Child Criminals. The rest would go to the vicar to help the local families.

Clayton looked up from the ledgers in front of him. "Remind me again why you convinced me to tell the emperor I wanted Arshun's lands as my reward for saving his life. Again."

She walked behind him and pressed a kiss on his cheek. "I thought you needed something more than camels in Siberia." But she knew Clayton didn't truly mind. Blin had been able to return to his family. And without Arshun's oppression, the land was proving remarkably productive.

"Are you going to open your letter?"

She nodded, turning the paper in her hands. She'd thought that this moment would be harder, but she'd gained so much more than she'd given up.

She broke the seal and scanned the contents. She froze, rereading.

She looked up to find Clayton grinning at her.

"*You* bought the mill?"

"For you. I thought you needed more to occupy that brilliant mind than a husband who adores you."

She set down the letter on the desk. They would need to figure out the best strategy for diverting business from the Steltham Mill. And Parliament was thinking of raising the tax on rags again. They'd need to make plans to—

Clayton's hand slid down her hip.

Tomorrow would be soon enough.

She settled herself in his lap.

"I never want you to doubt that I'm in awe of the woman you've become."

She lifted her lips to his. "I don't need a mill to know that."

His kiss was all the proof she needed.

Next month, don't miss these exciting new love stories only from Avon Books

Lord of Wicked Intentions by Lorraine Heath

Lord Rafe Easton never thought he'd want a companion, but when he sees Miss Evelyn Chambers—an earl's illegitimate daughter—he's determined to have her, if only as his mistress. For Evelyn, circumstance gives her little choice but to accept the lord's indecent proposal. But when dark discoveries threaten to destroy them both, what they find in one another may be enough to save them both . . .

Half Moon Hill by Toni Blake

A rugged loner and ex-biker-gang member, Duke Dawson is looking for some peace and quiet in the little town of Destiny, Ohio. But when Anna Romo comes wandering through his woods and into his cabin, she completely shakes his world. Their passion is palpable—but can she convince a man who has turned his back on life to take the biggest leap of faith of all and fall in love?

One for the Wicked by Karina Cooper

Dr. Kayleigh Lauderdale possesses the only cure for what's killing the city's witches. Desperate to acquire it, the resistance sends Shawn Lowe to retrieve it. He never planned on saving or *wanting* anyone—least of all, the daughter of his sworn enemy. But when the world turns upside down, it will take everything Kayleigh and Shawn have to hold on . . . to life, to hope, and to each other.

At Avon Books, we know your passion for romance—once you finish one of our novels, you find yourself wanting more.

May we tempt you with . . .

- **Excerpts** from our upcoming releases.

- Entertaining **extras**, including authors' personal photo albums and book lists.

- Behind-the-scenes **scoop** on your favorite characters and series.

- **Sweepstakes** for the chance to win free books, romantic getaways, and other fun prizes.

- Writing **tips** from our authors and editors.

- **Blog** with our authors and find out why they love to write romance.

- **Exclusive content** that's not contained within the pages of our novels.

Join us at
www.avonbooks.com

An Imprint of HarperCollins*Publishers*
www.avonromance.com

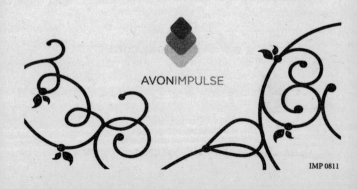